PRAISE FOR VICTORIA MALVEY AND

TEMPTRESS

"Victoria Malvey gives classic romance a fresh and exciting new voice."

—Teresa Medeiros, author of *Charming the Prince*

ENCHANTED

"A delightful and alluring romance. This is the kind of tale that brightens the day and brings back memories of first crushes and the wonderful feeling of falling in love." .

—*Romantic Times*

"Filled with wonderfully drawn characterization and dialogue that flows seamlessly, written with skill and humor, this is a compelling story about the endurance of love."

—*Rendezvous*

"An enthralling tale of mystery and intrigue.... Splendid."

—*Bell, Book & Candle*

PORTRAIT OF DREAMS

"A new star has burst on the romance horizon.... The spark that makes a book a bestseller is present on every page of this beautiful story. FIVE STARS."

—*Affaire de Coeur*

Books by Victoria Malvey

Portrait of Dreams
Enchanted
Temptress
A Merry Chase

Published by POCKET BOOKS

VICTORIA MALVEY

A Merry Chase

SONNET BOOKS
New York London Toronto Sydney Singapore

This book is a work of fiction. Names, characters, places and incidents are products of the author's imagination or are used fictitiously. Any resemblance to actual events or locales or persons, living or dead, is entirely coincidental.

An *Original* Publication of POCKET BOOKS

A Sonnet Book published by
POCKET BOOKS, a division of Simon & Schuster Inc.
1230 Avenue of the Americas, New York, NY 10020

Copyright © 2000 by Victoria Malvey

ISBN: 0-671-77525-1

First Sonnet Books printing April 2000

10 9 8 7 6 5 4 3 2 1

SONNET BOOKS and colophon are registered trademarks of Simon & Schuster Inc.

Front cover illustration by Alan Ayers

Printed in the U.S.A.

To my sisters—

To Jayne—the courageous way in which you face life's challenges amazes me. With a unique blend of pure grit and good humor, you overcome adversity . . . and remain strong and happy. I admire you greatly, Jayne—my sister with the brave soul.

To Linda—your irreverent humor never fails to make me smile. You add such color to my life, Linda, and without you, my world would definitely be less bright. You, Linda, are my sister with the incredible wit.

To Eileen—your sense of "family" has always overwhelmed me. Though life may be hectic, stressed, and not filled with enough hours, you always find the time to make everyone in the family feel important, Eileen—my sister who always helps me to understand what is truly important in life—family.

To Lynn—the unwavering generosity of your soul makes you a very special person. You share yourself— your heart, your love—without reservation. I have always thrived beneath your warmth, Lynn—my sister who knows how to make everyone in her life feel special and unique.

And lastly, to Cathy—you possess the biggest heart of anyone I've ever known. With abounding love, unwavering support and unquestioning loyalty, you show me how much you love me day after day. I can honestly say, Cathy, that I feel *blessed* to have you for a sister. You, Cathy, are my sister who truly understands the meaning of love.

A Merry Chase

Prologue

London, England
May 1813

"You *can't* be serious." Laurel Simmons struggled to understand what her fiancé, Archibald Devens, was telling her.

"I must say, Laurel, you're not taking this as well as I'd hoped," Archie drawled.

"That's all you can say? You tell me you're ending our engagement and you think *I'm* acting poorly?" she asked incredulously.

"I'm not ending our engagement," he pronounced shortly, "merely delaying our marriage for a few years."

Her emotions raced from sadness to confusion to rage. Unfortunately for Archie, it was rage that stayed with her. "I cannot believe you expect me to agree to sit back and wait patiently while you flit about Europe."

Archie released an exasperated sigh. "You are simply being difficult, Laurel. I've already explained to you that I need a few years to experience life."

"I thought you wished to experience life with *me,*" she said, unable to hide the pain in her voice.

"As did I," he agreed, "but now that I've inherited the title and estates, there is no need—"

Though Archie broke off his explanation, his meaning remained perfectly clear. "No need to marry for money now that you have inherited it, is there?"

His silence answered for him.

Closing her eyes, Laurel felt her heart split within her chest. From the moment she'd seen Archie, so handsome, so charming, she'd fallen in love with him and had decided in an instant that he was the perfect man for her. Though her father had urged caution, the heady taste of love proved too much of a lure for her eager seventeen-year-old heart.

Slowly, she raised her eyes to him again, seeing all too clearly the flush of agitation upon his features. The sweetness of first love began to harden within her. "I won't wait for you."

"Very well," he said stiffly, tugging down upon his vest. "If you are going to be so unyielding about this matter, Laurel, I'm not certain we'll be able to continue our relationship."

Laurel rose to her feet, facing Archie as an equal. "Consider our engagement over."

The flash of relief in his gaze chilled her to the core. "If that is your wish," he began smoothly, "then I shall make it known that you cried off, leaving you blameless and, hopefully, your reputation will remain unsullied."

"Does it really matter?" Laurel didn't understand how she could have been so silly, so foolish, not to have seen the shallow man lurking beneath the charming façade.

Archie cleared his throat. "No, I suppose it doesn't."

"Indeed," Laurel murmured, unable to keep from studying Archie. His true nature seemed so obvious to her now. Despite all of his flattery, all of his professions of undying affection, Archie was simply a fortune hunter.

A fortune hunter who now, having come into money of his own, had no need of marrying a fortune.

Slowly, Laurel turned away from him. "Goodbye, Archie," she murmured coldly.

"I wish you wouldn't be so difficult about this, Laurel," he protested, placing his hands upon her shoulders. "I've never had financial freedom before and I merely wish to experience some of the pleasures money can provide before I settle down to a staid, married life."

Stepping forward, Laurel shrugged out from beneath his touch. "What would you like me to say, Archie? Thank you for breaking my heart?" She drew back her shoulders. "It would be best if you left now."

Archie's heavy sigh feathered against the nape of her neck. "I shall miss you."

She flinched at his statement . . . and wished she hadn't. More than anything, Laurel wanted to cut out the softness inside of her, the innocent, gullible core that had believed in such an arrogant creature like Archibald Devens. Only one thought had the power to calm her.

She'd been saved from making a terrible mistake; she had time now.

Time to erase the mistakes of the past and to harden herself against ever making them again. Lifting her chin, Laurel glanced over her shoulder at Archie. "Good-bye," she said again, adding a harshness to her voice that brooked no argument.

"Au revoir, Laurel," Archie murmured in a tone which would have once melted her. "I wish you the best."

A moment later, Laurel heard Archie walk out of her life. He wished her the best, did he? A strangled sound rasped from her throat and she pressed her fingers against her mouth to keep from crying.

No, she would not spill any tears over that arrogant man. Instead, she would tuck the pain deep into her heart and never forget the invaluable lesson Archie had just given her.

After all, things could have been far worse.

She could have married the bastard.

Chapter

1

***

London, England
April 1816

*E*njoying a snifter of brandy at White's, Lord Royce Van Cleef relaxed against his leather chair, perfectly content to be alone. Suddenly, much too suddenly, his reverie was interrupted. His contentment disappeared as he watched his three friends approach.

"I say, Tewksbury, what are you doing here off by yourself?" asked Lord James Edridge, the boldest of the three.

"Wallowing in the solitude," Royce murmured, taking a sip of his drink.

Lord William Mull, an old friend from Oxford, shook his head, sending a lock of thick brown hair across his brow. "*You're* seeking solitude?" He snorted in disbelief. "Hardly likely. You've never been known for quiet reflection. Hell, Van Cleef, your wild exploits are legendary. Why, everyone knows that a party isn't considered complete without the ever-entertaining presence of the wicked Earl of Tewksbury."

"Yes, our dear Royce sets a standard of sowing those proverbial oats to which most men can only aspire. Being among that number, it only enhances my enjoyment of your company, Royce; I never know if I might learn some trick for charming the ladies," his friend, Steven Morris, finished in his usual verbose style. Smiling, Steven gestured to a nearby chair. "Do you mind if we join you?"

Holding back a sigh at the loss of his rare solitude, Royce accepted the company of his friends. "Not at all."

As the three men sank into their chairs, James murmured, "What a treat for me to be in the company of men." He leaned his head back against the leather chair. "Females can be so . . . vexing at times."

"Edridge is on the verge of an agreement with the lovely Miss Annabeth Porter," Steven explained to Royce. "From his tale of woe, I can only deduce the courtship is not progressing smoothly."

"Indeed not. Annabeth will make me crazed before I've even proposed to her," lamented James, his shoulders sagging forward.

"If you think she drives you mad now, just wait until after you've placed the ring upon her finger." William shook his head and laughed good-naturedly. "Only then will you understand the true meaning of misery."

"Misery? Excuse me, Mull, but aren't you the same chap who waxed on and on oh, so eloquently about the magical powers of love or some such foolishness. If I remember correctly, you even told us Meredith was your soul mate." Royce couldn't hide the derision in his voice. "What happened? Did your soul decide it didn't want a mate?"

Protesting swiftly, William waved Royce's words away. "Of course not. I still adore my Meredith . . . even if she *is* determined to drive me daft. It's simply that there is no end to the demands she makes of me." A horrified expression twisted his features as William confided, "I'm expected to dance attendance upon her night and day."

"I know *exactly* what you mean," agreed James. "Why, Annabeth asked that I accompany her on some dreadfully dull tour of our church gardens. Of course I didn't want to disappoint her, so I went." Glancing around, James leaned forward and lowered his voice to whisper, "I was mortified because I was the *only* gentleman in attendance. I felt quite the fool."

"The two of you are pathetic," Royce pronounced with a laugh. "You allow your women to lead you about as if you had rings through your noses."

Sitting up straighter, James began to sputter, "It's certainly easy for you to mock us, Van Cleef, because you've never fallen in love."

"That's true," Royce conceded with a grin. "I consider myself far too intelligent to ever believe in such rubbish."

"Are you calling us idiots?" asked William, his eyes narrowed in annoyance.

"Certainly not." Royce tipped his glass toward them. "Fools perhaps, but never idiots."

While James and William gasped with indignation, Steven burst into laughter. "Do stop teasing them so, Royce. It is most unkind," he said as he wiped at the corner of his eye.

"Oh, come now. Both William and James understand I'm jesting with them." Royce glanced at his two friends. "Don't you?"

"I'm quite certain you don't intend any offense, Royce, but I must say your attitude bothers me."

Royce lifted his brows at Willam's assertion. "My attitude?"

James leaned forward. "Yes. You know, Royce, it's the way you roll your eyes whenever we mention spending time choosing just the perfect gift for our ladies or how you scoff at us for swapping bits of poetry to enchant them."

Fighting to keep the grin off of his face, Royce replied smoothly, "I don't mean to insult you, James, but you're going about securing your lady in entirely the wrong way."

"Oh, do pray enlighten us," Steven urged, his voice lilting in sarcasm.

Both James and William nodded their agreement.

Looking at his friends' intent expressions, Royce was stunned that such a simple matter would escape their grasp. "It's quite obvious, really. Every time we meet, you are in the midst of concocting some sort of plan to enthrall your lady, yet you are always uncertain of her response."

"Well, of course we are," William sputtered, crossing his arms. "Ladies tend to be unpredictable."

"But that's just it, William; they shouldn't be!"

"So speaks the confirmed bachelor," James scoffed.

"Not true, James. I do indeed plan to marry." Royce took a sip of his brandy. "After all, every gentleman needs an heir."

"Oh, ho!" chuckled Steven. "Won't that be a sight

to see? The polished Earl of Tewksbury leaping through hoops for his lady fair."

Smiling over the laughter of his three friends, Royce waited until their sounds of mirth faded away before clarifying, "I will never resort to such nonsense, Steven. No, instead, I shall simply approach the matter logically and eliminate any foolishness."

"Oh, is that all?" William asked, shaking his head. "And how do you propose to do that?"

Royce sat his drink down on the table next to him. "It shall be very easy, really. Catching a bride is rather like . . . well, like a fox hunt."

"A fox hunt?"

James's exclamation made Royce grin. "Yes, indeed. Most of you expend many hours and tremendous energy toward pleasing your lady and capturing her interest with very little reward for your efforts." He paused, pointing a finger at his three companions. "And why? Because you've all forgotten the most important rule in fox hunting."

"And that would be what?" William asked dryly. "Don't forget to wear the proper attire?"

Laughing at his friend's quip, Royce leaned back in his chair, lacing his fingers over his lean stomach. "No, but I certainly wouldn't discount the importance of a gentleman's appearance. After all, it quite impresses the ladies when a man is turned out well."

"Then, pray tell us, Royce, for we can't stand the suspense much longer," James finished with a smile.

Royce eyed his friends. "The number one rule in fox hunting is—know your quarry." At their blank looks, he expounded upon his point. "Think on it for a moment. How often have you spent time and money on arranging for a romantic gesture only to have it ignored? But if you'd taken time to discover your chosen lady's interests, her passions, her amusements, then you would have chosen an item which would be certain to enthrall her."

"Know your quarry," retorted William, shaking his head. "You make it sound so easy."

"While you seem set on making it difficult."

Royce's quick reply brought a frown to William's face. "Words are easy, Royce. You'd find things weren't so neat and tidy if you ever set your cap upon a lady."

"I most certainly would not," Royce replied, conviction ringing in his voice. He'd spent far too many years observing the bumblings of his peers as they fell over themselves in order to please their ladies. No, he *knew* his way was far better . . . and a lot less wearying.

"You sound so certain of that fact," Steven pointed out.

"That's because I am."

"Are you confident enough to make a wager then?"

As ever, the idea of a challenge intrigued him. "A wager? About what? How often I can observe men behaving foolishly over their lady loves?" Royce rested his booted foot against the table before him.

"Hardly," snorted Steven. "I know that would be far too easy for you. No, instead I want to make a wager about whether or not your methods would be successful."

"Oh, I assure you the outcome would be most

satisfying." Royce lifted his glass toward Steven. "I wish you good hunting."

"Oh, not for me." Steven's mouth tipped upward. "I want *you* to prove it, Royce."

Royce's foot slipped off the table and thudded to the ground. *"Me?"*

Crossing his arms, Steven nodded firmly. "Of course. You've said that you intended to produce an heir, so why not choose your bride now?"

"Indeed," Royce murmured, struggling to keep his poise. Taking a deep breath, he forced himself to calm down even though the mere thought of chaining himself to one woman for the rest of his life caused panic to clutch at him. Royce exhaled heavily, focusing upon his future logically. After all, he had just admitted he intended to marry. So why not accept the challenge? He could choose his bride, then prove unequivocally that his method was far superior.

Warming to the idea, Royce sat upright in his chair. "You're quite right, Steven. It is time." He held out his hand. "I accept your challenge."

Steven swung his head side to side. "Oh, no, you don't. Not so fast, my friend, for I wish to make this challenge even more interesting."

Ignoring James and William as they shifted to the edges of their seats, Royce kept his gaze firmly fixed upon Steven. "And how do you propose to do that?"

"By choosing your wife for you."

Stunned, Royce didn't know how to respond until his sense of humor came to his rescue. He burst out laughing.

"I'm quite serious," Steven returned.

Royce caught his breath. "Yes, which is why you're grinning like a fool."

"That doesn't lessen my intent." Steven looked toward James and William. "Tell me, gentlemen, don't you think it only fair that we choose his bride for him? After all the boasting he's done about the ease of his method, he's made it clear that *any woman* would react to his approach. Therefore, I fail to see why Royce would hesitate to accept our choice."

Eagerly, James agreed. "Indeed, Royce. We promise to choose someone of good name and breeding."

"We'll even pick a lady who is easy upon the eyes," offered William. "Come on now, Royce. Don't be a dullard. Let's have a bit of fun."

"I don't know if you'd so eagerly embrace Steven's harebrained idea if you were in my place," Royce pointed out.

"Why should the woman matter to you as long as she is a lady of quality? You've already informed us that you don't believe in love," Steven pointed out.

"True, but I have no wish to marry a shrew."

Shaking his head, William patted Royce's shoulder. "We wouldn't condemn you to life with a harpy, my friend."

"I think Royce is afraid his method won't work, so he wants to choose a pliable female." James crossed his arms and leaned back.

Though he found James's challenge laughable, Royce decided to accept it anyway. What did he have to lose? "Very well then, you may choose my bride," Royce conceded smoothly. "However, I must agree with your choice and she must not only be a lady of breeding, but also one known for having an affable disposition."

Grinning like a fool, Steven thrust to his feet. "Excuse us for a moment, Royce, while my companions and I step over to the alcove to discuss our candidates."

Royce sipped at his brandy, smiling as he watched his friends argue. After only a few moments, all three men grinned and shook hands, then returned to their seats.

"Who is it to be?" Royce asked nonchalantly before taking another sip.

All three men answered in unison. "Lady Laurel Simmons."

Choking on his brandy, Royce proceeded to cough harshly. "You *can't* be serious," he finally rasped.

"And why not?" demanded Steven. "She meets all of your requirements: beautiful, well-bred, fine reputation, and affable."

"I easily concede those points to you, Steven, but she has also made it well-known that she has no desire to marry."

"What does that have to do with anything?" William asked, grinning like a jester. "You never made mention of their willingness to wed in your specifications for the perfect bride."

Split, gutted, and hung by his own words. Royce knew they had him.

"You must admit, Royce, everyone speaks well of her and with her beauty, it would not be a hardship to bed her," James added.

Looking at his friends, Royce considered their proposition. Laurel Simmons did indeed meet all of his specifications in a bride and from all accounts, her beauty was surpassed only by her wit. Certainly a self-confident, intelligent woman would breed strong sons.

Royce slapped the arm of his chair. "Very well, my friends. I accept your challenge." He paused, looking each man in the eyes. "With little effort and no heartache, I shall claim Lady Laurel Simmons for my bride."

"Well, then, old boy, let the game begin."

Chapter

2

It was happening again.

Laurel looked around the crowded ballroom, trying to catch sight of the person who was giving her the eerie feeling of being watched. While she didn't see anyone paying overt attention to her, the feeling lingered.

"Who are you looking for?"

Turning to face her dear friend, Harriet Nash, it took all of Laurel's concentration not to flush. "No one," she answered with a chagrined smile. "I'm simply allowing my vivid imagination too free a rein."

Harriet tipped her head to the side. "How so?"

"It's nothing, really," Laurel insisted, waving a hand in dismissal. "I'd feel silly even mentioning it."

"Then all the better." Harriet's lips twitched. "Feeling silly would be far preferable to suffering the boredom of this party, don't you think?"

Laughing, Laurel conceded the point with a nod.

"Very well, then, but you must promise not to laugh at me."

Harriet pressed a hand against her bodice. "You have my most solemn vow, my lady," she returned in mock seriousness.

"Jest all you like, but I *will* hold you to your word." Laurel took a deep breath before admitting, "For the past week, I've felt as if . . . someone was watching me."

Harriet's brows shot upward. "Truly?"

"Unfortunately, yes." Laurel glanced around the ballroom. "I'm certain it is my imagination playing games with me, but there are times when the feeling is quite . . . overwhelming."

"There must be something to your feeling, because you're not a woman prone to fanciful imaginings."

"That's very kind of you to say, Harriet," Laurel replied softly. "But I still tell myself that it's silly of me to . . ."

Her words trailed off when she caught sight of a man standing directly across from her on the dance floor and, something deep inside of her uncoiled as if she'd been waiting for this man to reveal himself to her.

Laurel's breath caught in her throat. "Oh my," she whispered breathlessly. Pressing a hand against her chest, she tried to steady herself, to remind herself that he was a stranger, yet her racing heart refused to calm. As if he could read her thoughts, the corner of his mouth tipped upward.

His intense gaze never faltered from her as he began to move across the room, uncaring of the couples weaving around the dance floor, unswerving in his path. The fluttering inside of her increased at his blatant disregard for the rules of polite society, but Laurel tried to squelch it.

Lifting her chin, she awaited his arrival.

Finally, he was standing before her, offering her his hand without greeting or introduction.

Instantly, Laurel was intrigued. Here she'd been expecting an introduction or a charming flirtatious remark, yet he'd given her neither. As she watched him, his mouth turned further upward, creating a small, seductive smile upon his handsome face.

His audacity tempted Laurel, making her wish she could accept his dare and place her hand in his outstretched one. Time seemed frozen as she waited for him to speak, to move, to drop his hand to his side. Instead, he remained silent, seemingly unaware of the attention his behavior was drawing.

Glancing about the room, Laurel saw how people looked at them, laughing at her apparent refusal to accept his hand. Chagrined, she returned her attention to the confident man standing before her.

Slowly, she placed her hand into his, accepting the bold invitation.

His smile spread into a broad grin as he twirled her into his arms and out onto the dance floor. The room spun about for Laurel as she clung to his shoulder, caught up in the moment. Though the urge to speak tempted her, Laurel remained silent, unwilling to disrupt the magic that flowed between them.

As she whirled about the room in the arms of a stranger, Laurel had never felt so unrestrained, so . . . wild. The challenge in his smiling gaze made her ache to throw caution to the wind, to shake free from the fetters of her past and allow this man, this wild, impetuous man, to shape her future.

Much to her disappointment the music died all too soon; she could have lived within that one magical moment forever. Escorting her back to Harriet, the man bowed to her, pressing a kiss to the back of her gloved hand.

As he straightened, Laurel couldn't resist saying, "I don't believe we've been introduced."

Smiling down at her, the gentleman held his tongue.

Dismayed, Laurel tried again. "Might I learn your name?"

"Perhaps in good time," he murmured, his voice low and melodious, before he turned on his heel and walked back across the room, fading into the crowd of people gathered there.

For a moment, Laurel could do no more than stare after him, too shocked to respond.

Turning toward Harriet, Laurel asked, "Do you know who that gentleman is?"

Shock widened Harriet's eyes. "You danced with a gentleman without even knowing his name?"

"Quite scandalous of me, wasn't it?" Laurel replied with a grin, still feeling the sweep of excitement. "Please answer my question. Do you know him?"

"Yes, I recognize him," Harriet acknowledged. "I was introduced to him earlier in the season."

"*Please*, Harriet." Laurel needed to know his name.

"Your charming new suitor is none other than the Earl of Tewksbury, Royce Van Cleef."

Lord Van Cleef. While she didn't know him, she certainly knew *of* him. His reputation as a bold rake was well established amidst society . . . a reputation that closely mirrored her ex-fiancé's. Archie had been known as a charismatic rake who all the ladies wanted to catch for their own. Lucky for her, she had the one thing the other ladies didn't—the largest dowry, Laurel thought darkly.

Making herself forget the tiny spark of excitement Royce had ignited, Laurel vowed she would be prepared if he ever tried to approach her again. No, she'd learned her lesson far too well to be taken in by a charming gentleman . . . regardless of how much he intrigued her.

Once was more than enough for her.

With a self-confident swagger, Royce made his way through the crowded ballroom into the seclusion of the empty library. Lighting a cigar, Royce waited for the arrival of his friends, who had undoubtedly observed the entire scene. An instant later, the door opened and William and James tumbled into the room. Trailing behind, Steven quietly shut the door.

"Welcome, gentlemen, and congratulate me on the first successful maneuver," Royce said, lifting his cigar.

William snorted derisively. "One dance doesn't warrant congratulations."

"Ah, but it was much more than a dance." Royce paused, remembering the bright shine of interest in Laurel's gaze. "It was an engagement of her senses."

"A what?" Steven asked with a laugh.

Taking a puff of his cigar, Royce smiled at his friend. "In other words, I've aroused her interest." He paused, staring idly at the glowing tip of his cigar. "All it took was a few discreet inquiries and I discovered that our dear Lady Laurel easily dissuades her ardent suitors with a friendly, albeit firm, rebuff." He glanced at his friends. "Since I had no desire to be added to that list of failures, I decided to capture her attention *before* advancing with my suit."

"And you believe a dance accomplished that for you?" James shook his head. "It is not a novelty for her to dance, Royce."

"True," he acknowledged swiftly, "but before I approached her, I made certain she felt my presence. I shadowed her every move and would catch her glancing about . . . as if she felt my gaze upon her."

"Which would only make her seek *you* out," concluded Steven with a nod. "Very clever, Van Cleef."

Bowing slightly, Royce answered, "Thank you, my friend." He lifted a finger. "But, there is more, gentlemen. Tonight when I approached her, I said not a word."

"No introduction?" William gasped, obviously shocked at Royce's behavior.

"None. And, after the dance when she requested my name, I told her she might learn it in time." Royce savored that tidbit, remembering her expression at his response. "Tonight when I saw her glancing about the room, I knew it was time to reveal myself, so I stood at the opposite edge of the dance floor and waited until she spotted me."

"Then you walked straight through the bloody dancers," James pointed out with a chuckle. "I'll admit, Royce, that when you stood there with your hand outstretched, I thought she would snub you."

"Not Lady Laurel," Royce replied softly. Observing Laurel this past week had given him great insight into her character, and he'd been positive that she couldn't resist the lure of the forbidden. "I knew she would accept."

"Without a proper introduction?"

Smiling at William's questions, Royce paused to draw upon his cigar. "Yes. You see, gentlemen, I don't believe this lady can be seduced with charm and sweet phrases." He shook his head. "The only way to entice her toward me is to tease her interest. By not revealing my identity, I made her wonder about me."

"And she will then seek out information about you," Steven finished, his eyes widening with comprehension. Tossing back his head to laugh, he finally managed to utter, "You are a clever one, Royce."

"Thank you," Royce accepted with a salute of his cigar.

Looking disgruntled, James pointed out, "Perhaps you did capture her attention this evening, but once she asks a few questions about you and discovers your reputation, the game won't be so easy for you."

"And I shall welcome the challenge." Royce thought back on the feel of Laurel in his arms. "Indeed, I shall."

"Where are you off to this fine day?"

Laurel glanced up from her morning repast to smile at her father. "Harriet and I are attending Lady Perry's lawn party today. Would you care to join us?"

Lord Percy Simmons shook his head vehemently. "Good God, no. Lady Perry makes my head ache with her endless chatter."

"You're terrible," Laurel chided with a laugh.

"No, merely honest."

"Perhaps, but regardless of the truth of your statement, that's not the reason you refuse to attend the party. If you were completely honest, you'd admit that Lady Perry scares you." Laurel shook her head. "No one would ever guess that the Earl of Sewley is *afraid* of Lady Perry."

"Poppycock," scoffed Lord Simmons, pointing at Laurel with his fork. "If you so much as whisper in jest about my avoidance of Lady Perry, I vow you'll not see the light of day for a year."

Rising to her feet, Laurel walked around the table to press a kiss upon the top of her father's graying head. "I swear your secret is safe . . . even though I don't believe your threat for a moment."

"Disrespectful daughter," Lord Simmons said in a mock grumble.

"So true, so true." Laurel patted her father's shoulders before moving toward the door. "I'm off. Remember we promised to attend Miss Andrews' musicale this evening."

Her father groaned in response.

Laughing, Laurel paused at the door. "Come now, Father. This evening shall be enjoyable. Miss Andrews has a most agreeable voice."

"For a tortured cat, perhaps," he mumbled, scooping up a forkful of kippers.

Smiling at his grumblings, Laurel hesitated over her next question. "Father," she began, trying to sound casual, "what do you know about the Earl of Tewksbury?"

Her father's fork stopped in midair as he jerked his head up to gaze at her. "Van Cleef? Royce Van Cleef?" He set down his fork with a clatter upon his plate. "You're asking me about a *gentleman?*"

Despite the fact that she was flushing, Laurel tried to act calm. "Why does that surprise you so?"

"Because you haven't shown even the slightest inkling or asked the vaguest question about any man in years. Not since that bast—" Lord Simmons broke off his reply, but his meaning was clear.

Royce Van Cleef *was* the first man she'd inquired about since Archie had broken their engagement. Why had she asked about him? Laurel didn't have an answer, but she didn't like the fact that she couldn't seem to get him out of her thoughts.

Shaking her head, Laurel told her father, "Don't bother answering that question. It was silly of me to even inquire about him." She smiled brightly, hoping it didn't look as forced as it felt. "I'll see you this evening."

Before her father had a chance to respond, Laurel stepped quickly from the room.

"Now isn't this an interesting development," murmured Lord Simmons as he decided to keep a closer eye upon his daughter and her interest in the Earl of Tewksbury. It was deuced difficult acting both mother and father to a headstrong girl, but since her mother had died during childbirth when Laurel had been three, Lord Simmons hadn't been given a choice. He only prayed he'd given Laurel all she needed to thrive. Her steadfast avoidance of men had alarmed him, so her interest in Lord Van Cleef was telling indeed. Perhaps his Laurel simply needed a little guidance in the matters of love.

And, after all, wasn't that the role of a father?

At the discreet knock on his study, Royce paused in his work. When his butler entered, anticipation swept through him. "Do you have any news for me?"

"Indeed, my lord," Giles answered, coming to stand in front of Royce's desk. "The Earl of Sewley's cook was most forthcoming."

"After you graced her palm with a few shillings," Royce said with a laugh.

"Quite so." Giles looked pointedly at Royce. "However, I believe you will find the information purchased well worth the cost."

Royce waited for his butler to continue.

"The lady will be attending Miss Andrews' musicale with her father this evening."

Leaning back in his chair, Royce steepled his fingers together. "Excellent. Thank you, Giles."

Giles bowed before retiring from the room.

Tapping the tips of his fingers together, Royce tried to decide how best to approach Laurel this evening. The thrill of the chase rushed through him as he imagined different ways to corner his quarry.

The boredom that had plagued him for so long was suddenly gone, swept away by the excitement of the hunt. Suddenly, Royce was fiercely glad that his friends had offered him such an intriguing challenge. Applying his theory toward catching a bride, Royce had found it easy to capture Lady Laurel's interest. Still, anticipating her next move sparked his imagination, making him feel more alive than he had in a very long time.

She'd felt soft and womanly in his arms last night and he found it all too easy to picture her in his bed.

Yes. This time, winning would be very sweet indeed.

It was all she could do to keep from squirming in her seat.

Laurel refused to glance behind her . . . despite the fact that she felt Lord Royce Van Cleef's eyes boring into her. The sweetness of Miss Andrews' voice did nothing to lessen her agitation, yet Laurel vowed not to let on that the Earl's attentions affected her in the least.

Instead, she focused all of her attention upon Miss Andrews as she trilled out the final note of the aria. Clapping loudly, Laurel glanced at her father, only to find him looking behind her. "Father, you should applaud now," she pointed out quietly.

"Hmmm?" Lord Simmons blinked, suddenly realizing what was happening around him. "Oh, yes," he murmured, clapping in appreciation.

"Whatever is on your mind tonight?" Laurel prayed he hadn't been looking at Lord Van Cleef.

Her prayers went unanswered.

"I couldn't help but notice that the Earl of Tewksbury has not taken his eyes from you all evening." As the singing began again, he leaned closer to Laurel. "It struck me as particularly interesting since he was the very same gentleman you inquired about this morning."

Fanning herself quickly, Laurel wished she could

control the telling color that flooded her face. "The only reason I asked after him was because of his behavior last night." She took a calming breath. "I ask you, Father, what manner of man sweeps a lady into a dance without so much as a word of introduction."

"One who wishes to capture a lady's interest," Lord Simmons replied with a grin. "It would appear he was quite successful."

"That issue is neither here nor there," she insisted firmly. "Lord Van Cleef's unwanted attention this evening is drawing far too much notice from everyone here."

"By tomorrow, a rumor that he is enamored of you will be on everyone's lips," her father predicted with a nod.

Narrowing her eyes, Laurel rasped, "There's no need to be so delighted about it."

"I beg to differ." Lord Simmon's smile dimmed. "It's been far too long since I've seen you take even the faintest interest in a gentleman. This does my old heart good."

Laurel shook her head. "Most fathers would be appalled at the Earl's blatant attentions, yet you seem ready to ask him into the library for a cigar and brandy."

"Not a bad idea."

Unable to hold in her smile, Laurel laughed softly. "You really should try not to be so overprotective, Father. It's quite trying."

"You, my darling Laurel," he began, flicking a finger against the tip of her nose, "have set up enough walls around yourself that it worries me far more that no gentlemen will persevere with you." He glanced back at Royce. "In fact, Tewksbury's tenacity is most admirable."

"Oh, Father, you really—"

"Shhhh."

The long hiss came from the matron sitting behind them. Flushing at the reminder of her surroundings, Laurel sank into silence, returning her attention back to Miss Andrews.

Regardless of her father's opinion, Laurel knew she needed to put an end to the Earl's behavior. As soon as Miss Andrews ended her performance, she would seek out Lord Van Cleef and dissuade him from ever bothering her again.

Rising the moment Miss Andrews finished singing, Royce moved toward the hallway. He glanced back once to make certain Laurel had taken his bait. Excitement flooded him when he saw her rising to her tiptoes, her face turned toward his empty chair.

Her expression of vexation only increased his enjoyment. Confidently he watched Laurel glance around the room and waited until her gaze fell upon him. Lifting her hand, she silently beckoned him to remain still as she began to work her way out of the room.

Chuckling to himself, Royce ignored her request and slipped down the hall. He paused once more, waiting for her to appear at the entranceway to the corridor, before easing into the Andrews' empty study. A chuckle broke from him as he neatly turned the tables upon Laurel, turning her into the pursuer.

He composed his features into a pleasant smile as she sailed into the room. "Good evening, Lady Laurel," he murmured before she could utter a word. "I must say I'm pleasantly surprised that you sought out my company this evening."

Tapping her fan against her hand, Laurel stepped closer. "It could hardly come as a surprise, my lord. Surely this was the precise reaction you sought."

A clever little fox, Royce thought, holding back his smile. "I'd hoped," he admitted softly.

Satisfaction warmed her features. "I'd surmised as much." Tilting her head to the side, Laurel said, "The only part that confuses me is why you're behaving in such an odd manner."

"Odd?" The corners of his mouth inched upward, forming a quizzical grin. "And here I thought I was being *intriguing.*"

"Even if you were, it is certainly not something to which I would ever admit."

Sighing lustily, Royce nodded his head. "Most certainly the wisest course, my lady. There is no telling what an arrogant scoundrel like me would do with a little encouragement."

"A truer word has never been spoken."

Royce couldn't help but appreciate the lovely sight she made, all flushed and flustered. His plan was progressing perfectly.

"At the risk of being blunt, my lord, I *must* ask that you desist in your unwavering attention."

"Why?"

His question took her aback. "I should think that rather obvious," Laurel asserted. "I find it most uncomfortable."

"Bravo for me then, for life would be terribly dull if one never felt unsettled."

Her brows lifted. "I believe I would survive."

"Perhaps, but you would merely be existing, not really living." Shrugging, Royce continued, "As for me, I'm thoroughly enjoying all that life has to offer. You should try it sometime, Laurel."

"I don't believe I gave you leave to address me so informally," she replied stiffly.

Closing the distance between them, Royce reached out and fingered the lace upon her sleeve. "We could easily remedy that," he pointed out.

Laurel lifted her shoulder, dislodging his hand. "That will not be necessary as I don't plan on spending time with you."

Not discouraged, Royce rubbed his jaw. "And why not?"

"Because we have *nothing* in common," Laurel pointed out.

"Of course we do," he denied, moving around the side of Laurel, circling her in the manner of hunter to prey. "Deep within your gaze, I see a spark of wildness . . ."

Laurel parted her lips, drawing in a swift breath.

". . . a burning urge to let yourself experience life to the fullest . . ."

Biting her lower lip, she looked lost within the seductive spell he was weaving.

". . . to indulge in your every fantasy . . ."

Instantly, she stiffened, and the spell was broken. Squaring her shoulders, Laurel stepped back from Royce and walked toward the door.

With her hand upon the knob, she glanced back. "I

learned a long time ago never to believe in fantasies, Lord Van Cleef, so in the future I would appreciate it if you would focus your attentions elsewhere."

Lifting his eyebrows, Royce remained silent as she walked from the room, her head held high. So, his bride-to-be was pricklier than he'd anticipated. Still, he was quite pleased with his results so far.

There could be no doubt that he was affecting her senses . . . despite her efforts to ignore them.

Chapter 3

⌘

"I vow, Harriet, if he approaches me this evening, I will be completely and utterly cool to him."

Tapping her toe in time to the music, Harriet slanted a glance at Laurel. "And your reason for rebuffing him is . . . what again?"

"Because he is an arrogant wastrel by reputation and action and I want nothing further to do with him," Laurel explained, wishing it were true. It worried her that she'd been unable to stop thinking about the rakish Earl. Indeed, she'd lain in bed and heard his whispers over and over again, enticing her, beckoning to her. Pressing a hand against her stomach, Laurel refused to allow herself to think of him any further.

The turmoil this man aroused proved an undeniable fact. Royce Van Cleef was dangerous to her state of being. She'd worked too hard to overcome her vulnerabilities to forget them even for a moment.

"You'd best prepare your rebuff, Laurel, for here Lord Van Cleef comes now."

At Harriet's whisper, Laurel jerked herself from her thoughts, lifting her head to watch Royce work his way toward her. The very instant their gazes met, Laurel recognized the terrifying, overwhelming, yet somehow intriguing emotions soaring through her.

While she knew in her head that she should avoid him, the way her heart leapt at the very sight of Royce made it impossible to remember *why* she should avoid him.

"My lady," he murmured, reaching out to clasp her hand before bowing to press a kiss onto her glove-encased fingers. "It is always a pleasure."

"My lord," she replied, proud of the coolness in her voice.

But Royce didn't seem to notice. Instead, he turned smoothly toward Harriet. "Ah, Miss Nash, how delightful to renew our acquaintance."

At Harriet's giggle, Laurel widened her eyes pointedly at her friend, but Harriet was too busy staring at Royce to notice. It would appear that he affected *every* lady's composure in the same manner as he affected hers.

"My lord," Laurel began briskly, "you are not honoring the bounds of our agreement."

"Agreement?" Shaking his head, Royce tilted one side of his mouth upward. "I never agreed to anything, my lady."

Knowing he spoke the truth, Laurel stood her ground nonetheless. "While that might be true, I still expected you to grant my request like the titled gentleman you are."

"Titled, yes. As to the gentleman part . . ." Royce shrugged lightly, grinning at her.

That made her laugh. She couldn't help herself, despite her determination not to yield to Royce's charm. If only he weren't such an appealing rogue, Laurel thought with a sigh.

"Excuse us, Miss Nash," Royce murmured as he caught Laurel's hand and tugged her onto the dance floor.

Before she could even utter a protest, she was in Royce's arms. "I believe I made myself quite clear," Laurel finally said as Royce twirled her into position.

"Perfectly," he agreed amicably, clasping her against him once more. "But I'm afraid I can't accommodate your request."

"Can't? Or won't?"

"Both." Caressing the small of her back, Royce slowed their steps. "I consider it my duty, as a gentleman, to teach you how to dream once again."

If he'd said that he was going to toss her onto the floor and kiss her madly, he couldn't have shocked her more. "Excuse me?"

"You heard me perfectly well the first time," Royce returned, tapping his fingers against the back of her hand. "Everyone needs fantasies, Laurel."

Stiffening in his arms, she retorted, "That's not true. I am perfectly content to keep myself firmly set in reality. Living in a dream world, my lord, is a foolish thing to do."

"Ahhhh," he sighed dramatically. "A realist, I see."

"Exactly."

"What a shame."

Laurel stumbled slightly. "A shame? I hardly think so."

"But it is," Royce protested lightly. "After all, fantasy is what gives life color, what makes the ordinary seem special."

His words created a yearning within Laurel. Once, she'd believed as he did, and then Archie had shown her how painful it could be to have your dreams shattered.

"Outside I have a magical carriage awaiting, one fit for a princess." His hand tightened upon her waist. "Come take a ride around the park with me, Laurel, and we'll pretend we're royalty taking a tour of our properties. Or we can even imagine that I'm a dastardly fellow who's abducted you and is intent on carrying you away to Gretna Green."

Oh, how he tempted her. Part of her yearned to accept the offer, to fall into his fantasy, but the other half demanded her to remember all she'd once been through. Feeling torn, Laurel shook her head slowly. "I . . . I . . . can't," she finished in a rush, regret sweeping through her.

"Cant? Or won't?" he asked, mimicking her.

The dance ended and Royce escorted Laurel back to Harriet's side. Bowing low, he pressed a kiss to the back of her hand. Yet as he straightened, he didn't release his hold. "I'll be waiting outside," he whispered softly. "Don't allow fear to control your destiny."

As Royce turned and walked toward the garden doors, she longed to race after him, yet still she held back.

Don't allow fear to control your destiny.

Was that what she was doing? Laurel's heart

pounded within her chest as the answer became all too clear. God help her, it was true. By allowing fear to dictate her actions, she'd inadvertently given Archie such power over her future. Yes, he'd taught her a lesson, but surely that didn't mean that she couldn't occasionally indulge in a harmless fantasy. As long as she went into it with a level head, she would be fine.

There was no way in heaven or on earth that she would allow Archie to defeat her.

"Laurel?" Harriet asked hesitantly. "Is everything all right? You look so . . . so . . ."

"Certain?" Laurel nodded once firmly. "I hope so, because that is exactly how I feel. Now if you'll excuse me for a moment, I'm going to take in a bit of fresh air."

Touching Laurel's arm, Harriet asked, "Would you like me to join you?"

"No thank you," she replied with a smile. "I'll see you in a short while."

Laurel took a few steps before turning around to grin at her friend. "Oh, and by the way, Harriet, for this evening you may address me as *Your Highness.*"

Laughing at Harriet's perplexed expression, Laurel spun around and hurried after Royce.

She wasn't coming.

Pacing before the gilt carriage he'd borrowed for the evening, Royce struggled to keep faith in his plan. He'd been quite certain that Laurel wouldn't be able to resist his challenge, yet with each passing moment, he grew increasingly less confident.

He'd planned these encounters so very carefully,

trying to ensure that he would spark her interest
without too much attention lest he scare her off.
And if she fell into the trap he'd laid this evening,
then he knew he had her. One romantic spin
around the park and Laurel would accept his offer
without hesitation.

And that would be that.

All nice and neat, tied with a gilded ribbon. Being
married to Laurel would be sweet indeed, Royce
thought as he remembered the feel of her in his
arms as they'd danced. Not to mention how pleasant it would be to lord over his friends the fact that
his was the far superior method for catching a wife.
A few strategically planned meetings and voilà!—a
marriage made of compatibility without any tedious
emotions mucking up the works.

"Well, my lord, this is indeed quite a fantasy
you've produced here."

At Laurel's teasing voice, Royce turned to face
her, relief flooding him along with excitement. Taking in the lovely picture she made in her evening
gown of silk and lace, he could imagine tasting her
sweet lips, molding her body against his, and satisfying the curiosity burning within him.

"What seems to be the problem, Your Highness?
Have you misplaced your royal scepter?"

"Now that's something I'd never misplace," he returned with a laugh, doubting if Laurel caught the
double entendre.

Tapping a finger against her cheek, she smiled at
him. "*That* is very reassuring."

Her quick wit left him with no doubt that she had
understood his teasing all too well. Pleasantly sur-

prised, Royce swept into a low bow, demonstrating
his best courtly manners. "Might I have the honor
of your company whilst we tour the royal gardens,
Your Highness?"

Mimicking Royce's gesture, Laurel dipped into a
curtsey. "It would be my pleasure, sire."

Quickly, Royce stepped forward, offering his arm,
and escorted Laurel over to the festooned carriage.

Pausing, Laurel eyed the purple and gold ribbons
decorating the horses' harnesses, her gaze sweeping
over the ornate gold scrolling that rimmed the roof
of the carriage. "This is most impressive, Royce."

"It belongs to a friend of mine," he admitted with
a wry grin. "It's a bit overdone for my tastes."

Laurel trailed her fingers down the etched panel
on the door, the languid movement echoing within
Royce until he yearned to feel that delicate stroke
against his skin. With a small shiver, he reined in his
thoughts.

Lifting her chin, Laurel pronounced grandly,
"Still, it is a most fitting ride for a personage such as
my royal self."

"Indeed it is," Royce agreed, handing her up into
the carriage.

Once ensconced within the plush velvet interior,
Royce sat back, entranced by the picture Laurel
made against the lush surroundings. "Might I say
that your beauty astounds me," he admitted quietly.

Smiling brightly, Laurel dipped her head regally.
"Your praise is most appreciated, sire," she said as
she brushed out her skirts. "However, I will admit
that I'd prefer it was my wit or my sense of fairness
or even my direct manner that attracted you."

Royce lifted an eyebrow. "I fear you do not understand my definition of beauty . . . for only a woman who possesses all the characteristics you mentioned can be considered truly beautiful."

"Ah, yes, the perfect response," she replied softly.

"Did you expect less from your courtier?"

Tipping her head to the side, Laurel smiled at him. "I thought you were His Royal Highness."

"I was, but I decided to switch," Royce admitted, shrugging lightly. "It's far more amusing to be your favorite admirer."

"Ahhh," Laurel murmured with a laugh. "Then why aren't you bowing at my feet?"

Without a moment's hesitation, Royce slipped onto his knees.

Laughing at his silliness, Laurel tugged at his sleeve. "Come up off of there, Royce, before you hurt yourself."

"Far better to bump my head than to offend your personage." He braced himself against the seat cushion for balance. "However, if it were a royal command—"

"It is," Laurel returned, tapping the seat beside her. "Now please get up before we hit a rut and send you flying."

"I would never disobey a royal decree," Royce murmured as he slid onto the seat next to Laurel. Tapping his fingers against his leg, he glanced around. "I must say, Your Highness, the view from your side of the carriage is far nicer than mine."

"Of course," Laurel sniffed, her lips twitching with suppressed laughter. "What else would you expect?"

"True enough." Royce leaned his head against the cushions, openly studying Laurel. "Seriously though, I am pleased that you decided to indulge in my little fantasy, Laurel."

Glancing away, Laurel shifted restlessly. "I almost didn't," she admitted in a whisper. "But then I decided not to allow myself to be robbed of pleasure simply because of past . . . disappointments."

"Past disappointments?"

She lifted an eyebrow. "There is no need to be so polite, my lord. I'm quite certain you know of what I'm alluding to."

"My name is Royce," he said firmly. "And if you refer to the incident with Lord Devens, then I am indeed acquainted with the subject."

"Incident?" Laurel smiled over the word. "Is that what they're calling a broken engagement these days?"

It was Royce's turn to raise his eyebrows. "Engagement? It was my understanding that no formal announcement had ever been made."

"Then you were misinformed."

Slowly, Royce lifted his hand to stroke one finger along the taut curve of her cheek. "It's rather a miracle that you accepted my invitation at all," he observed softly. "I shall consider myself quite lucky."

Holding still beneath his touch, Laurel finally let free a shaky laugh. "A gentleman as persistent as you, my lord, creates his own luck."

"Royce."

Laurel sobered, meeting his gaze with her own. "Royce."

Her soft whisper swept inside of him, tightening his chest, making him catch his breath in wonder at the odd sensation. Shaking his head, Royce struggled to pick up the thread of their conversation. "I do believe you're right," he murmured as he regained his balance. "The world belongs to those who make their own luck."

His fingers fell away from Laurel's cheek as she tipped her head to the side. "That sentiment is one you share with Archie, for he used to say the very same thing."

Stiffening, he took offense to her comparison. "I am *nothing* like that pansy-waist, Devens. Any gentleman who would cry off upon a lady deserves nothing but scorn."

"That's true," Laurel acknowledged. "Please accept my apology, Royce." Placing her hand upon his forearm, she continued softly, "I know you have far too much honor to ever deceive a lady."

Swallowing uncomfortably, Royce shifted in his seat. He was *nothing* like that dullard Devens and yet . . . he *was* deceiving her. His intent to marry her did nothing to lessen his culpability in the wager he'd made. Lord, if Laurel ever discovered the reason he'd begun this courtship, she would undoubtedly dismiss him without a word, cutting him off as quickly as she once did Devens.

Glancing away, Royce swallowed hard, determined to never let her discover the intent behind his courtship. "While I appreciate your sentiment, please don't place me too highly in your esteem. Like many gentlemen, I often feel the end justifies the means."

"Really?" Laurel leaned toward him. "When would that be the case?"

"I can't think of any particular instance at the moment," he evaded smoothly. "I'm simply trying to point out that, like most men, I believe that honor is more often than not a matter of opinion."

"I should think it would be rather black or white." She shifted her shoulders. "By its very definition, honor is a steady ideal, not a fluid notion."

"By whose definition?" snorted Royce.

Laurel tilted her chin upward. "By mine."

"While I find the concept admirable, Laurel, I also find it utterly improbable." Tugging on a ribbon dangling from her sleeve, Royce continued his argument. "For instance, if you have a friend who arrives at a formal affair wearing the most dreadful of gowns, what do you say if she asks your opinion about her attire? Honor would dictate that you answer honestly, thereby hurting your dear friend's feelings. Whereas, if you allow personal emotion to color your perspective toward honor, you would simply ease your way around the direct question by admiring the fabric or the color of the gown."

Blowing out her breath in a huff, Laurel leaned back against the cushion. "I do so hate it when you're right," she grumbled in mock ferocity.

"You'd best get used to it."

"Arrogant jackanapes," Laurel retorted with a laugh.

"Quite true." Grinning at her, Royce leaned closer. "And you enjoy my company for precisely that reason."

"Rubbish. The only reason I'm in your company

at all is because you bedeviled me until I agreed to spend time with you."

"What happened to your honor, my lady, to spout such a bald lie? You are in this carriage at this precise moment because of your pride."

"My *what?*"

"I believe you heard me," he returned, thoroughly enjoying their repartee. "If I hadn't dared you to meet me, I'm quite certain you would still be cowering in the ballroom."

"*Cowering!*" Laurel exclaimed, twisting in her seat to face him. "I assure you, my lord, I have never *cowered* in my life."

Meeting Laurel's affronted gaze, Royce leaned even closer. "Royce."

"The braying coxcomb," she added, her eyes sparkling with life.

Her sweet scent drifted upward, tickling his nose, teasing his senses. Dropping his gaze onto her lips, Royce longed to indulge in his private fantasy, to see if Laurel could possibly taste as wonderful as he imagined.

Unable to resist, he bent toward her.

❦

*L*aurel's breath caught in her throat as she watched Royce lean closer, his gaze fixed upon her now parted lips. Uncertainty mixed with desire within her as she struggled to remain still. Part of her wanted to turn away from his kiss, but the other half ached to experience it, to satisfy her burning curiosity.

Having found Royce fascinating from the first moment he'd approached her, Laurel wanted . . . no, needed, to ease her desire for this man. Perhaps then she could treat him as a friend instead of finding herself constantly plagued with unwanted passion for him.

Mere inches from her mouth, Royce stopped, his warm breath feathering across her lips, making her heart pound in anticipation.

"Laurel," he whispered, his voice achingly soft. With his gaze capturing hers, Royce grasped her hand, slowly lifting it to his lips. His eyes darkened as he pressed sweet kisses upon the tips of her fingers, the soft touch of his lips sending shivers of delight down her body.

Gasping, Laurel watched, transfixed, as Royce slipped the tip of her index finger into his mouth, his tongue curling around the sensitive flesh, before freeing it to the warm night air. All conscious thought escaped her as she quivered beneath Royce's expert touch, willing him to continue his sensual torment of her senses.

Turning her hand over, Royce pressed his lips against her palm, the softness of his mouth making her crave more. She leaned closer, wanting to feel his lips upon hers. Slowly, he lifted his head, bringing his mouth a breath away from hers. Anticipation washed over her as she awaited his kiss.

"I want nothing more than to kiss you at this moment," Royce rasped. "May I indulge in *my* fantasy, sweet Laurel?"

Only one answer sang in her blood. "Yes."

His expression held sensual promise as Royce closed the distance between them. Waiting breathlessly, Laurel watched him come closer, wetting her lips in anticipation. The first gentle sweep of his kiss caused her fingers to curve around his, holding him fast. Desire fluttered downward when he settled his mouth over hers, his lips tasting, searching for a deeper touch.

Groaning softly, Royce lifted his free hand, stroking across her cheek to hold her steady, before delving into her mouth, his tongue sweeping forward to claim her. Unknown delights soared through Laurel as she fell into the kiss. She'd never experienced such passion with Archie, never burned for more, never craved his touch the way that she craved this man's.

As if sensing her desire, Royce slid his hand along the curve of her jaw, stroking downward, until his fingers rested at the base of her throat. Breaking off their kiss, Royce pressed kisses along the path his hand had taken as he made his way toward the edge of her bodice.

Toying with the lace of her dress, Royce lifted his head to recapture her lips, swallowing her moan beneath his hungry kiss. When his fingers curved along the edge of her breast, molding the flesh into the palm of his hand, Laurel pressed eagerly against him, craving surcease from the burning torment within her. Her hands clutched at his waist as she arched upward, offering herself to him.

Disappointment flooded Laurel when, instead of accepting her invitation, Royce drew back slowly, ending their kiss in a light brush of his lips. A soft moan escaped her.

Lifting his hands to cup her face, Royce shook his head. "Laurel, my love, we must stop now . . . before I forget myself."

"But . . . but . . ." she stammered, before falling silent. How could she protest when she knew Royce had followed the wisest course? This man, this wonderful, infuriating, enjoyable man, had made her forget all she'd ever learned, all she'd experienced. The heady thought was also a frightening one.

In Royce's arms, she had lost control.

Even more disconcerting was the fact that Royce had obviously not been as affected by their kiss. He was, after all, the one to break it off. Gathering her composure, Laurel straightened and forced a smile onto her face. "I must thank you for retaining a hold upon your senses."

"I'd accept your thanks if that were true, but I must confess it was only the rapping on the door that brought me to my senses."

That thought warmed Laurel. "Rapping on the door?"

Sliding a velvet drape aside, Royce motioned toward the carriage window. "Our coachman was merely letting us know that we've arrived back at our party."

Only then did Laurel realize that the carriage was no longer moving. Giddiness and relief welled inside of her. "My goodness, Royce, you certainly do know how to treat a lady to a fantasy."

The intensity of his gaze made Laurel gasp. "Not everything was a fantasy, Laurel," he whispered softly. "With a reality like the one we just shared, there's no need for enhancement. Our reality is better than most people's dreams."

She couldn't deny it. Somehow, some way, this man had pushed past all of her defenses and safeguards and gifted her with a dream come true. Unbidden, she arched toward him.

"As much as I'd like nothing more than to kiss you again, it might be best if I accompany you back to the ball now." Grinning rakishly, Royce leaned forward to whisper, "After all, everyone always notices when the Royals step out for a few moments."

Their game reestablished, Laurel tapped Royce lightly on the arm. "So very true, my humble servant." She lifted her chin. "And because I'm in a generous mood, I shall even forgive you your liberties with my person."

"Most generous, indeed," Royce replied thoughtfully, before opening the carriage door.

Gazing at Royce where he stood in the doorway, offering her his hand, Laurel felt happiness well up inside her. For the first time in years, her future looked bright once more.

With a smile, Laurel accepted his hand and allowed him to assist her from the carriage . . . and back into reality.

Satisfied.

Yes, if he had to pick one word to describe how he felt at this very moment, it would be satisfied, Royce decided as he stepped back into the ballroom. Automatically, he searched for Laurel, spying her across the room where she stood conversing with her friend, Henrietta . . . or was it Harrietta? Shrugging away the unimportant question, Royce instead focused in upon Laurel, noticing her heightened color.

A finger of desire curled inside of him at the realization that he'd put that flush upon her face. Memories of their passionate embrace cheered him; her sensual nature simply enhanced the prospect of marriage, an added bonus to an already wise decision.

Royce tried to keep the smile of triumph from his face. The task proved difficult as he considered how easily he'd snared his quarry. Tomorrow he would call upon her father and formally ask for her hand in marriage. After their lovely carriage ride, Royce had no doubt that his strategy would proceed as planned.

"Your methods appear to be failing," James observed as he handed Royce a glass of port.

Glancing at his friend, Royce lifted a quizzical brow. "Excuse me?"

"I said that your theory about catching a bride was off the mark." James tilted his head toward Laurel, who stood across the room. "Proximity does count in these matters."

"I must agree with James," William added as he joined them. "You can hardly get the job done if you're on different sides of the room."

Crossing his arms, Royce allowed a smile to ease onto his face. "I'm sorry to disappoint you, gentlemen, but the trap has already snapped and the vixen has been captured. All that remains is claiming the prize."

"Come now, Tewksbury. Wishful thinking there, isn't it?"

"Not in the least." Royce returned his attention toward James. "Have you ever heard of the Earl of Hath's penchant for elaborate carriages?"

"Who hasn't?" replied James with a shake of his head. "But what does that have to do with attracting Lady Laurel's attention?"

"Patience, patience." Shaking his head, Royce grinned at his companions. "That is part of your problem, gentlemen. You are so quick to question, so eager to act, that you forget to take time to *strategize* your attack."

"Strategize?" exclaimed William. "Good God, man, you're proposing marriage, not a bloody war."

"When you compare the two logically, there's not much difference. In both cases, the best way to accomplish your goal is to treat it like the conquest it is and plan for success."

Rolling his eyes, James muttered, "You make the entire business sound so . . . cold-blooded."

Again the memory of Laurel's embrace shimmered in his mind. No, what he had created with Laurel in that carriage was anything but cold. Shrugging, Royce answered, "Not at all. I'm merely applying my intelligence, gentlemen, to accomplish the task in the most efficient manner." Swiftly, Royce told them of the carriage ride, omitting, of course, the passionate kiss. Some things weren't meant to be shared. "So by challenging Laurel, I made her come to me, allowed it to be her decision to accompany me, thus, perhaps in a small way, overcoming her antipathy toward marriage and males in general."

William glared at him. "Does everything come so blasted easy for you, Tewksbury?"

Brushing his hands together, Royce nodded succinctly. "Usually," he admitted cheerfully. "I've found that whenever a gentleman applies logic to a problem, the solution is easily discovered." Royce took in the disgruntled stares of his friends and smiled. Lord, it felt wonderful to be proven right.

"Excuse me, gentlemen, but I need to see about returning a carriage," Royce murmured as he moved off, secure in the knowledge that the night's work had been most profitable.

"The bastard's too smug by half," grumbled James as he took another swig of brandy. He'd joined William at White's to lament their friend's good fortune.

"He's got good reason to be," William pointed out glumly. "He usually succeeds where we mortal men fail miserably."

Swirling the brandy around in his glass, James nodded in agreement. "Personally, I think it high time he learned a lesson in humility and discovered what life is like for the rest of us."

"We already tried that." William sank back into his chair. "And all we did was hand him yet another victory."

"Hmmmm," murmured James, rubbing a finger along his eyebrow. "Lady Laurel proved a disappointment. I thought for certain she would make Royce run circles 'round her before granting him her hand in marriage."

"You can hardly blame her. After all, she doesn't realize she's the quarry in Royce's sights."

"No, she doesn't—" Bolting upright in his seat, James slammed his glass down onto the table. "That's *it!*"

"What the devil are you talking about?"

Slapping a hand onto William's shoulder, James crowed, "I'm talking about a way to bring our illustrious friend down a notch and to make this wager of ours into an actual challenge."

William shook his head. "I'm afraid I still don't follow you, James."

"What I am proposing, my friend, is that we let the lady in on the wager."

William's eyes widened. "You want to betray Royce's confidence?"

"I'd rather do that than give him the upper hand once again." Sitting forward, James tried to convince William to agree to his plan. "Think on it, William. If Lady Laurel were to *overhear* us discussing the wager, then we wouldn't be betraying Royce. After all, we can't control who hears us speaking, now can we?"

"I don't know," William hedged. "It seems rather underhanded to me."

"And what if it is? Would you rather look upon Royce's bloody smug face as he waltzes the lady down the aisle? Besides," James continued, "you know Royce well enough to realize he'll enjoy the challenge. He's easily bored these days, so we'll actually be *helping* him . . . in a fashion."

"Well." Slowly, William nodded. "Perhaps you're right. If Royce convinces Lady Laurel to marry him so quickly, he'll soon tire of her. Yet if she resists his charms, it might make him appreciate her more. So, your plan might help her as well."

James smiled as he listened to William try to convince himself that the entire plan was for Royce's own good. Hell, he wasn't above admitting that he wanted to see Tewksbury taken down a notch or two. But if William needed to justify their actions, then so be it.

"All right," William agreed finally. "I'm in."

"Wonderful!" James cried as he raised his glass in a salute.

"What do we do now?"

"Why, we follow our chum's advice—apply our intelligence to the matter, and devise a strategy." James was more than ready to increase the stakes in the game. "It's time we set a trap of our own for the spirited Lady Laurel."

Chapter 5

"You're awfully quiet today, Harriet," Laurel observed as she set down the hat she'd been admiring. "Is something bothering you?"

After a moment's hesitation, Harriet murmured, "Well, no. Everything is perfectly . . . fine."

Placing her hands upon her hips, Laurel turned her full attention to her friend. "That lackluster response was hardly convincing, which only makes me even more curious as to why you're not being truthful."

Harriet's gaze darted around the milliner's shop. "Excuse me?" she squeaked before clearing her throat and reclaiming her composure. "Are you insinuating that I am *lying* to you?"

Seeing the guilt in Harriet's expression, Laurel nodded firmly. "Indeed I am," she replied with a laugh.

"Well!" Harriet sniffed. "I never—"

"Don't waste your efforts on me, Harriet Nash." Laurel waved her hand, dismissing Harriet's protest. "You won't be able to distract me by acting affronted. We both know it's simply an attempt to change the subject." Leaning closer, Laurel looked into Harriet's face. "Now tell me what is bothering you."

Fiercely, Harriet shook her head. "I don't want to tell you. It will upset you far too much."

"Believe me, Harriet, nothing could upset me on this wonderful day." Memories of the previous evening, of her delicious kiss with Royce, were still with her. "Absolutely nothing."

"I know you're still excited from your adventure . . ."

"My *grand* adventure."

If anything, her correction made Harriet look even paler. "Indeed," she replied weakly.

Something in Harriet's voice caused Laurel to pause. "Whatever is wrong with you, Harriet?" But before her friend even had a chance to respond, a horrible thought struck Laurel. "Does your distressing news have something to do with Royce?"

Glumly, Harriet nodded.

"Well?"

"I don't want to tell you," Harriet moaned, placing a hand upon Laurel's arm. "I was so very happy for you last night when you told me about your carriage ride and I don't want to spoil anything for you."

Unwilling to continue the argument, Laurel didn't say a word; she merely looked at her friend. Beneath her steady gaze, Harriet shifted in discomfort.

"Very well," Harriet said with a sigh. "Before I called upon you, I went to the park to feed the swans."

"As you do every day..." Laurel prompted, wondering where Harriet was leading.

"Yes, indeed, but this morning there were two gentlemen already feeding the swans as I arrived. Even though I stood a few feet away, I could hear their conversation quite clearly."

"Obviously they said something that upset you." Suddenly, Laurel connected the two pieces of their conversation. "Did they see me in the carriage with Royce?" she gasped, alarmed at the thought that someone had witnessed her intimate embrace. She'd hoped that everyone would simply assume she'd stepped out for a bit of fresh air. After all, she and Royce had left and then returned separately. But perhaps someone had noticed both of their absences and pieced it together. "Did they?" Laurel asked again.

"No."

Laurel released her indrawn breath. "Thank heaven."

"It was *much* worse," Harriet said softly.

With four words, Harriet had destroyed her sense of relief, making her tense once more. "I can't stand this any longer, Harriet. You need to tell me what you overheard."

Straightening her shoulders, Harriet nodded. "It's far better that you hear it from me than from... someone else." She took a deep breath, before blurting out, "Royce Van Cleef is spending time with you... on a wager."

Laurel struggled to make sense of Harriet's words. "I don't understand," she whispered through a suddenly tight throat.

Harriet's gaze darkened in sympathy as she

placed her hand upon Laurel's shoulder. "I'm so sorry, Laurel, but it's true. I overheard Lord Edridge and Lord Mull discussing it this very morning. It was quite clear from their conversation that Royce Van Cleef has been spending time with you in order to win a bet."

Drawing herself up, Laurel fought to retain a hold upon her emotions. She'd made a dreadful mistake by trusting Royce. He'd already stolen her hard-won faith; she wouldn't allow him to take her dignity as well.

Lifting her chin, Laurel quietly asked, "Exactly what is the wager?"

"Apparently, Lord Van Cleef felt that finding a bride would—"

"*Finding a what?*"

"A bride," Harriet repeated. "He decided it was time to marry and remarked to his friends, the two gentlemen I overheard, that they'd gone about the business of securing a wife in the wrong fashion."

"The *business* of securing a wife," Laurel murmured as anger began to simmer inside of her. "And did the two gentlemen say anything *else* about this lovely wager?"

"Only that Lord Van Cleef had applied the rules of fox hunting to catching you and felt the battle was won. He intends to call upon your father to finalize his plan." Squeezing Laurel's arm, Harriet tried to smile. "At least this time you uncovered Lord Van Cleef's true nature *before* you agreed to marry him."

Bitterness swelled within her. "There shouldn't have been a 'this time' at all, Harriet. I foolishly allowed myself to forget the most important lesson of my life." Memories of Royce's touch flittered through her mind, but Laurel pushed them aside. "I *won't* forget ever again."

"Royce!" murmured Elizabeth Van Cleef as she set down her quill. "I wasn't expecting you to call upon me."

"Hello, Mother." Bending down, Royce pressed a quick kiss onto his mother's cheek in their traditional polite greeting. Cool and polite described their relationship to perfection. "I apologize for coming around unannounced, but I have some important news I felt I should share with you."

His mother lifted her brows.

"Within a few days, I shall propose to Lady Laurel Simmons."

Slapping both hands on her desk, Elizabeth pushed to her feet. "You *can't* be serious."

"It seems I am destined to disappoint you, Mother, for I assure you I am most serious," Royce replied, bracing himself for her response.

"Laurel Simmons has neither the reputation nor the breeding for her to become the next Countess of Tewksbury." Rounding her desk, Elizabeth placed herself directly in front of her son. "I must insist that you rid yourself of this nonsensical decision and choose a more appropriate bride."

"You insist?" Royce asked, his voice low and steady.

"As your mother, it is my right. If your father were alive, naturally he would have guided you in this choice, though I doubt if he would have been of much assistance. However, it is now up to me to help you make a wise decision."

"I *have* made a wise decision, Mother," Royce said firmly. "Lady Laurel is a fine, well-bred lady who will do our family name proud."

"She has a scandal in her past, a broken engagement."

"Yes, I know."

Her eyes widening in amazement, his mother shook her head. "You *know?* Yet you still consider her worthy of the title I have struggled to protect?"

"I fail to see how the matter of her broken engagement would in any way affect the honor of our family name," Royce countered calmly, far too accustomed to his mother's rigid stance to become upset. "Lady Laurel has many fine qualities which are more than befitting the station."

"I won't allow you to do this," Elizabeth said, setting her jaw. "It would not be in your best interest."

How could his mother possibly know what was in his best interest? She didn't even know him.

Sadness touched him at the realization that his relationship with his mother had never allowed for warmth or acceptance. His entire life had been filled with lectures on duty, reminders of his obligations, and stern repercussions when he failed. Early on, he'd learned to strategize in order to outwit his mother.

However, this time, for the first time, he wasn't going to mince words.

"I wasn't asking your permission, Mother," Royce said softly, meeting his mother's glare without flinching. "I was merely informing you of my decision."

Despite her protest, Royce bowed in farewell,

turned on his heel, and strode from the room, leaving his mother sputtering behind him.

Fox hunting!

Fuming at the very arrogance of the man, Laurel vowed to teach him a lesson. When Archie had betrayed her, she'd allowed him to simply walk away, leaving her to face the gossip and innuendos.

And she'd survived.

But she'd made the mistake of trusting Royce and relearned the most painful lesson of her life. While she'd allowed Archie to walk away unscathed, Royce would not be so lucky.

All she needed to do now was figure out a way to hand Royce his comeuppance. After all, any man who tried to "capture" a wife by using the rules of fox hunting deserved—

Fox hunting.

That was it! She would turn the tables on Royce by countering all of his maneuvers, twisting him around until he didn't know who was the hunter and who was the prey. It was a perfect plan. She would go home and question her father about the strategy behind the hunt. Then, she'd apply her newly learned strategy on Royce and see how *he* enjoyed being the quarry for a change.

If Royce wanted a hunt, then she was more than willing to accommodate him.

Let the game begin!

Chapter 6

≈

Despite the people milling about the opera hall, Laurel was aware of the instant Royce entered the room. Fighting every instinct to flee, Laurel did her very best to keep her mind on the conversation at hand and to ignore Royce's determined strides toward her. "You are quite the charmer, Lord Morris," she murmured before tapping his forearm with her fan. "I vow I'm in danger of losing my heart around you."

Steven laughed at her quip. "If only that were true, my lady," he returned smoothly.

Coming to a halt next to her, Royce clasped Laurel's hand and bowed over it. "Good evening, Laurel," he said, his tone low and intimate. Barely looking at his friend, he continued, "Hello, Steven. I wasn't expecting to see you at the Opera this evening. I thought you were still in the country."

"No, I decided to rejoin society for a bit." Steven smiled brightly at Laurel. "And it's a lucky thing I did too. Otherwise I wouldn't have been afforded the pleasure of this lovely lady's company."

Royce's smile grew strained. "My Laurel is a delight, isn't she?"

"*Your* Laurel, my lord?" she asked with a forced laugh. "How you jest, sir."

A slight frown etched Royce's brow. "I wasn't trying to be amusing."

"There you go again," Laurel replied playfully. "Pretending to be serious as if we have some sort of arrangement or understanding. You're going to give people the wrong impression, my lord."

Royce grew very still. "Might I have a word with you?" he asked quietly, before glancing at Steven. "In private."

Before Laurel could refuse Royce, Steven took the decision out of her hands.

"Subtlety was never your strong suit, old boy," Steven remarked dryly. "But nevertheless, I do believe I'll . . . take a stroll."

"There's no need for that," Laurel said as brightly as she could manage while reaching out to clasp Steven's arm. "I was so enjoying our conversation."

Lifting her hand to his mouth, Steven pressed a kiss onto her fingers. "As much as I'd love to keep you company, I'm afraid that I'm far too much of a coward." He glanced at Royce. "You see, I've seen Royce practice his fisticuffs . . . and he has quite the right hook." Fingering his jaw, Steven added, "And I rather like the way I look."

Smiling at Steven's quip, Laurel drew in a deep, steadying breath before she turned to face Royce. "Your friend is utterly charming, my lord."

"How did we get back to 'my lord'?" Royce asked, clearly puzzled.

Touching her hand to her forehead, she apologized prettily. "How foolish of me," she replied with a laugh. "Naturally, I meant to say Royce. Perhaps my mind is still spinning with all of Steven's compliments."

Royce looked nonplussed. "I notice you have no trouble remembering to address my friend by *his* first name."

She broadened her smile, deciding to let him make of her response what he would.

Apparently, the conclusion he drew was not favorable. Frowning, Royce took a step closer, ensuring their conversation wouldn't be overheard. "I'm afraid I'm at a loss, Laurel. After our carriage ride, I thought we understood one another. I thought we were becoming . . . intimates."

Immediately a spark of fury ignited within her. He'd *lied* to her! That's the only thing that Laurel understood, the one thing of which she was certain. "Of course we're friends, Royce." She fluttered her fan toward him. "In fact, I owe you a great debt of gratitude."

"You do?"

"Most certainly," she replied. "I do so appreciate you encouraging me to indulge in my fantasies, to allow myself to be swept away. I now realize that I'd been shutting myself off from all sorts of eligible men." Laurel kept her tone light and airy. "I can't thank you enough for encouraging me to let go of the past."

Royce visibly relaxed. "It relieves me to hear that,

Laurel. In fact, there's a private matter I wish to speak—"

"Is there?" she interrupted. "That is quite the co-incidence, then, for I wanted to ask you a question as well." Leaning in even closer, Laurel glanced around the room. "Is Steven courting anyone?"

She watched with great satisfaction as Royce clenched his jaw so tightly that a little tick started jumping in his cheek. "Steven?" Royce hissed. "Why the devil are you making inquiries about *him?*"

Shifting her expression into one of disbelief, Laurel sent another quick glance around the room, knowing her drifting attention would upset Royce further. "I should think that would be rather obvious, Royce."

His shock was clear. "You're interested in that lech, Steven? Is that what you're insinuating?"

"Shhh," she whispered, silently pleased at his anger. "I don't know why you find it so hard to believe that I could be intrigued by your friend. He's really a lovely gentleman. But please don't worry overmuch about him. I'm not quite ready to settle upon any one gentleman. I'm finding flirting all too enjoyable at the moment."

A vein in Royce's temple began to pulse alarmingly.

"And I have *you* to thank for my new-found pleasure. If you hadn't encouraged me to revisit my dreams, I never would have even *considered* marriage again." She reached out and patted Royce on the arm. "You're a wonderful friend, Royce, and I'll never forget all you've done for me."

Looking pale, Royce just shook his head, obviously at a loss for words.

Extremely pleased with herself, Laurel decided it was time for her grand exit. Glancing around again, she gave a quick wave to Harriet, who stood across the large foyer. "Oh, good. There's Harriet," Laurel began, glancing at Royce. "You wouldn't mind if I joined her, would you, my lord? I've got *so* much to tell her!"

Tossing him a grin over her shoulder, Laurel felt his eyes upon her as she walked across the room.

Victorious.

If she had rapped him across the face with her fan, she couldn't have shocked him more. Royce watched Laurel saunter away, too stunned to call her back. Hell, he wasn't even quite certain he could speak.

What the devil had happened? He'd been so certain that his plan was progressing perfectly, never once considering this outcome. What the devil did she think she was doing, flirting with Morris and Lord knew who else? He'd wanted, yes, he'd *urged*, Laurel to forget her past, to cut off the shackles of fear that had burdened her for far too long. But never once had he imagined that she would embrace her freedom with such . . . enthusiasm.

Dear God, he'd created a monster!

Rubbing two fingers against his temple, Royce tried to set his annoyance aside. What he needed to do now was come up with another plan to overcome this setback.

If he didn't devise a new strategy . . . and quickly, he just might lose the prize. There was no way he could think properly while watching Laurel flirt outrageously with every man in the room. He'd head over to White's and enjoy a drink while concocting his next move, then, in the morning, he'd pay a little visit to his old friend, Steven . . . and dissuade the man from pursuing any interest in Laurel.

He only hoped he wouldn't have to visit every eligible gentleman in London before the game was won.

"I can see quite clearly now that I handled the entire situation incorrectly," Royce admitted, handing a brandy to William. "My only excuse is that she took me completely by surprise." He gestured toward James, who sat next to William. "I ask you, how is a man supposed to respond to his lady announcing she's going to put herself on the market?" Snorting once, Royce shook his head. "No gentleman worth his salt could use charm in that situation."

"Indeed not," William concurred. "The fact that you were able to handle the matter as well as you did is commendable."

Mollified, Royce sat back in his chair. "I thought so as well."

"What are you going to do next?" James asked as he gestured for another drink.

"Obviously I'm going to have to shift my plan . . . as my quarry has proven more elusive than I first thought."

Shifting in his chair, William asked, "And does that worry you?"

Royce considered the question. "At first her evasiveness did, but now I'll admit that I find her skill at countering my every move quite challenging."

"I knew it!" James crowed, clapping his hands together.

When William kicked at James's booted foot, Royce wondered at their peculiar behavior. What was wrong with the two of them? But before he could voice his questions, James began to speak again.

"What I mean is, I knew you'd enjoy the added challenge."

William nodded eagerly. "Indeed, you're quite the hunter."

"Thank you, William. It's amusing that you say that, because it ties in so neatly with the new plan I've devised."

With a gleam in his eyes, James leaned forward. "Oh?"

Smiling at his friends, Royce took a sip of his brandy before responding, "I'm going to enlist the aid of another hunter." He took in his friends' befuddled expressions and hoped the change in strategy would affect Laurel in much the same manner. "After all, it's a well-known fact that a fox hunt is far more successful when it is a group activity."

"Well, I'm certainly willing to help," William piped up, his response seeming a tad too energetic to Royce.

"As am I," James chimed in.

"Thank you both, but I believe the aid should come from someone close to Laurel." Folding his hands onto his lap, Royce wondered at their unexpected enthusiasm. "Someone she'd never suspect."

"Come now, Royce, you can't leave us dangling." James glanced toward William, the furtive look striking Royce as odd. "Give us a name."

Deciding that his friends were merely worried that he'd win their wager, Royce finally answered, "Lord Percy Simmons, The Earl of Sewley."

William's brandy sloshed in his glass. "Lady Laurel's own father?"

"One and the same."

"What makes you so certain that he'll help you?" James asked.

Folding his arms across his chest, Royce answered easily, "What father doesn't wish to see his daughter married?"

"Brilliant," whispered William with a shake of his head.

Royce called for another round of drinks as he basked in his friends' astonishment and praise.

The game was about to get very, very interesting.

"I appreciate you seeing me, sir," Royce said as he took a seat in Lord Simmons' study.

Inviting Royce to call him Percy, Laurel's father offered Royce a drink. "I know it's a bit early yet for spirits, but I'll happily join you if you care for a nip."

With a grin, Royce accepted.

After handing Royce his glass, Lord Simmons claimed the seat across from him. "I do believe this is the first time you've ever called upon me, Van Cleef," he said, his tone pleasant. "And since my daughter has mentioned you in the past few days, I assume you're here with regard to Laurel."

Admiring the older man's directness, Royce knew he'd made the right choice in seeking Laurel's father's aid. "Indeed I am." He set down his glass and leaned forward, resting his elbows on his knees. "I wish to ask for Laurel's hand in marriage."

Lord Simmons choked on his sherry. "Good Lord, Tewksbury, you should warn a man when you're about to shock him like that." Taking a deep breath, he regained his composure. "I thought you were here to ask permission to call upon her. It seems a bit premature for talk of marriage."

Stiffening, Royce stated, "I assure you my intentions are completely honorable."

"Of course they are," Lord Simmons replied without hesitation. "That was never in question. I'm merely stunned at the impetuous nature of your proposal. After all, it's not as if you've known my daughter long enough to become smitten with her."

The tension inside of Royce released a bit. "While it's true we haven't known each other very long, the time has been sufficient to assure me that Laurel and I have quite a bit in common. I believe we would suit well. Indeed, I greatly admire your daughter."

Lord Simmons lifted his brows. "Admire? Hardly the emotion one wants when entering into a marriage."

"I beg your pardon, sir, but I disagree. I believe a solid relationship is based upon companionship, loyalty, and respect."

"With your chums, true, but not with your wife!" exclaimed Lord Simmons with a shake of his head.

"Why not?" Royce challenged. "If more marriages were approached in a logical fashion, then there wouldn't be so many affairs or indiscretions."

"There would be *more*. A man would swiftly grow bored in a marriage to a woman he *respected*," Lord Simmons nearly spat the word. "Thus increasing the rate at which he seeks . . . female companionship."

Warming to the subject, Royce sat back in his chair. "I disagree, sir. After all, if a man is not only physically but mentally satisfied within a marriage, then he will be less apt to look elsewhere for companionship." He spread his hands wide. "After all, why should he? He has everything he could ever desire right in his own home."

Chuckling, Lord Simmons lifted both of his hands, warding off further argument. "All right, you win. I'm not about to get embroiled in a long discussion about the merits of marrying for passion as opposed to marrying for compatibility. That is your business."

"Not if your daughter accepts me, then it becomes yours as well."

"No," Lord Simmons clarified, "it becomes my daughter's business."

Lord Simmons' response left Royce exasperated, but he quickly checked the emotion. It would hardly do to yell at his future father-in-law. Keeping his voice calm, Royce asked, "Might I ask for your daughter's hand in marriage?"

Lord Simmons shrugged. "It is perfectly fine by me."

"Then can I count upon you to encourage her that I would make the ideal husband? I believe your opinion would matter greatly to her."

Lord Simmons shook his head. "I'm sorry, Tewksbury, but this is something you'll have to do on your own."

"But don't you wish to see your daughter happily settled?"

"Of course. Any father wants that for their daughter, but I also have to leave the choice up to her."

Lord Simmons' response baffled Royce. "Why? I'd think after her troubled experience with Devens, you would be eager to nudge her toward someone you know has the best intentions."

"Don't you think it's a bit presumptuous of you to assume that you are best for Laurel?" Lord Simmons leveled a sober gaze at Royce. "*I* can't say that for certain. I don't doubt your honor, nor your sincerity, but I do wonder if your approach to marriage would best suit my daughter."

Royce watched as his well-laid plan began to disintegrate before him. Desperately, he struggled to keep it from disappearing completely. "What can I do to convince you?"

"I'm afraid there's nothing at all." Lord Simmons glanced away. "Even if I wanted to help you, I couldn't."

"Why ever not?" Royce asked, feeling slightly insulted by Lord Simmons' lack of trust in him as a gentleman.

Sighing heavily, Lord Simmons admitted. "I'm the one who introduced Laurel to Archibald Devens."

Suddenly, all of Simmons' reticence made sense. After that fiasco, it was little wonder Lord Simmons didn't want to help him. The burden of guilt obviously weighed heavily upon the older man's shoulders.

"When Laurel spoke to me about Devens, she said that before she'd even met him, she'd heard all the other ladies sighing over his exceptional charms and listened as they exclaimed that he would be the ideal husband. Because of this, I believe Laurel thought Devens the perfect match before she even met him," Royce said quietly. "So, whether it was you or someone else who introduced them doesn't seem to be the issue." A side of his mouth tilted upward. "And knowing your daughter, I can say without hesitation that she would have somehow found a way to meet him. So, you see, you weren't at fault, sir. No, it was simply that your daughter made a poor choice."

Lord Percy's gaze sharpened upon him. "Perhaps you might be best for Laurel after all," he murmured softly.

"Then you'll help me?" Royce asked with hope coloring his voice.

Chuckling, Lord Simmons shook his head. "No, but your persistance is admirable."

"Funny, your daughter said almost the exact same thing to me."

Chapter
7

I hope you don't think me overly bold for inviting you to join me on a ride through the park," Laurel said as she slowed her horse to a walk. "It's just that I enjoyed our conversation last night so much and I hoped we might have a chance to continue it."

"I would never think you anything but the lady you are," Steven pronounced as he changed his horse's gait. "Quite honestly, I was preparing to call on you when your invitation arrived."

A twinge of apprehension fluttered within her. Perhaps she was carrying this flirtation a bit too far. Yet Royce had reacted so splendidly to seeing her with Steven the evening before, she couldn't resist taunting him again. Since she knew Royce went for a ride in the park every morning, it was the perfect opportunity to bump into him with Steven at her side.

Still, it hardly seemed fair to Steven. He certainly

didn't deserve to be used so callously. Guilt raked through her until she realized she needed to confess her actions to him.

Drawing in a deep breath, she began, "Steven, I need to tell you something."

He tossed a smile at her. "Are you going to confess that your only interest in me is to make Royce jealous?"

Stunned, she couldn't form a response.

"Didn't think I knew, did you?" he asked with a laugh.

"No . . . I mean . . ." Laurel brought her stutterings to a halt. Closing her eyes for a moment, she calmed herself. When she was composed, she said smoothly, "I can only apologize for using you so dreadfully and . . ."

"Oh, there has been nothing dreadful about it," Steven replied, leaning forward to smooth his horse's mane. "You've made me quite glad that I returned from my country estate. I wouldn't want to miss the taming of the Earl of Tewksbury."

"I don't believe *taming* is the right word," returned Laurel tartly. "Replace taming with tormenting and then you'd have it."

"Ah, an evil woman," Steven drawled with a grin. "Are you quite certain all you want from me is to drive Royce insane?"

It was odd how easily she could resist Steven's charm . . . especially since she hadn't been able to resist Royce's even a little. Smiling at Steven, she nodded her head. "Sorry, but I'm quite certain. In fact, I believe I'm swearing off all men."

"Now *that* would be a shame."

Laughing at his retort, Laurel glanced around, hoping to catch a glimpse of Royce.

"If you're looking for Van Cleef, I'm afraid you will be sorely disappointed." Steven ducked beneath a tree limb.

"But he always rides in the park at this time of the morning." She knew. She'd paid one of Royce's servants enough money to uncover that bit of information.

"That's true," Steven agreed, "but this morning I have it on the best authority that he had a far more important errand to run."

Disappointment flickered through her; she'd been eagerly anticipating Royce's reaction. "Oh, I didn't know."

"There's no way you could have," Steven said easily. "Since his errand is of a most personal nature, he wouldn't have mentioned it to any of his staff, nor would the information be fodder for the gossips."

Intrigued, Laurel urged Steven to continue. "So how do you know?"

"Because Royce shared the information with two gentlemen who I also consider friends . . . and they told me." Steven tilted his head to the side and looked at Laurel. "Aren't you the least bit curious about where he is?"

"Of course," Laurel replied, trying to hide her disappointment. "Now, why don't you be the gallant and tell me?"

"How does telling you my friend's secret make me a gallant?"

"Please, Steven. Just tell me."

"Very well, I'll tell you," Steven replied with a

smile. "At this very moment, my dear friend Royce is undoubtedly sitting in your father's study . . ." He paused, giving Laurel a steady look. ". . . asking for your hand in marriage."

Laurel didn't reply. She was far too busy kicking her horse into a gallop, hoping against hope that she'd reach home in time.

Racing into the foyer, Laurel didn't even spare a moment to smooth out her wind-tossed attire. Instead, she marched straight over to the door of her father's study and opened it without knocking.

"Laurel, my dear," Lord Simmons began as he and Royce rose from their chairs. "I thought you were out riding."

"I was, but I returned early," she said simply. "Might I have a word with Lord Van Cleef in private?"

Her father's mouth twitched. "Most certainly." Glancing at Royce, he added, "And I do believe the Earl has a matter he wishes to discuss with you."

Laurel could barely contain herself until her father left the room. As soon as the door shut behind him, she turned on Royce. "Whatever are you *doing* here?"

Holding her gaze, Royce moved closer. "Surely you can guess why I'm here, can't you, my dear?" Stopping a few feet from her, he lifted his hand to lightly stroke one fingertip down her cheek. "You're a very intelligent woman and I'm confident you can reach the proper conclusion on your own."

For a moment, one brief moment, Laurel allowed herself to be lulled by the lilting tenor of his voice. But once she reminded herself of his foul wager, it was easy to shake off the seductive promise she heard in his voice.

"But that's just it, Royce. I don't wish to draw any conclusions." She stepped back, breaking off contact with him. "I believe we said everything we needed to last night."

"Not quite."

Laurel heard the determination in his voice, yet she would not let down her guard. Again.

"I didn't come here today to speak with you," Royce continued, a sensual smile curving upon his lips. "I came to ask your father's permission to marry you."

Of all the arrogant assumptions he could have made, Royce's belief that she would be overjoyed at his news annoyed her the most . . . because if she hadn't learned the truth, she might have reacted just that way. Drawing in a calming breath, Laurel stated, "I believe I made myself quite clear last night, Royce. While I appreciate all you've done to open my eyes, I believe we're better suited to being friends."

"*Friends?*" Royce's voice vibrated with disbelief. "Aren't you forgetting about this?"

And before he finished his question, he'd advanced upon her and swept her into his arms. Lowering his head to bring his mouth inches from hers, Royce rasped, "How can you say you want to be friends when I can make you explode with passion?"

Without a moment's hesitation he closed the distance, his mouth capturing hers. Her overheated emotions reacted fiercely to the desire in his kiss, her anger shifting into passion in an instant. Moaning softly, Laurel pressed her body against his as she gave herself up to the moment.

Royce held her tightly as he parted her lips and deepened the kiss. Eagerly, Laurel met him, accepting all he had to give and returning it in full measure.

Breaking off the kiss to press his mouth against her neck, Royce ran his fingers along the curve of her back. "I don't kiss my *friends* this way, Laurel."

No, he makes wagers with them.

The thought broke through the sensual haze fogging her mind, freeing her from the grip of desire. Stiffening within his arms, Laurel twisted away from Royce's embrace. "Please, don't," she murmured coolly.

"My dear . . . whatever is wrong?"

"Nothing is wrong . . . *except* that you persist in calling me by that annoying appellation," she said, smoothing her hair back as she moved away from him. "I just thought it was time to end our kiss before we got carried away." She touched two fingers to her lips. "Though I do so enjoy being kissed."

Following her, Royce grasped her arm, gently turning her around to face him. "Who else has kissed you besides me? Was it Devens?"

She smiled pleasantly at him. "Yes . . . among others."

"Others? Just how many men *have* you kissed, Laurel?"

Patting him on the chest, she removed his hand from her arm. "I'm not quite certain, Royce. There were far too many to keep count."

The expression on his face was priceless. Her victory secured, Laurel turned on her heel and left Royce to contemplate her taunting words.

If that bastard Steven kissed Laurel, then he'd have to toss him into the Thames, Royce decided as he headed toward the scoundrel's townhouse. How could his study of Laurel have left out such an important detail? *Too many to count?* Everything he'd learned about Laurel had led him to believe that she'd avoided men. Even he'd had to—

Royce skidded to a stop as his thoughts suddenly cleared like sun chasing away fog.

Laurel had tricked him.

He *had* done his research on Laurel. He'd studied her habits, her friends, her responses to others. Smacking himself on the forehead with the heel of his hand, Royce wondered how he hadn't seen through Laurel's strategy sooner. Thoughts of her sweet response to his kiss began to surface, bringing a smile to his face. After so many years of shutting herself off from the male populace, Laurel was undoubtedly alarmed by her response to him.

Still, Royce knew she had nothing to fear from him, and in time she would learn to trust that he would always honor her. All that remained now was drawing her in close enough to convince her of that fact. What he needed to do now was find another hunter to assist him in securing the prey. It was quite a shame that Lord Simmons wasn't willing to go along with his plan.

Perhaps he would pay Steven a visit after all. It was obvious that his friend had managed to garner

Laurel's trust, so perhaps Steven could help him sneak beneath her defenses.

His confidence increased with every step as he headed toward Steven's townhouse.

A soft knock sounded on the door to Laurel's bedchamber. She continued to gaze out her window at the sunset as she called out, "Enter."

"I hope you don't mind my meddling, dear," Lord Simmons began as he walked into the room. "But I wanted to see how your visit with Lord Van Cleef went."

Holding back a sigh, Laurel turned around to face her father. "It went as you probably suspected it would."

Lord Simmons nodded. "You turned down his proposal then?"

"Of course," Laurel replied as she glanced away. "I hardly know the man." But she thought she had. Laurel fought back her tears as she realized that if she'd received Royce's proposal a mere two days ago, she probably would have accepted it. That knowledge only increased her anger toward him.

Approaching his daughter, Lord Simmons reached out to stroke his hand down the length of her hair. "Have you considered giving yourself a chance to get to know him? I know how badly you were hurt by Archie, but perhaps it's time to overcome your fears."

"But that's just it, Father. I did," Laurel admitted as tears spilled down her cheeks. "What I said is true, I hardly know Royce . . . but I thought I did. I spent time with him and felt connected to him." Her heart tightened as she confessed, "I thought I was falling in love with him."

Lord Simmons looked down at her, concern darkening his gaze. "Then what happened?"

"I discovered the only reason he was showing any interest in me at all was because he'd made some sort of wager. Apparently, he declared that the way to find a wife was to treat the courtship like a hunt. And the bride like a . . . f . . . fox." Laurel swiped at her tears.

"Ahhh, so that's what all the questions about fox hunting were about," Lord Simmons murmured as he gathered Laurel in his arms.

Leaning against her father's strength, Laurel let herself cry for the first time over her bitter disappointment.

"Everything will turn out just fine," her father said softly. "You'll see."

Her tears subsiding, Laurel nodded against her father's chest. "I know it will," she agreed with a tear-stained voice. "Especially when Royce finds himself captured by his own trap."

"You're planning on marrying him then?"

"Of course not." Laurel pulled back to give her father a wavering smile. "But I do intend to make him crazed."

Laughing softly, her father pressed a kiss upon her forehead. "I've always admired your sense of fairness."

Laurel joined her father in laughter as the sweet image of Royce, frustrated and annoyed, danced in her head. She'd teach him a thing or two about placing a horrid wager on a lady, toying with her emotions as if she were a . . . a . . . furry little creature.

Yes, it was past time for the high and mighty Lord Van Cleef to be taught a lesson on how to treat a lady.

Chapter
8

"Royce paid me a visit today," Steven said as he swung Laurel around the dance floor.

Stumbling slightly, Laurel fought to regain her balance. "Did he tell you he proposed?"

"Naturally." Glancing pointedly down at her, Steven slowed their steps. "Though I suspect he left out a few details."

A flush darkened her cheeks. "Why would you think that?"

"Oh, just the way he seemed to drift off occasionally, losing his train of thought, all the while wearing a secretive smile." Steven shrugged. "Little indications like that."

Laurel felt an odd sense of satisfaction. She'd trusted Royce to keep their conversation confidential and in this, at least, he hadn't disappointed her. "What else did he say to you? Anything of importance?"

"Only that he wants me to help lure you to him."

Smiling brightly, Laurel responded pertly, "Too bad for him that I got to you first."

Steven twirled her toward the edge of the dance floor, and, before she could utter a word, she'd been spun around, straight into Royce's arms.

Whirling her away, Royce gave her a rakish grin. "Do you mind if I cut in?"

"It's a bit late to ask, don't you think?" Laurel glanced back at Steven, who stood on the side of the room wearing a sly, knowing grin. "The least Steven could do is look a bit disappointed."

"Even if he did, *I'd* still be wearing a smile," Royce said smoothly. "After all, you're dancing with me now."

"For the moment," Laurel warned, watching as Steven began to move closer. "It appears that Steven is getting into position to cut in."

Grinning boldly, Royce immediately twirled her around, angling them away from Steven.

"What are you planning on doing? Make Steven chase us all around the room?"

"Not at all," Royce replied. "He's an intelligent fellow, so he'll quickly realize that his efforts are futile and give up the chase."

Sobering, Laurel looked up at Royce. "And what will it take to make you realize the same thing?"

"That I'm wasting my time chasing you? I don't think that's possible. For you see, my sweet Laurel, I've looked past your protests and found the truth."

Gazing at him coolly, Laurel asked, "And what would that be?"

"Despite all these men you claim to have . . . entertained," Royce began dryly, "you're still intrigued by me for one simple reason." He paused for a moment, before saying, "You enjoy my company."

"Not lacking for confidence, I see," she retorted quickly.

"If I did, I could never hope to win over a strong-willed lady such as yourself." Royce turned them toward the middle of the dance floor, moving them away from Steven once again.

Laurel wanted to rail at Royce, to tell him that she wouldn't be the prize in a wager or the finish for any game, but she held firm in her resolve not to give him the upper hand again. As long as she knew his secret, she could counter his moves, but once he knew that she'd learned about the wager, then the entire game would shift once more.

"If your hope is to win me, I fear your efforts will all be in vain," Laurel murmured, forcing an apologetic note into her voice. "I'm having far too grand of a time entertaining my . . . options to settle upon one choice so quickly."

"By options, I assume you mean gentlemen," Royce said dryly.

"To put it plainly, yes." The look upon Royce's face gave Laurel pause and she began to wonder if she wasn't enjoying this sparring with Royce just a bit too much.

"Ah, but if I am the most persistent, I can easily wait out the other suitors." His gaze burned with intensity. "I'll persevere and in the end, when all the other gentlemen have given up, I'll claim you for my prize."

Lifting her chin, Laurel met his challenge. "That will be your downfall, my lord, for I am no man's prize to claim. When and if I settle upon someone to marry, it shall be my choice and mine alone." She waved her hand airily. "So, you see, you would be far better off settling upon some other lady to court."

Royce drew her in closer. "I've settled upon you."

The flutter his words caused inside of her angered Laurel. Royce's vow would have thrilled her . . . if she didn't know about the reason behind his determination to have her for his wife. A man like Royce hated to lose a wager.

Laurel was determined not to be taken in by his words. "Perhaps you need to consider other options as well," she suggested softly, feeling a sense of relief as the music finally came to an end. "Thank you for the dance, my lord. I found our conversation most . . . enlightening." Without giving him a chance to respond, she pulled out of his arms and hurried away.

Fearful that Royce would follow her, she headed toward the private chamber set aside for the ladies to repair their attire. Laurel breathed a sigh of relief as she entered the crowded room, knowing that even a man as bold as Royce Van Cleef wouldn't dare to enter. Sinking down on a stool, she pressed her gloved hands against her overheated cheeks.

What was she going to do? Despite her resolve to teach Royce a lesson, it seemed as if every time they were together he would charm her into forgetting his dreadful wager . . . only for a moment, true, but what if, in time, she began to soften toward him? What if her pain at his betrayal began to lessen? Would she start to trust him again?

Slowly lowering her hands, Laurel gazed into the mirror and prayed for a way to distract Royce from the chase.

Just then, the answer to her prayer walked through the retiring room door. "My Maribeth is having a *marvelous* time this season," announced Lady Pennigrove as she sat down with a huff. "Though I must say there seems to be quite a lot of heiress-hungry rabble sniffing around the marriage mart these days."

"I know precisely what you mean," agreed Lady Harding, who fluffed her skirts before returning her attention to her companion. "My Emily has been plagued with offers from untitled gentlemen all season."

Laurel listened with half an ear to their conversation. If only that were her problem, she thought with a sigh. Instead, she had to handle a persistent—

Her thoughts stumbled to a stop as inspiration struck. Holding back her chuckle, Laurel turned toward the two women. "I believe I can help you," she began in a casual tone, "for I know of one fine, titled gentleman who is currently seeking to marry."

The two women turned on Laurel, the gleam in their eyes reminding Laurel of two hungry cats stalking a fat, juicy mouse. Or, even better, they reminded her of two determined hunters after a particularly fine fox. Laurel smiled over her last thought, then promptly tossed Royce over to the two eager mothers.

* * *

Leaning against the column edging the doorway, Royce waited for Laurel to emerge from the ladies' chamber. He knew he was gaining ground with her and he would do whatever it took until she admitted that he was the man she wanted.

And then, he'd make her regret ever having taunted him with the thought of her with other men. Luckily for her, he would accept a sweet kiss as an apology.

The door to the ladies' chamber opened and Royce eagerly looked around the corner to see if Laurel was exiting. No, only Lady Pennigrove and Lady Harding bustled back to the ballroom where they would release their unappealing daughters upon countless unsuspecting young gents.

"How fortunate that we should meet, Lord Van Cleef," cooed Lady Pennigrove as she came to a full stop directly in front of him. "It's been so long since we've had an opportunity to chat."

If "so long" meant never, then he'd have to agree with the old biddy. Royce kept that thought to himself and instead accepted her proffered hand. "Far too long indeed."

Slipping to the side of him, Lady Pennigrove looped her arm through his. "While I'd simply adore to hear all about your recent escapades," she began as she tugged him forward, "we simply *must* find my daughter so that you can renew your acquaintance with her as well. You remember Maribeth, don't you, my lord?"

It took all of his concentration not to shudder as the image of Lady Pennigrove's near-sighted, gap-toothed daughter filled his mind. "While I would dearly love to accompany you, my lady, I'm afraid now isn't the proper time."

"Nonsense," pronounced Lady Pennigrove. "That is the entire function of these affairs."

Not allowing her to tug him more than two steps, Royce stood firm. He didn't want Laurel to slip away from him unnoticed.

"I agree completely with Lady Pennigrove," added Lady Harding as she took hold of his other arm. "In fact, I see Maribeth standing across the room with my own daughter, Emily." She smiled brightly at him. "I would be more than happy to introduce you, my lord."

Lady Pennigrove tightened her grip upon his arm until Royce felt certain he'd have welts in his flesh when she finally released it. "Of course you can introduce him to your daughter, Prudence, but only *after* he's spent some time with my Maribeth."

Yanking his arm downward, Lady Harding held on tightly. "But if they're both standing together, Ann, don't you believe we could introduce them at the same time?"

Royce was perplexed. Whatever was wrong with these two ladies? Why were they suddenly treating him as if he were the rarest treasure on earth? Hearing the door to the ladies' chamber open once more, Royce glanced over his shoulder, hoping Laurel would come to his rescue.

It was Laurel all right, but from the smug expression she was wearing, he knew no help would come from her quarter. In that instant, he pieced together why these two matrons were fighting over him like a coveted prize.

Laurel had set them on him.

Walking past, Laurel sent him a cheery little wave and a victorious smile as she strolled away with a decidedly cocky spring in her step. Royce couldn't help but admire her cunning.

What a clever little vixen he was after.

"I believe it's time for you to hold another grand affair, Mother," Royce announced as he stepped into the library.

Snapping her book of poems shut, Elizabeth looked up at him. "I beg your pardon?"

"I need to speak privately with a certain young lady, and the best way to arrange that is to invite her to our home," Royce replied stiffly, wishing he'd been able to devise a plan that didn't require his mother's cooperation.

Her eyes grew frosty. "Lady Laurel Simmons?"

"No," Royce replied, shaking his head. "Her best friend actually, Miss Harriet Nash."

"Dear Lord, you've gone from bad to worse." Elizabeth laid her book on her lap. "Surely you can't mean to propose to an *untitled* nobody!"

"I doubt if Miss Nash would appreciate being called a nobody."

"Why would her opinion affect—"

He held up both hands. "Enough, Mother. I have no wish to delve into this conversation." He gave her a steady look. "Will you hold a party and invite Miss Nash?"

Elizabeth lifted her chin. "Why should I? You've come into my home these past few days in an adversarial mood and I must tell you, Royce, you've done nothing that makes me want to help you."

"I'm sorry that you feel that way, Mother, but I'm afraid I shall have to insist you hold a party."

Her features turned stony. "You *insist?* Where did I fail in your instruction? You are ever the disappointment to me," she finished.

Ignoring the scrape of pain, Royce answered calmly, "I've tried in the past to be what you wanted, but only met with failure. I've accepted the fact that I am destined to disappoint you and have learned to live with that knowledge." He braced himself against the mantel. "What I will not accept, however, is your continued disrespect toward me and the title I bear. Whether you like it or not, I *am* the Earl of Tewksbury and, as such, hold the position of power within this family. While I honor you, Mother, I will not allow you to dictate my actions."

"You make me sound like a shrew."

He didn't deign to respond to her observation. Instead, he said, "Let's not allow this conversation to degenerate into insults. Please ask your secretary to arrange for the party, Mother."

"And if I refuse?"

Looking at his mother, he wished futilely that things could be different between them. "Then I shall be forced to think twice about paying the extravagant bill I just received from your dressmaker."

Her lips tightened. "Very well, Royce. You shall have your party."

"Thank you," Royce murmured. "I do appreciate your assistance."

"What option did I have?" she asked bitterly.

"What option indeed," Royce returned, regretting that she'd forced his hand.

"I am *so* honored that you invited me to your party, my lady," gushed Miss Harriet Nash, as she took in the elegance of the room.

Sending a glance over at Royce, who stood a few feet away, Elizabeth responded smoothly. "The honor is mine, Miss Nash."

"You are too kind."

"May I get you some refreshment?" Pressing a hand to her throat, his mother added, "I vow I am parched."

"No, thank you," Harriet replied with a shake of her head.

"Then please excuse me while I fetch myself a nice cup of tea." Elizabeth took one step away, before stopping. "Oh, but I shouldn't leave you alone. You are, after all, my guest."

"I shall be perfectly fine, my lady."

"Nonsense," Elizabeth replied, waving him forward. "My son shall keep you company. I believe you met him earlier—Royce Van Cleef, the Earl of Tewksbury."

Royce joined them before Harriet had a chance to respond. Bowing to both ladies, he murmured, "Miss Nash. Mother. How may I be of assistance?"

"Would you mind entertaining Miss Nash while I get some refreshment?"

Ignoring the sarcastic edge to his mother's voice, Royce smiled politely. "Would you like me to get it for you, Mother?"

"No, thank you," she said in perfectly polite tones. "What young lady wouldn't prefer the company of a young gentleman?"

With a smirk at him, his mother moved off before anyone could reply. The moment his mother left their little group, Harriet stiffened and her expression grew stony.

Perhaps he'd been wrong. Perhaps Harriet wouldn't be able to explain Laurel's coolness of late. "Good evening, Miss Nash."

"My lord."

Ouch. The frost in her tone could maim him if he weren't careful. "I'm pleased that you could come to my mother's affair. We haven't had a chance to converse in quite some time," he added, taking a page out of Lady Pennigrove's book of untruths.

But Harriet wasn't impressed. "We have *never* conversed, my lord."

Flinching at the tart reply, Royce decided to plunge on. "Alas, that is true, but perhaps we can remedy that today," he said, applying his charm in full measure. "I'd very much like to become better acquainted with you, Miss Nash."

Though he would have thought it impossible, her expression grew even stonier.

Her lack of response answered clearly for her. Releasing his breath in a huff, Royce decided to try a different tact. "You don't like me very much, do you?" he asked in brutal honesty, knowing he was tossing aside all the rules of polite conservation.

Shock reflected for a brief moment in Harriet's gaze, before her eyes narrowed once more. "Not particularly, if you must know."

Finally they were getting somewhere. Eagerly, Royce leaned closer. "Why? We don't even know each other."

"Perhaps your reputation precedes you," she said briskly.

Furrowing his brow, Royce shook his head. "That's it? Because you've heard a bit of gossip about me, you've now concluded that I'm a horrid person?"

"It wasn't gossip," she retorted, her voice ringing with conviction. "The things I know about you came from a most reliable source."

"Precisely what do you know, Miss Nash?" He was beginning to get a sickening feeling that this had something to do with Laurel.

"Nothing I care to repeat, my lord." Harriet lifted her chin in a movement that reminded him of Laurel. "Though I will tell you that in the future you should consider a lady's tender feelings far more closely before you begin any childish games."

It *was* about Laurel. "I don't know what—"

"Good evening, Lord Van Cleef," Harriet declared, effectively cutting him off at the knees. As she strode away, she hit him with one parting blow. "Happy hunting."

Happy hunting? What the devil did she mean by that? And what was that muck about considering a lady's feelings before beginning childish games? What could—

Dear God. Laurel knew about the wager.

All the pieces fell into place, every exchange, every sentence uttered over the past few days. Somehow, some way, she'd found out the truth . . . and was furious about it.

The way she'd taunted him with tales of a thousand kisses and thrown Lady Pennigrove and Lady Harding at him, it all made sense to him now.

Of course. It all seemed so obvious he couldn't imagine why he hadn't reasoned it all out before. But how had she learned the truth?

Like a bolt of lightning, he knew who had informed Laurel about the wager. Steven. That wily bastard. His first instinct was to confront Steven, but common sense prevailed.

A smart man, one who applied strategy to accomplish his goals, would use the knowledge he'd just gained for his own purpose. After all, if Steven were secretly handing information to Laurel, it might prove interesting to see just how well it would work if he gave Steven false information.

Royce almost laughed aloud at the thoughts dancing in his head. The adventure of claiming his bride kept getting better and better.

Chapter
9

*L*ining up her shot, Laurel swung her croquet mallet just as a raspy whisper caught her attention, causing her to knock her ball in the opposite direction.

"Laurel."

Glancing around, Laurel tried to see who had whispered her name. Everyone appeared to be engrossed in the game of croquet that Lady Needham had organized at her garden party. Deciding it must have been her imagination, Laurel went to retrieve her ball.

Swinging back, she hit the ball back toward the playing field just as she heard the demanding whisper once again.

"Laurel! Over here."

She frowned as her ball went careening off to the left, coming to rest far from the wicket. Turning around, fully prepared to rail at the person who broke her concentration, Laurel found herself facing nothing but a hedgerow.

"Over here!"

Automatically, she glanced toward the sound. "Royce?" Taking a step closer, she could now see him clearly. "What are you *doing* back there?"

In response, Royce simply reached out and pulled her through the break in the bushes, whisking her skirts away from the clawing branches.

Amused, Laurel glanced around the secluded arbor. "Now that you have me in your lair, what do you intend to do?" The moment the teasing question left her mouth, Laurel wished she could take it back. Perhaps she *had* been flirting far too much lately.

"Now there's an interesting question," Royce murmured, his eyes gleaming. "What *should* I do with you? After all, it's your fault that I'm stuck hiding behind these blasted bushes."

"My fault?" Laurel squeaked, taking a step backward.

"Indeed." Advancing on her, Royce narrowed his eyes. "Do you realize that I can't attend any social functions without being surrounded by a horde of anxious mamas and eager chits? Now that you've made it common knowledge that I'm seeking a bride, I've received more introductions to giggling females and more questions about my background, my habits, and even my wealth, then ever before."

A giggle escaped her. She couldn't help it. The look of vexation upon Royce's face tickled her.

Grasping her by the shoulders, Royce drew her closer. "To my way of thinking, there is only one way out of this mess you've created, Laurel."

Trying to ignore the sudden racing of her heart at

his touch, she stood still beneath his hands. "And how is that?"

"Marry me."

Two words. Two little words that brushed against her very soul, making her yearn to say yes, to accept what he offered. But she had far too much pride to sell herself so cheaply. Instead, she lifted a hand, patting it over her yawning mouth. "Don't be tedious, Royce. We've already discussed this."

"Very well," he agreed without argument.

The ease with which he gave up made Laurel suspicious. It was a very un-Royce-like thing for him to do.

"But I would then ask you to assist me in dissuading these persistent ladies."

Ah, here was the angle. She'd known he wouldn't defer so easily. "And just what would you like me to do?"

"Spread vicious rumors about me."

Her mouth dropped open. Of all the things she'd expected him to say, this wasn't one of them. If he'd said that they needed to pretend to be engaged or that she should stay at his side to give the impression that they had reached an understanding, then she wouldn't have flinched. But this? Laurel fought to apply logic to his request. "Why on earth would you ask something like that of me?"

"Because it's the most expeditious manner in which to dissuade my ardent admirers," Royce pointed out calmly. "No one will consider me marriage material if there are nasty murmurings rumbling around about me."

"No one would believe anything even remotely devilish about you," Laurel said firmly. "Your reputation as an honorable, albeit lusty, gentleman is well established."

Grinning broadly, Royce patted her on the arms before releasing her. "I leave it entirely up to you to convince the masses otherwise."

Uncomfortable with the entire idea, Laurel hedged. "I have no wish to ruin your fine name, Royce."

"Then you should have thought of that before you made my life a living hell," he argued, leaning toward her. "If you don't aid me, I shall be forced to hide in bushes for a very long time." Straightening, Royce tapped one finger against her chin. "It's the least you could do for me."

Guilt flickered through her. While she'd succeeded in her attempt to make Royce far too busy to pursue her, he was right—she'd also created havoc in his life. "Very well," she said reluctantly. "I'll try to start a few rumors that will hopefully send all of your prospective brides fluttering away." A thought struck her, making Laurel pause. Frowning at Royce, she asked, "But if I accomplish my goal, how will you *ever* find a suitable bride?"

His smug smile set off warnings bells inside her. "Don't worry about me, Laurel."

"Fine, then. And, in return for doing you this favor, I'd appreciate it if you would grant me one as well. Please stop seeking me out at public functions. I've made myself very clear, Royce. I do *not* desire your attentions," she said finally, clasping her croquet mallet in both hands. "Now, if you'll excuse me, I'm in the middle of a game."

Holding up her skirts, Laurel ducked through the narrow opening in the hedgerow.

As he watched her go, Royce allowed a smile of pure satisfaction to creep upon his face. "You are indeed," he murmured, pleased with how easily she'd agreed to his plan. Little did she realize that as soon as she'd chased away all of the other prospective ladies, he'd play upon her guilt and finagle her into marrying him.

After a day or so, he'd also put Steven into play and add yet another layer to his strategy. Tucking his hands into his pockets, Royce strolled away, happy with the day's outcome.

"Laurel, where have you been?" Harriet called to her as she approached the other players on the lawn. "It's your turn to hit."

Still flustered, Laurel tried to concentrate on the croquet game . . . and found it extremely difficult as thoughts of Royce filled her. How could she keep her promise to him? Everything within her revolted at the idea of publicly denouncing Royce.

It was one thing to toss him to the title hungry mamas and quite another to speak ill of him. Forcing a smile onto her face, Laurel lined up the ball and hit it straight through the wooden arch.

"Wonderful shot," remarked Lady Winthrop as she joined them. Patting her gray hair, she continued, "Then again, I well remember your father's astounding ability when it came to matches of skill."

Squelching her grin, Laurel shot a glance at Harriet before remarking politely to Lady Winthrop, "So true, my lady. My father is quite the competitor."

Suddenly, her promise to Royce shimmered through her. As Harriet moved away, Laurel knew she'd been presented with the perfect opportunity. Swallowing, Laurel leaned forward, reluctantly planting the first seed of suspicion. "Luckily, my father is most honorable in his wagers . . . unlike some gentlemen I could name," she finished with a whisper.

Lady Winthrop's eyes widened, an eager gleam brightening them. "Such as?"

"It wouldn't be proper to say," Laurel murmured, glancing away.

"Of course it would, my dear. After all, we ladies must protect one another." Placing a hand on Laurel's arm, she urged, "Do tell."

"Perhaps you're right."

"Indeed I am," pronounced Lady Winthrop.

Nodding her head, Laurel sent another look around, trying to convince Lady Winthrop of her reluctance. "It's been said that the Earl of Tewksbury is far from a gentleman where wagers are concerned."

A frown creased Lady Winthrop's face. "Pshaw," she muttered. "Van Cleef might be a rake, but he's far from a cad."

"That is precisely what I thought until I found out about his most recent wager."

Curiosity shifted into Lady Winthrop's expression. "Wager?"

Blending truth with deceit, Laurel wove her tale, casting shadows upon Royce's fine name, all the while praying she was doing the right thing. "Apparently Lord Van Cleef made a very public wager at his club, stating that he could 'catch' a wife. In fact, a certain young lady was even named as his prey."

Pausing, Laurel waited expectantly. At Lady Winthrop's silence, she emphasized her point. "He made the wager without any regard to the poor woman's feelings. And as you well understand, any young lady who honors her reputation would not appreciate being the subject of such speculation."

"No, no, of course not," agreed Lady Winthrop, enjoying every word Laurel fed her. "It's most distressing that he would bandy about a young lady's name in such a public forum. I must say I'm shocked to learn what a cad the young man has turned out to be—quite unsuitable for polite society, I'm sure." Tsking as she shook her head, the older woman expressed her displeasure at Royce's actions.

The muscles in Laurel's stomach tightened as she watched Lady Winthrop feast upon the latest gossip. "Now you can understand my concerns toward Lord Van Cleef. He has proved himself to be no gentleman."

"Indeed," Lady Winthrop agreed automatically, before asking, "Tell me, Laurel, who is the lady?"

"That's just it," Laurel began in a confidential tone, "No one seems willing to say. It could be any one of the ladies present today."

Drawing herself up, Lady Winthrop sniffed loudly. "Well, then, I see nothing left to do but to make it my personal mission to inform each and every one of them about the Earl's plans."

"It might be for the best," Laurel said slowly, holding back a shudder.

"Excuse me, Laurel, while I attend to this matter immediately."

Watching her stride away, Laurel prayed she'd done the right thing.

"What was that all about?" Harriet asked, as she approached. Placing a hand upon Laurel's arm, Harriet pointed out, "You're looking a bit peaked."

"Is that all?" If she looked even half as good as "peaked," then she'd disguised her feelings quite well . . . for she felt positively sickened. Now that she'd accomplished her half of the bargain, what if Royce kept up his end?

What had she done?

The hunt had suddenly intensified . . . yet not in his favor. Royce couldn't quite understand how the tables had been turned, but he knew with certainty who had turned them.

Laurel.

Hiding in the Hathaways' alcove, Royce couldn't tear his gaze away from Laurel. In a frothy gown of sea foam green lace, Laurel floated around the room in the Viscount of Hathaway's arms like an ocean goddess risen from the depths of the sea.

Shaking his head, Royce thrust away the fanciful thought, disturbed far more than he cared to admit by how often his thoughts returned to Laurel. Royce narrowed his gaze upon her as she spun past him. He wondered if she'd be able to tear herself away from the dance floor long enough to do as he'd asked.

"So this is where you disappeared to, my lord."

Wondering if he'd ever again find a moment's peace from inquisitive females, Royce slowly turned to face Miriam St. John, yet another mother intent on introducing him to her daughter.

"When I saw you earlier this evening, I knew I simply *must* introduce you to my darling Margaret."

Knowing there would be no escape, Royce smiled at Lady St. John before glancing at her daughter. "I welcome the opportunity," he murmured politely, wishing he had chosen a better hiding spot.

A triumphant expression flitted across Lady St. John's face. "Wonderful," she gushed before drawing herself up to her less than formidable height. "Lord Van Cleef, it is my honor to present my daughter, Lady Margaret."

Automatically, Royce accepted the proffered hand and bowed low over it. "It is a pleasure," he said smoothly, taking in the delicate blond beauty of Margaret.

Offering him an insipid little smile, Margaret dipped into a curtsey, flashing him a view of her generous bosom. "The pleasure is all mine, my lord."

Royce strained to pick up the breathy words. Glancing back at the dance floor, he wished Margaret and her mother would hie themselves off from whence they came. It was difficult to keep an eye on Laurel and her latest dance partner while carrying on a conversation.

Stepping forward, Margaret fluttered her lashes at him. "Pardon my boldness, my lord, but I must tell you that I do admire the fine cut of your jacket."

"Thank you," he replied, before giving her a pat response. "Might I return the compliment by telling you that your gown is quite stunning."

"Oh, Lord Van Cleef," Margaret said with a giggle, pressing a hand to her cheek. "Your charm overwhelms me."

Holding back a sigh, Royce forced a smile onto his face. "My apologies, Lady Margaret, for I fear I shall find it impossible to ignore such beauty as you possess." For some reason, the once familiar words of flirtatious pleasantries seemed trite and tired. If he even tried to impress Laurel with such useless phrases and compliments, he was confident that she would, quite simply, laugh in his face.

With her delicate features, blond hair, clear blue eyes, and sweet demeanor, Margaret was precisely the type of lady he'd once sought out for companionship. Unfortunately, she was also exactly the sort of lady who now bored him to tears with inane conversation and lack of wit.

Taking another glance at the dance floor, Royce searched for Laurel, but, try as he might, he couldn't spy her. Without conscious thought, he turned toward the center of the room, twisting away from Lady Margaret and her mother. Out of the corner of his eye, he caught a flash of green disappear into the garden.

He excused himself with barely a glance at his companions before making his way toward the veranda. Courtesies be damned; he had a vixen he needed to run to ground.

The instant Royce strode from the alcove, Margaret allowed the sweet expression she'd perfected in front of countless mirrors to slip away.

"Oh, dear," fluttered Lady St. John, patting her hand against her chest. "Lord Van Cleef certainly took himself off in a most impolite manner."

"Thank you for pointing out the obvious,

Mother," Margaret snapped, shooting a glare at her mother.

Placing a hand upon her arm, Lady St. John tried to pacify her daughter. "Now, Margaret, don't let his actions upset you."

"I thought you told me he was searching for a wife," Margaret said petulantly.

"It's true," Lady St. John swore. "According to the rumor, the Earl has already chosen his bride."

"Apparently, it isn't me." Margaret crossed her arms with a harrumph. "That doesn't please me, Mother."

Waving her hand, Lady St. John begged, "Please, Margaret, don't fret."

"I'm not fretting, Mother," she replied through gritted teeth. "Indeed not." Turning toward the room once more, Margaret watched Royce slip out into the garden. "I'm simply making my plans."

"Plans?"

Rolling her eyes at her mother's inability to keep up with the conversation, Margaret didn't bother to hide the scorn in her voice. "Yes, Mother. Do try to follow . . . my plans are quite simple, really," she said, ignoring the wounded expression on her mother's face. "I want him . . . and I'm going to *get* him."

"How?"

Margaret's cheeks flushed with heat. "What do you mean 'how'? Do you doubt my abilities to ensnare Lord Van Cleef?"

"Of course not," rushed Lady St. John, a nervous smile wavering on her lips. "You've always managed to get everything you've ever desired."

Her mother's reassurance calmed Margaret and

she took a deep breath, pressing her hands against her middle. "You're most correct, Mother." Gifting her mother with a smile, Margaret tossed back her head. "I've always managed to get what I desire . . . and I've decided I desire the Earl."

"The *nerve* of the chit!" gasped Elizabeth. "The Simmons girl has been spreading nasty rumors about my son?"

"Shocking ones." Lady Herold shifted closer. "Not that I'm a gossip, mind you, but apparently the girl said that your son mishandled a reputable lady."

"No, no, no; you've got it all wrong," chided Lady Worth, flicking her fan impatiently. "The Simmons girl said that our dear Royce was a philanderer with no sense of *honor* or *duty.*"

Pursing her lips, Elizabeth searched the ballroom for the lying little miss. Suddenly, she saw Laurel disappear through the glass doors . . . with her only child in pursuit. Disgraceful, she thought with a sniff, that the Earl of Tewksbury should be chasing after that brazen girl with flapping lips.

Elizabeth vowed to find a way to dissuade her son from his foolish pursuit of such an unsuitable bride. Go ahead, Royce, and chase your precious Laurel, Elizabeth thought as she watched him disappear outside.

In a few days, Lady Laurel Simmons would no longer be a problem. Getting rid of impudent females was an easy matter . . . if one knew the angle from which to approach the problem.

Satisfied, Elizabeth sat back and fed upon the gossip.

* * *

Lord Simmons watched Royce trail after his daughter and wondered what the man was up to. He'd heard the rumors flying about in the billiard room while he'd enjoyed his cigar, and though he'd never been a man to put stock in gossip, he suspected this particular tidbit was true; and he knew just who the unsuspecting lady in question was as well.

Lord Simmons now wondered if he'd made a mistake in not aiding Van Cleef in his courtship of Laurel. Perhaps Royce had been correct in urging him to nudge her a bit. From all accounts, Lord Van Cleef was a respected man among men . . . in spite of, or perhaps because of, his reputation for being a favorite among the ladies as well as a skilled gamester.

But it was the expression upon the young lord's face as he marched after Laurel that finally convinced Lord Simmons to intercede on the man's behalf. For only a strong man could ever hope to partner his daughter, and if Royce's dogged pursuit was any indication, he was more than up for the challenge.

Rocking back on his heels, Lord Simmons decided it wouldn't hurt anyone if he gently guided Laurel in the right direction . . . straight into the arms of the Earl of Tewksbury. After all, what was a father for if not to help his daughter?

Chapter 10

"Thank you so much for escorting me outside," Laurel said with a smile. "It was overwhelmingly hot on the dance floor and I was convinced that if I didn't get some fresh air, I'd faint in your arms."

"There are worse fates," Steven returned, grinning down at her.

Laughing at his quip, Laurel squeezed his arm, grateful to have made such a fine friend. "Then I won't trouble you next time. I'll simply allow myself to breathe in all the heady scents and perfumes until my head spins, then I'll promptly collapse into your arms."

"Must they be Morris' arms you collapse into, Laurel, or will any old pair do?"

Holding in a gasp, Laurel turned to see Royce approaching along the garden path. Quickly, she gathered her wits about her. "Well, my lord, I suppose any pair but *yours* will certainly do."

"Ah, ah, Laurel." His grin slashed across his face.

"Don't be too hasty. You never know what the future holds."

"Quite true," she retorted. "I don't know what the future holds, but I know what it *doesn't* hold . . . and that would be you, my lord."

"I do so admire a confident lady."

"Really? Now I find that a surprise, for I would have imagined that you would feel . . . threatened by such a woman."

Royce tried valiantly to hold his laughter inside and Laurel couldn't help but smile herself at his effort.

"Why do I have the feeling that no one even remembers I'm here?" Steven asked dryly.

"Oh, Steven, I am so . . ." Laurel began.

"Please, don't apologize," he said, holding up both hands. "The only thing that could make this any more awkward is an admission that you did indeed forget my existence."

"Not your existence—"

"No, merely your presence," Royce said, interrupting Laurel's protest. "So do be a good fellow and go find another lady to entertain, will you, Steven?"

Shaking his head, Steven had the good nature to laugh. "It's a lucky thing we're friends, Royce. Otherwise, I'd be forced to take offense at your condescending manner."

With Laurel looking on, Royce sobered. "Perhaps if you met another lady you found entertaining, we could return to our old selves."

The seriousness of Steven's response baffled Laurel. "Sorry, old boy, I don't think that's possible."

"I suspected as much," Royce muttered, a muscle in his cheek beginning to pulsate.

While she wasn't entirely certain of what she was witnessing, Laurel could feel the tension between them all too easily. Seeking to diffuse the situation, she offered Steven a smile. "It might be best if I speak to Royce alone."

Drawing his brows together, Steven placed a hand upon her arm. "Are you quite certain?"

"Quite."

"Very well then," Steven said after a long hesitation. Bowing slightly to Laurel, he excused himself and exited down the garden path, leaving her alone with Royce.

Drawing in a deep breath, Laurel returned her attention to the Earl and went on the offensive. "Why have you sought me out after I specifically asked you not to?"

"Because we had an agreement and you didn't keep your end of it."

"I most certainly did," she replied, affronted that he would suggest such a thing. "In fact, I accomplished the distasteful task of spreading rumors about you not ten minutes after you made your request."

Royce reached out to finger the lace on her gown. "Then I must not have made my wishes clear. I'm not certain *what* you told people, but, if anything, the matrons are even more determined to have me . . . or rather, my title and monies, for their daughters."

"How could that be?" The sight of his strong hands sweeping over her fragile lace disturbed her senses, making it difficult to concentrate. Taking a step backward, she broke off the contact and forced her mind back to the matter at hand. "I swear to you, Royce, I did tell a nasty bit of gossip about you.

Just as *you* requested," she added, ensuring her displeasure at being given the task was clear.

"Exactly what did you say?" he asked, closing the distance between them.

Feeling much like prey within the sights of a hawk, Laurel struggled to remain cool, unaffected by his probing gaze. "I informed a notorious gossip, Lady Winthrop, that you'd made a wager about an unnamed lady, betting that you could claim her for your bride with a minimum of fuss. And, I might add, I was most disparaging about the appropriateness of your actions. After all, wagering on a lady hardly behooves an *honorable* gentleman."

For a moment, Royce was silent, then he let forth a bark of laughter loud enough to make her jump.

"I fail to see what is so amusing," she said stiffly.

"Don't you understand what you did?" he finally asked. "You've declared me tender meat before the pack of hungry dogs."

Lifting her chin, Laurel held her ground as Royce took yet another step forward. "I did nothing of the sort."

"I beg to differ, my dear," Royce returned. "Don't you realize that Lady Winthrop probably didn't hear anything other than I'd chosen my future bride?"

"Don't be ridiculous. Of course she heard me."

Royce's eyes darkened as he searched her face in the moonlit garden. "Can you truly be that naive, Laurel?"

Something in his look made her catch her breath, even though his question annoyed her. It seemed easier to focus in upon the anger than upon the other, more disturbing emotions he aroused within her. "I assure you, my lord, I am no longer the innocent girl I once was."

"How often do you need to tell yourself that before you believe it?"

His soft whisper reached down inside of her, stroking an unwilling response. Still, she denied it. "Once is enough, because it is nothing less than the truth."

Slowly, he lifted his hand, trailing the backs of his fingers down her cheek. "That is precisely what you'd like everyone to believe," he murmured in low, even tones. "Yet deep inside of you is a vulnerable woman searching for a way to be free from all the locks you place upon your emotions."

His words jarred her, but it seemed far too difficult to concentrate on them, to make sense of what he was saying. "No," she rasped finally as his hand curved against her cheek, the gentle touch making her want to close her eyes and give herself up to the delicious desires swirling within her.

"Why don't you spare us both this game, Laurel, and surrender to your feelings?"

The question slammed into her. Jerking back, Laurel drew herself upward. "A game," she repeated, her voice reverberating with her anger. "That is precisely the reason that I will never surrender to you, my lord. You're simply playing a game, uncaring that you toy with emotions and feelings." Knowing she'd revealed far too much, Laurel broke off. With much effort, she forced a smile onto her face. "Consider our agreement null and void, Lord Van Cleef. In fact, I shall do everything in my power to make certain that you're tormented by every title hunting mother in all of England."

Royce scowled at her. "You wouldn't dare!"

Tossing back her head, Laurel placed her hands upon her hips. "Would you care to make a wager on that?"

His frown deepened. "If that is an attempt at humor, you fell short of the mark."

"I beg to differ," she replied lightly. "Only one thing will prove more amusing to me." Stepping forward, she patted Royce upon the cheek, her manner condescending and insulting. "I shall very much enjoy watching you be hunted to the ground. Let us see how you like it."

And with that, she strode away.

At this point, Royce wasn't certain if he wanted to marry Laurel or strangle her. Undoubtedly a little bit of both. The past few days had been horrid. He'd been unable to go anywhere without hordes of eligible beauties surrounding him. Feeling as if a thousand eyes lay trained upon him, Royce entered White's through the servant's entrance, unwilling to take a chance that some overeager mama might catch sight of him before he could escape inside. Quite a few servants glanced at him askance as he wound his way through the narrow corridors up into the main salon.

Sighing deeply, Royce lowered himself into a chair, relishing the respite. At least here, he'd be safe . . .

"Ho, Tewksbury, mind if I join you?"

The moment he laid eyes upon Lord St. John he wondered if he'd spoken too soon. The fellow's daughter, Margaret, had been most persistent in her pursuit, but then Lord St. John would hardly press her interest. Not here in White's. Forcing himself to relax, he waved his hand toward the empty seat opposite him.

"I've been hoping I might spot you today," began Lord St. John, settling onto the stiff brocade.

"Oh?" Wincing at the weak answer, Royce tried to strum up more enthusiasm for the conversation . . . but failed miserably.

"Indeed." Lord St. John tugged at his cravat. "Normally, I wouldn't dream of being so bold, but as my little Margaret has cried her eyes out over the past few days, I feel it is my duty as a father to—"

"Excuse me," Royce interrupted. He knew he was being rude, but he wouldn't, no, he couldn't, listen to any more. "I hate to cut you off, St. John, but I see Lord Simmons across the way and since I had arranged to meet him here, I feel it only right that I greet him immediately."

"Perhaps I can walk you over," Lord St. John said, moving to rise from his chair.

"No!" The word burst from Royce before he could help himself. Trying to soften his response, he smiled down at the older man, patting him on the shoulder. "What I mean is that you look so comfortable here and I'd hate to disturb you."

"But it's fine if—"

"No," Royce repeated. "I'm afraid I'll have to insist. It's not often that a man is afforded an opportunity to relax."

"True, but I had wanted an opportunity to speak with you."

"Perhaps later."

The vague promise seemed to settle Lord St. John, who nodded briskly. "Very well, then."

Feeling like a belabored man finally tasting freedom, Royce hurried over to Lord Simmons and swiftly took the seat across from him.

As Lord Simmons glanced up in surprise, Royce leaned forward to whisper, "I hope I'm not interrupting you, sir, but I fear I'm in need of rescuing." He tilted his head toward Lord St. John. "It would appear I'm not safe anywhere these days."

Chuckling, Lord Simmons leaned back in his chair and folded his arms across his chest. "I believe that is the doing of my sweet Laurel."

"I beg your pardon, but I would choose other words to describe your daughter," grumbled Royce under his breath, far too put out at the moment to hide his annoyance at Laurel.

"I imagine you would."

Flushing, Royce straightened in his chair. "Forgive me, sir. I spoke out of turn."

"Never apologize for the truth, Van Cleef." Lord Simmons grinned at him. "I can only imagine the torment my daughter has caused you."

"It is acute, I assure you."

"Knowing Laurel, I would expect nothing less."

Royce leaned back. "I knew you'd understand my problem, which is why I sought shelter with you." Rubbing a hand against his temple, he tilted up one side of his mouth. "I must say I find it ironic that the one person from whom I'd welcome matchmaking efforts is the only one not in the least interested in me as a prospective son-in-law."

"I never said that," Lord Simmons said with a shake of his head. "I merely told you I wouldn't help you court my daughter."

"I wish you'd reconsider, sir, for Laurel is proving most elusive."

"Out of respect for my daughter, I feel it best if I stay out of the matter." Lifting his hand, Lord Simmons began to study his fingernails. "However, if I happened to mention, in the normal course of our conversation, mind you, that Laurel is attending Hammington's weekend party at their country estate, I couldn't be held accountable." His lips twitched as he paused. "Now, could I?"

"Absolutely not," Royce agreed with a slow grin. "Not at all."

Sipping at her tea, Laurel chatted with the other ladies sitting with her in the Hammingtons' garden. The inconsequential conversation soothed her ragged nerves. After her confrontation with Royce, she'd felt the need to escape the city, so she'd accepted the Hammingtons' invitation without hesitation.

"I'm so happy that you could join us this weekend, Lady Laurel," Lady Hammington said brightly. "How fortunate for us that your schedule freed up enough for you to get away from the city."

"I am the lucky one," Laurel corrected. "And I do so appreciate you finding rooms for both Miss Nash and me."

Waving a hand dismissively, Lady Hammington rushed to reassure Laurel. "Don't worry one moment about it, my dear. I was more than happy to rearrange the rooms." Reaching out, she patted Laurel on the knee. "Besides, you're not the only one who decided to come at the last minute."

"That makes your effort no less appreciated."

Lady Hammington took a sip of her tea. "You are most gracious, Lady Laurel. It is an attribute sorely lacking in most young ladies these days," she finished with a pointed look at the other three women in their circle.

"I beg to disagree," Royce murmured smoothly as he stepped into the garden bower. "Most of the ladies of my acquaintance are quite gracious, though it hardly comes as a surprise to me. After all, when they have an example like you to follow, it could only stand to reason that they are paragons of womanly grace."

Once she got over the shock of seeing him, it was all Laurel could do to keep from rolling her eyes at Royce's flattery. Still, she found Lady Hammington's response amusing. "Ah, my," the older woman fluttered, pressing a hand to her bodice. "With such charm, my lord, it is little wonder that you are the most eligible catch of the season."

He lifted his gaze to Laurel. "I fear my intentions are already well and truly caught."

Lady Hammington's expression danced with curiosity. "By whom?" she asked, leaning forward in her chair. "Do tell."

Holding her breath, Laurel prayed Royce wouldn't be so foolhardy as to claim his intentions. Lord, what would it take to dissuade the man from following her?

"Yes," urged Lydia Chapel as she shifted so close to the edge of her chair that Laurel was surprised that the ninny didn't fall upon the ground. "I'm positively dying to hear who you've settled upon for your wife."

Royce tilted one of his eyebrows upward as he caught Laurel's attention once more. The gleam in his eyes didn't bode well. "Yes, Lord Van Cleef, do tell us who you've chosen for your bride," she said softly, forcing her lips into a smile. "We've all heard the rumors about your intentions and, as Lady Hammington pointed out, you are *quite* the catch. Why, with your title and charm, you could choose anyone."

"However my tastes are *most* discerning," Royce replied, one side of his mouth quirking upward.

"I would expect no less." Rising from her chair, Laurel moved to stand behind Lydia, Juliana, and Millicent, her three young companions. "You might have even chosen one of these lovely ladies, isn't that so, my lord? Each one possesses beauty, grace, and a fine pedigree."

"Pedigree?" squeaked Juliana. "That pertains to hounds and horses, not people."

Crossing his arms, Royce grinned at her. "I do believe Lady Juliana is correct."

Flushing, Laurel forged onward. "A slip of the tongue," she replied blithely. "I meant to say lineage."

The three ladies nodded, appeased.

"Anyway, my point is that Lord Van Cleef could have chosen one of you." Placing her hands on the back of their settee, Laurel bent down to urge them. "So, I do believe it would be in your best interests if you informed him of your unblotted reputations."

Eagerly, they bounded up from their seats, pressing forward. Satisfaction filled her as she watched the three hopeful brides plead their case with Royce. Wiggling one finger of farewell at him, Laurel slipped quietly from the garden as Lady Hammington began to chastise the girls, begging them to show a bit of decorum.

Late night shadows arched in the deserted hallway as Royce crept toward Laurel's door. Since she'd avoided him during the day, he had no other recourse but to seek her out after she'd retired to her room. Not wanting to be discovered, he tried to make as little noise as possible as he placed his hand upon the doorknob to Laurel's room.

Hearing footsteps coming around the corner, Royce darted across the hall, pressing himself into a doorway, hoping the darkness of the hallway would shelter him. As soon as he spotted the man in his long dressing gown, Royce knew he didn't need to worry about being discovered lurking outside Laurel's room. The man appeared preoccupied; obviously he'd arranged a little midnight rendezvous.

The shock that rippled through Royce when the other man stopped in front of Laurel's door soon grew into outrage. "You there," he rasped harshly, careful to keep his voice low. "What are you doing at that door?"

A muffled curse reverberated down the hallway as the man knocked his elbow against the doorjamb. His startled expression darkened into dread. "You," the man whispered, obviously recognizing Royce.

Between the darkness of the corridor and the tilt of the midnight caller's nightcap, Royce couldn't identify the man. "Just what do you think you're doing, entering that chamber?" he demanded, stepping forward.

Hastily, the man shook his head and took a step backward, tripping slightly on his robe.

Before Royce could question him further, the man turned and ran back around the corner and down the hallway. Royce watched him flee and promised himself that he would find out the man's identity. What bloody business could the man have had with Laurel—and in the middle of the night, no less—Royce wondered as he opened the door to Laurel's room and slipped quietly inside.

The sound of frenzied whispering, angry whispering at that, froze Laurel in her tracks. It would hardly do to be found traipsing down the hallway in nothing but her nightclothes. Though she'd only been exchanging the days events with Harriet, she'd been unwise to slip down the corridor without first redonning her gown. Still, it was too late for regrets now.

Hesitantly, Laurel peeked around the corner to see who was lingering about the hall. The sight of Royce entering her room stunned her. What did he think to accomplish by sneaking into her room at night? The sheer audacity of the man amazed her. Hurrying back to Harriet's room, Laurel entered without a knock. "You won't believe what I just saw."

Putting down her hairbrush, Harriet hurried toward Laurel. "Are you all right? You're positively pale."

"Fine," Laurel said quickly. "Though I can't say that would be true if I'd stayed in my room this evening."

Harriet's eyes widened in anticipation.

"I just saw Royce sneaking into my room."

"No," Harriet returned, disbelief coloring her voice. "He wouldn't dare."

"Well, he did." Moving forward to the bed, Laurel sank down upon the covers. "What can he be thinking?"

"That he wants to win this game of his . . . regardless of how he accomplishes that goal," Harriet said solemnly.

"I don't know what he'd hoped to accomplish, but I won't allow him to go sneaking around sullying my reputation. Can you imagine if anyone had seen him?" Just the thought of that horrid possibility sent Laurel to her feet. She needed to put a stop to his outlandish behavior. Now. "Do you have something I can write on?"

Harriet searched the lady's desk for some foolscap. "What are you going to do?"

"Find someone to roust that irksome man from my room."

Where the devil could she be? Was it possible that all her talk of kisses and enjoying the charms of suitors had been true? Did she get impatient waiting for her midnight caller? Who was that blasted man anyway? When he imagined some other man kissing Laurel, tasting those delectable lips, stroking that silky flesh, well, he just wanted to—

Breaking off his thoughts, Royce forced himself to unclench his fists before he gave in to his desire to smash something. Besides, it would hardly win Laurel over if she saw him pummeling the wall. He already had enough black marks against him; he didn't need to add more.

The creak of the doorknob turning caught Royce's attention. As the door slowly opened, Royce clasped his hands behind his back, and began, "Good Evening, Laurel. How lovely—"

His words choked him. "What in the bloody hell do you think you're doing?"

"I could ask the same of you," Steven returned as he quietly shut the door behind him.

"You could, but I wouldn't answer." Royce took another step forward. "I know my intentions are honorable, but I doubt I can say the same about yours."

"I hate to disappoint you, old friend, but I'm here at the lady's request." Lifting his hand, Steven waved the missive he held within his grasp.

"Let me see that," Royce muttered as he grabbed the note. As he read Laurel's letter, Royce's first reaction was relief—relief that she hadn't sent Steven an illicit invitation. The feeling, however, was short-lived. "She sent you to 'roust' me?"

"Indeed," acknowledged Steven, tugging on his jacket. "Apparently I've been enlisted as her shining knight this evening."

Royce chuckled aloud.

"What's so amusing? Can't you see me as a brave knight come to rescue the maiden fair from the hands of the evil villain?" asked Steven with a broad smile.

Eyeing his friend, Royce shook his head. "No, if the truth be told. I don't suppose that you mentioned to Laurel how often I've trounced you in the sparring ring at Minton's."

Steven's smile quickly turned into a frown. "What the devil does that have to do with anything?"

"Only that you couldn't 'roust' me if you tried," Royce pointed out.

"I beg to differ," Steven sputtered indignantly.

Royce didn't even answer the protest, settling instead on simply crossing his arms and allowing his silence to speak for him.

Annoyance flashed in Steven's gaze. "Don't get too cocky, Royce, for the moment you do, you'll be caught unawares."

"I highly doubt that—"

Before Royce could finish his sentence, Steven lunged at him, causing Royce to shift to the side and shove Steven toward the bed. On his way down, Steven reached out and grabbed hold on Royce's shirtfront, effectively dragging Royce onto the bed right after him.

Landing on top of Steven, Royce shifted to the side just as the door opened.

"Dear God!"

Lord Hammington's exclamation brought Royce stumbling to his feet, fully aware of the picture he presented while sprawled on Laurel's bed with Steven.

". . . so when Lord Hammington burst in upon Royce and Steven and caught them laying together in your bed, he demanded an explanation of what they were doing and *why* they were doing it in your room. So, Royce calmly explained everything to Lord Hammington."

Leaning forward, Laurel urged Harriet to continue. "What did he say?"

"From what Lady Hammington gathered, Royce told Lord Hammington that he'd exchanged rooms with you earlier in the evening as you complained of noises in the walls." Her gaze danced with mirth as she paused. "He then suggested that Lord Hammington have his rodent problem addressed."

She couldn't help but laugh at Royce's audacity, even as she admired his quick thinking. "How did he explain being found on the bed with Steven?"

"He's truly quite clever, your Royce," Harriet murmured.

"Harriet, please."

"I know, I know," said Harriet with a wave of her hand. "I truly am not encouraging you to reconsider Royce's proposal, but you must admit there is something appealing about his persistence."

"I imagine you find his persistence appealing because you're not the one forced to outwit him," Laurel pointed out, not all together pleased about her friend's change of heart. "Now, please, Harriet. I'm dying to hear how Royce explained his delicate . . . position . . . to Lord Hammington."

Grinning, Harriet leaned closer. "He told Lord Hammington that you believed you'd seen a rat scamper under the bed, but before he could look for it, Steven called upon him to see if he would like to have a late night brandy."

"That still doesn't explain how they both ended up on the bed."

"I'm getting to that part," Harriet said with a

tinge of exasperation. "As I was saying before I was so rudely interrupted—"

"Sorry," Laurel mumbled.

"Royce told Lord Hammington that when he and Steven bent down to look for the creature, Steven lost his balance and knocked both of them onto the bed."

"Of course he puts the blame squarely upon Steven's shoulders."

"Naturally," Harriet agreed with a laugh.

Smiling over the image, Laurel settled back in her chair. "One thing that still confuses me, Harriet, is why did Lord Hammington burst into my room in the first place."

Harriet's discomfort was obvious. "You won't like the answer, Laurel."

Gazing warily at her friend, Laurel urged, "Tell me anyway."

"Lord Hammington received a note saying that you needed immediate assistance."

"But who would send Lord Hammington a note—" A horrid thought took hold of Laurel. "That *cad*," she whispered.

"What was that?" asked Harriet.

But Laurel knew there was no other logical explanation. "It was Royce," she said grimly.

"Who sent the note?" At Laurel's nod, Harriet frowned darkly. "Impossible. He wouldn't do such a thing."

"What other explanation can there be? How many times do I need to be disappointed by that man in order to learn not to trust him?"

Reaching out, Harriet placed a comforting hand

upon Laurel's knee. "You don't know for certain it was he."

"It had to have been," Laurel said, trying to hide her disappointment. "Think upon it, Harriet. What would have happened if I *had* been in my room? I would have been *discovered* with Royce. At that late hour, I would have been thoroughly compromised."

"Then he could have announced your engagement to save your reputation and you would have had no choice but to accept his marriage proposal," Harriet concluded, her eyes widening with every word. "He *is* clever, isn't he?"

"Not nearly clever enough, for I managed to escape his nasty trap," Laurel pointed out, allowing her fury to burn away any thoughts of Royce being anything but a scoundrel. "I will admit that it surprises me that Royce would seek to accomplish his goals in such a dishonorable manner, but perhaps I underestimated his desire to win." The last spark of hope buried deep inside of Laurel flickered out. "Next time, I won't be so naive."

"I heard about last night's debacle, Royce, and I'll have you know it displeases me greatly," Elizabeth Van Cleef announced coldly.

Responding in kind, Royce said, "Then it is a good thing that I don't live my life to gain your praise."

"Don't snipe at me, Royce. If you'd stayed clear of that girl, none of this would have occurred."

Royce wanted to do nothing more than to walk away. Still, her position demanded respect, so he forced himself to act politely. "Let's remain pleasant,

Mother," Royce murmured, crossing the sitting room in his mother's chambers.

Taking a seat near the window, Elizabeth tapped her fingers against the arm of her chair. "I wish to discuss this situation, Royce."

"Well, I don't," he countered, keeping his voice light. "I must say that I'm surprised to see you here. I thought you avoided country affairs like this."

"I usually do, but I decided to enjoy the out of doors for a bit." Pausing briefly, Elizabeth gave him a chilly smile. "While I appreciate your attempt to change the subject, it will not dissuade me from expressing my displeasure with your behavior."

"Then feel free to natter away to your heart's content," Royce offered as he bowed to his mother. "I, on the other hand, shall take my leave."

Thrusting to her feet, Elizabeth snapped back her shoulders, a gesture Royce had seen more times in his youth than he cared to remember. "We need to speak about this."

"I think not," he replied breezily. "At the moment, I need to find 'the situation,' as you refer to her."

"I forbid you to see her again."

His mother's pronouncement brought a bitter laugh from Royce. "Sorry to disappoint you yet again, Mother, but the days of you monitoring my actions have long since passed."

Elizabeth scowled at him. "The Simmons chit is utterly unsuitable to become the next Countess of Tewksbury."

Royce's long held patience snapped and he took a step forward. "Allow me to point out that as the present Earl of Tewksbury, it is my privilege to decide just who is suitable to become my Countess. And no one . . ." Royce murmured, pausing for effect, ". . . no one will speak out against my choice. Not even you, Mother."

Lifting her chin, Elizabeth glared at him. "I shall say whatever I want to anyone I please. You cannot dictate my actions to me."

"True," he said in a silky voice, "but I can dictate how much you receive for your monthly stipend."

"You wouldn't dare!"

Shaking his head, Royce walked toward the door. "Don't force my hand, Mother," he warned softly before leaving her alone in her rooms.

Laurel was still stewing when Royce came upon her in the gazebo.

"There you are," Royce called, strolling into the glass-enclosed house. "I've been looking everywhere for you."

She'd retired to this seldom-used gazebo, hidden deep within the garden, precisely so he *wouldn't* find her. "Why?" she asked with a weary sigh.

A side of his mouth quirked upward. "Not mincing words, I see," he murmured. "Am I to presume that you heard about last night's events and are upset with me?"

Crossing her arms, Laurel faced Royce. "Very astute of you."

"I've been wondering how you knew I was in your room." Royce paced around the edge of the gazebo.

"As I was returning from Harriet's room, I heard whispering in the hall and I thought I'd interrupted a midnight tryst, but when I peeked around the corner I only saw you slipping into my room," Laurel explained, shifting to face Royce. "Naturally, it took a few minutes for me to trust my eyes, because I never would have imagined that you'd do something so despicable."

Lifting both his brows, Royce stopped pacing. "Despicable? Don't you think that's a bit harsh?"

Staunchly, she ignored the twinge of hurt she saw in his eyes. "Not at all. What would you call it when a *gentleman* comes uninvited to a lady's room late at night?"

"A manner of courtship perhaps?"

"*Courtship?*" Stepping forward, she poked at Royce's chest with her finger. "Perhaps in some backward civilization that would be considered an act of courtship, but I assure you, Lord Van Cleef, that in civilized company, you gravely insult any female unlucky enough to catch your eye."

Grabbing hold of her finger, he tugged her closer. "Forgive me if you find my technique a bit rusty, but I'm unaccustomed to chasing down a female in order to speak with her privately."

"So you resort to trickery?" she demanded, trying not to quiver beneath his touch.

"If you'd ceased your stubborn refusal to talk to me, I wouldn't have been forced into drastic measures."

"Oh, so now it's *my* fault." Fury bolstered her courage and Laurel moved closer, glaring up into Royce's face. "The least you could do is take responsibility for your own actions."

"You continually challenge me, daring me to

chase you, yet the moment I make a bold move, you accuse me of taking this game of ours too far."

Tilting her head upward, Laurel nudged him with her hand. "I don't wish to 'play' anymore, Royce. You took it too far when you arranged for us to be discovered by Lord Hammington."

"I did nothing of the sort," Royce protested. "Which is precisely why I searched for you today. I wanted to warn you that someone tried to arrange for your disgrace."

"Yes," she ground out, "you."

Annoyance flashed in his eyes as he tightened his hold upon her. "I just told you that I didn't send that note to Hammington."

Sniffing in disbelief, Laurel gave him a look of scorn. "As if I could believe anything you said."

"When have I ever given you reason to doubt me?"

"When haven't you?"

With his free hand, Royce grasped her shoulder. "Though I'd like nothing more than to shake some sense into you, Laurel, it is more important that you listen to me. Last night as I was about to enter your room, another man tried to go in before me, but I startled him and he fled before I could find out his identity."

She allowed her disbelief to color her features.

"It's the truth," Royce protested. "The whispering you heard was the two of us arguing."

Her laugh sounded bitter even to her own ears. "So now you're trying to convince me that a complete stranger, for some nefarious reason, wanted to disgrace me."

"Yes." Royce closed his eyes for an instant, before meeting her gaze once more. "I know it sounds a bit—"

"Implausible," she supplied.

"I was going to say far-fetched."

"Either way, you're quite right." Laurel tried to take a step backward, but Royce held her tight. "Please release me. I've had enough of your fairy tales."

"You must believe me, Laurel. Your reputation might be in jeopardy."

"It is," she conceded smartly. "Thanks to you."

Immediately, Royce pulled her against him and lowered his head until his face was mere inches from hers. "Trust me, Laurel, I've had a very trying day already, so tread lightly and listen carefully. I had nothing to do with the note Lord Hammington received." As Laurel opened her mouth to protest, Royce cut her off. "You must believe that someone has attempted to soil your good name."

"If I believed that, then I could just as easily believe all sorts of fantastical tales," Laurel returned swiftly. "Who knows what could happen then? There are all sorts of fairy tales I could believe in . . . such as the idea that you might be interested in me simply because you find me enchanting." Widening her eyes, she feigned a look of excitement. "Or perhaps I could even make myself believe that you wish to marry me because you, oh, I don't know, let's say because you love me."

An odd expression crossed Royce's face. "You are the most bedeviling woman I've ever met," he said finally.

"Then leave me alone!"

"I wish I could," he rasped, so low she barely made out the words.

A strangled sound echoed from his throat as Royce lowered his head toward her, closing the distance between them. The world spun on its axis as Royce pulled her against him and melted her with the touch of his lips.

She was lost.

Chapter 11

Elation soared through him as Royce satisfied his raging hunger for this delectable woman in his arms. Laurel Simmons frustrated him, challenged him, excited him in a fashion no other woman had ever done.

Needing to meld with her, Royce deepened the kiss, swept away by the intense cravings stirring within him. He curved his hand around her shoulder, wishing he could tug the offending material off her soft flesh, freeing her to his touch. Desire flamed within him as Laurel melted into him, her full breasts pressed against his chest.

This woman made him want things he'd never before imagined. He didn't know why and didn't care; all he knew was that life with her would be the stuff of fantasy. A shiver coursed through him as her fingers curled into his spine, eliciting a desire to feel the scrape of her nails along his flesh.

Driven with passion, Royce angled his head, parting her lips once more. Then, just as he moved, Laurel broke off the kiss and yanked herself out of his arms.

"No," she whispered hoarsely, wiping the back of her hand against her mouth.

"Laurel." Royce moved to hold her again, to kiss away any lingering doubts she might have about his motives.

"Don't touch me."

The wavering in her voice brought him to a halt. "Please, Laurel, I need to reassure you."

Her eyes had grown round, almost as if shock had taken hold of her. "No more," she said with a shake of her head, before she spun on her heel and ran from the gazebo.

He wanted to race after her and demand an explanation, but he knew she wouldn't thank him for his effort. Knowing Laurel as well as he did, he guessed she'd soon regret showing him any weakness at all and the fact that she'd stood before him with tears in her eyes would be more than she could bear.

Letting out a defeated sigh, Royce walked to the door and gazed down the now deserted garden path. He couldn't understand what had just happened. One moment Laurel had lost herself within his arms and the next she'd broken down in front of him, begging him not to touch her. Vexing, Royce decided with a firm nod. It was the perfect word to describe the woman.

While Laurel was far more intriguing than any other female of his acquaintance, there was little doubt that she, along with the rest of her species, was a complicated creature that delighted in tormenting the male species. Whether it be through their flirtatious ways or by direct manners, women knew how to reach inside of a man and twist him inside out.

Taking a deep breath, Royce tried to remain focused upon the facts. Despite his determination, he found claiming Laurel as his own was proving to be far more challenging than he'd ever imagined. Perhaps James and William were correct after all. Perhaps women, by their very nature, were troublesome creatures that required much care and time in order to keep them happy. Royce doubted if women understood that everything in life had a natural order and they were simply a part of a man's life, not the whole of it. However, it was the burden of a man to make their lady understand that simple fact and until he did, his life would be chaos.

Perhaps he should begin to blend his theory with the tried and proven courtship techniques of his friends, James and William. Then, once Laurel had wed him, he could consider all the trouble he'd gone through well worth the effort.

Satisfied by his reasoning, Royce felt he could now dismiss the ache he felt whenever he saw Laurel as purely natural. No, he no longer had to be concerned by the amount of time he spent thinking of her or about the way his heart tightened whenever he saw her.

Undoubtedly it was simply a result of all the energy he was expending when he devised new strategies to capture his bride.

Tucking his hands into his waistcoat, Royce strolled back toward the house, wondering when he'd be able to speak with Laurel and discover exactly what was bothering her. Until the chance arose, he would keep a close eye on her and try to discover just who had threatened to ruin his lady's reputation.

And once he did, he would destroy the bastard.

"Why did you leave the Hammingtons' party in such a hurry?"

Flinching at the question, Laurel splashed a bit of tea onto the table. "I'm sorry I didn't let you know I was heading back to London, Harriet, but I'd just seen Royce and was so upset I wasn't thinking straight."

"I suspected as much," Harriet replied, reaching forward to accept her tea. "What happened? Did you confront Royce with your suspicions?"

"Yes and he denied he'd sent the note to Lord Hammington." Wiping up the spill, Laurel set the dampened cloth on the tray. "He was most adamant about it."

"Did you believe him?"

"Part of me wanted to," Laurel admitted, trusting Harriet with the truth, "but, logically he was the only one who had a motive ... despite his tale about another man who'd tried to enter my room."

Harriet took a sip of her tea. "What are you going to do now?"

"Nothing."

An incredulous expression shifted onto Harriet's face. "You can't be serious."

"I most certainly am." Setting down her teacup, Laurel leaned forward. "I've given the matter a great deal of thought, Harriet, and I realized that while I accused him of playing games with me, I was just as guilty." She splayed her hands wide. "After all, I countered every move he made, twisting his plans, and, by my actions, encouraged him to continue his pursuit. If I had simply let the matter drop, he would have soon tired of his attempts and let me be."

"So no matter what he does, you plan on acting cool."

"Exactly." Laurel nodded firmly, sitting back in her chair. "Cool, yet polite." Smiling, she lifted her cup in a toast. "Here's to the end of the game."

Royce felt like snarling at William and James as they approached him. Couldn't a man enjoy an evening in peace? he wondered. It had been a week since his return from the country and, with his lack of response from Laurel, he was hardly in the mood for their crowing.

Wearing satisfied grins, the two men flanked him.

"Your grand theory seems to have gone astray," James said, clasping his hands behind his back.

"There is a certain satisfaction in knowing that capturing a bride is difficult even for someone like you." William's eyes sparkled. "Welcome to the world of mortal men."

Royce glared at William. "I'm ill-humored tonight and not interested in entertaining you lackwits."

"Lackwits, he calls us," James said, leaning forward to speak with William. "Did you hear that?"

"Indeed I did," William affirmed, his tone filled with mock surprise. "Amazing how unpleasant our friend becomes when things don't fall neatly into place."

Though he knew they were right, Royce could do little to lighten his mood. Laurel had refused to see him and he hadn't even had the opportunity of bumping into her at a social function, since she'd remained at home the entire week. Frustration had eaten away at his patience until he felt like a seething coil of nerves.

Knowing that he would regret it if he gave in to his urge to knock James onto the floor, Royce decided it was past time for him to leave. "I'm off to White's," he said, trying hard not to spit out the information.

"You're leaving already?"

Nodding, Royce answered, "I'm not certain why I came in the first place."

"Really?" James shrugged lightly. "I assumed it was because you wished to snatch the ever lovely Lady Laurel off on another grand adventure." Glancing around, James asked, "Do you have a stately carriage awaiting in the wings? Or perhaps a bower of freshly strewn rose petals?"

"Since the lady in question has gone into hiding, my plans would be for naught," Royce answered in spite of himself.

With a smile playing upon his lips, William tilted his head to the side. "If it's 'hiding' she's up to, then she's picked an odd way to play the game, for she's just entered the room with her father."

In the blink of an eye, all of his frustration fell away, leaving behind a stirring excitement.

"If you'll excuse me, gentlemen, I believe my lady awaits."

Both men chuckled as Royce stepped toward Laurel and her father. "Good evening," he murmured, grasping Laurel's hand and bowing over it.

"Good evening, my lord."

Her even tone revealed nothing. Lifting his gaze to her face, he could detect none of the vulnerability she'd exposed during their previous meeting. "I was wondering if I might have the honor of this dance."

"I'm afraid I'll have to beg off," Laurel replied, removing her hand from his clasp. "I'm feeling somewhat fatigued this evening and am going to refrain from dancing."

Her response set him aback. "Certainly you can manage one spin around the dance floor," he replied smoothly, injecting his voice with a confidence he was far from feeling.

"You're undoubtedly correct, my lord, but it would be best if I rested."

The polite smile she offered chilled him. He'd far prefer her anger, her frustration, her tears, over this treatment. It was as if she'd decided to freeze him out with blandness.

All at once, he recognized her odd behavior as the evasive tactic it was. His only problem now was to try to figure out how to combat it.

Feeling her move away from him, Royce reached out to take hold of Laurel's arm when she suddenly paled. No, that wasn't the right word to describe the look that came over her. All the color had drained from her in an instant as if she'd seen her own death foretold. Noticing her gaze fixed over his shoulder, Royce glanced behind him, wondering what could have caused such a reaction. The answer stood in the foyer, looking about him like royalty come to pay a visit amongst the peasants.

"Archibald Devens," Royce murmured, instinctively knowing the man's return would affect him profoundly, though he didn't yet know how.

Turning to face Laurel once more, Royce watched as her face suddenly flushed with color. Her reaction reassured him that she didn't hold any feelings for the man but anger. Settling back on his heels, Royce crossed his arms and waited for the explosion to start.

It would be wonderful to see Laurel turn her bedeviling displeasure toward someone else for a change.

Blinking twice, Laurel struggled to convince herself that her eyes weren't deceiving her.

He was back.

The heiress-hunting deceiver had finally returned from his extended European tour. Too bad, Laurel thought sourly, for it would have been wonderful to never see his lying-with-every-breath person again. Unfortunately, he'd come back, so she'd have to deal with him . . . right after she took care of Royce.

Inhaling deeply, Laurel returned her attention to Royce. "Pardon me, my lord, but a matter has just come up and I need to excuse myself."

"A matter?" Royce's eyes gleamed. "An interesting way to describe the return of a dishonorable ex-fiancé."

Coldness settled into her. "I hardly think you're qualified to judge a man's honor," she muttered under her breath.

But Royce heard her clearly. An affronted expression slipped onto his features as he straightened his spine. "Are you comparing me to that ... that ... popinjay?"

"Well, yes, I believe I am."

"I am nothing like him," Royce hissed, reaching out to clasp Laurel's elbow.

Slowly, she pulled herself free. "I'm quite certain you'd prefer to believe that to be the truth, but you, Lord Van Cleef, have more of Archie's characteristics than you would ever care to admit."

Indignation radiated from Royce, but she didn't allow him a chance to argue the point. Instead she hurried away, needing to escape the room before Archie confronted her. Her hopes of avoiding him were dashed when, mere feet from the ladies' withdrawing room, Archie closed in and cornered her.

"Hello, Laurel." His silky voice grated against her ears. "It's been a long time."

Not nearly long enough, she thought. Yet she kept the retort to herself as she didn't want to make Archie believe he'd affected her one way or the other. "Has it?" she said, pleased at the airy tone she'd managed.

He blinked. "Well, yes, yes, it has," he stuttered, before catching himself. Clearing his throat, he began again. "I see you've gotten over our ... less than cordial parting."

"Oh, that?" Waving a hand, Laurel laughed breezily. "Trust me, Archie, I managed to get over you sheer moments after you left." She tilted her head to the side. "In fact, I should probably thank you for breaking it off."

"Why is that?" he asked, his brows drawing together in confusion.

Delighting in Archie's reaction, Laurel continued, keeping her voice light. "Because we would have been miserable together." She held her arms out to the side. "And as you can plainly see, I am doing perfectly *fine* without you."

The minute his expression changed, she knew she'd said the wrong thing. "Indeed you are," he murmured softly, allowing his gaze to drift over her.

Laurel shivered, disgusted by his look. "If you'll excuse . . ."

"Do you see everyone watching us, Laurel?" Archie asked, amused. "Come along and let's give them something to talk about." Grasping her hand, Archie dragged her to the dance floor.

"No, Archie," Laurel protested, trying not to make a scene. She'd been the brunt of the ton's jokes for years because of this man; she wouldn't allow him to turn her into a laughingstock a second time. "No, Archie," she said again, firmer this time.

"Be a love and dance with me . . . for old times sake."

"She should slap you . . . for old times sake."

Laurel spun to face Royce. Reaching out, he helped Laurel break free from Archie's grasp. Without another word he escorted her to the dance floor, leaving an astonished Archie behind.

"Arrogant fellow, isn't he?" Royce grumbled, frowning back at Archie. "Comes back and immediately expects you to be at his beck and call."

"And that won't do at all since you want me there," Laurel replied.

"As a matter of fact, I do." Royce's fingers tightened upon hers. "But I won't ever toss you aside or treat you poorly."

But he already had when he'd made his wager. "And I suppose that should make a difference?" she asked calmly.

"Of course," said Royce, sounding quite affronted. "You already know that I want you to be my wife."

"So did Archie," she pointed out.

"Yes, but I'm willing to actually go *through* with the wedding."

"As I'm certain he would have been if he hadn't inherited a fortune." Tilting her head to the side, Laurel looked at Royce. "Who knows? Perhaps he's run through the monies already and is again seeking another source."

Royce jerked beneath her fingers. "I'll be damned if it's going to be you!"

So would she, but Laurel kept that thought to herself. Instead, she simply smiled.

"Laurel," he said warily, "you wouldn't entertain Devens again . . . would you?"

Again, she allowed Royce to draw any conclusion he wished from her silence.

"Laurel—"

Before Royce could finish his protest, Laurel was spun out of his arms and into Archie's. Laurel nearly tripped at the unexpected move, and Archie caught her up against him, pressing against her tightly. One glance over her shoulder revealed an extremely annoyed Royce standing amidst the other dancers.

"Rather nasty fellow, isn't he, Laurel? How could you have ever hooked up with him?"

Gazing up into Archie's still handsome face, Laurel wondered how she ever could have thought there was more depth to him. "That's my personal business and I have no wish to discuss it with you."

"Fair enough," Archie conceded, yet in the next breath, he said, "but you really must tell me what you saw in him. From what I remember of his reputation, Van Cleef was known as a man who enjoyed the ladies . . . *all* the ladies."

Laurel lifted her chin. "You've been gone a long time, Archie. Things are greatly changed."

"Yes, they are." A bittersweet smile curved upon Archie's lips. "You're no longer the sweet innocent I left behind, are you?"

For a moment, Laurel didn't know how to respond, but then, as always, humor came to her rescue. Tossing back her head, she laughed aloud at Archie's remark. "No, Archie, but I have you to thank for that. I do so appreciate your efforts in educating me."

Wearing a look of chagrin, Archie seemed at a loss for words.

An instant later, Laurel felt someone whirl her out of Archie's arms. She bumped against Royce, who began to lead her into the dance again, but she'd had enough.

"No!" she cried, not caring that everyone in the room suddenly stilled to watch them. "Enough."

"Laurel—" Royce and Archie chimed in unison.

Lifting her hands, Laurel cut off their protests. "I'm not a prize to be fought over, nor am I a marionette to dance to your tune. What I am, gentlemen, is tired of being chased for the wrong reasons." She glared fiercely at them. "Please feel free to dance with each other, because my time is no longer going to be wasted on either one of you."

She felt like spitting out the last words, but miraculously retained control over her fury. Thoroughly disgusted with the actions of both Archie *and* Royce, she turned on her heel and began to stride away.

"Laurel—" Royce began again, only to be cut off by Archie.

"Just what are we supposed to do now?" he called after her.

Twisting to face them once more, she shook her head. "I don't know and I don't care. Just keep me out of the entire mess." Wiping her hands together, she smiled at them. "I'm wiping myself free of you both."

As she left the room, Laurel was aware of the hushed whispers flying about the dance floor . . . and she couldn't have cared less. If having the ton gossip about her was the price she'd be forced to pay, she'd gladly do it if it would keep both Royce and Archie away from her.

She couldn't afford to allow either one close to her again, for Royce could cause her pain and Archie, well, he just *was* a pain.

Chapter 12

"There is a young lady here to see you," announced Giles, disapproval reverberating in every word. "Without a chaperone," he added with a sniff.

Eagerly, Royce leapt up from behind his desk, scattering papers in his haste. "Thank you," he said as he rushed past the butler and into the foyer.

His excitement died at the unwelcome sight of Margaret St. John. "Lady Margaret," he said, swallowing his disappointment. "This is . . . unexpected."

"Like all surprises, sometimes it is the unexpected ones that turn out to be the most pleasant," Margaret said, stepping closer.

While Royce agreed with the sentiment, he certainly wouldn't apply it to this particular surprise. Nonetheless, he smiled wanly and said, "True enough."

Aware of Giles's disapproving gaze, Royce escorted Margaret into his study and shut the door firmly behind them. "How may I be of assistance, Lady Margaret."

Instead of answering him, she launched herself against him. "There's no need to play coy, Royce. We're alone now."

Holding his arms akimbo, Royce looked down at the woman pressed against him, scrambling to decide what to do with her. "Lady Margaret, *please.*"

"There's no need to hide your passion from me," she whispered, lifting her face to him. "I know I'm the woman you've chosen."

"What's that?" He must have heard her wrong.

Cuddling against his chest, she lowered her lashes, then gazed up at him soulfully. "Don't try to deny it, Royce. When I heard what happened at the Hammingtons', I *knew* you wanted me."

He shook his head in confusion. "I'm afraid I'm still not following you."

"It's all over town that you were found in Laurel Simmons' bedchamber."

For the life of him, he couldn't follow her logic. "And this bit of gossip pertains to you . . . how?" he said, grasping her shoulders, trying to gently extricate himself from her embrace.

"Oh, you silly," she teased, clinging to him like a barnacle on a boat. "You know very well that I was assigned that room until I was forced to cancel my visit. Lady Hammington told me that everyone knew Lady Laurel was merely a last minute addition to the party." Rubbing against him, Margaret dropped her voice to a purr. "I only wish I hadn't been hosting a dinner party for my father. If I had attended the Hammingtons' party, we could have had a bit of sport before we announce the banns."

Again, he pushed her away from him, this time succeeding in his efforts. Holding her at arm's length, he attempted to reason with her. "I don't wish to disappoint you, Lady Margaret, but I'm afraid you're mistaken."

"There's no need to be shy with me," she cooed, reaching out to place her hand upon his cheek.

"I assure you, you *are* mistaken." Royce removed her hand from his face. "The reason I was in Lady Laurel's room that night was because I'd switched rooms with her after she heard rodents in the wall."

His explanation brought a halt to Margaret's squirming. "You weren't seeking me out then?"

"While I find your company pleasant, no, I did not intentionally seek you out."

An unattractive flush darkened her cheeks as she stepped back from him. "Then I have made a fool of myself."

"No," he hurried to reassure her. "Not at all. In fact, no one need learn of this visit. It will go no further than this room."

"Don't be naive, Royce. Haven't you learned yet that even the walls have ears?"

He wished he could deny her assertion, but he could not. "Then I shall simply inform my staff that you came to call upon me with concerns about my mother."

"Very well," Margaret agreed stiffly. Walking to the door, she paused with her hand on the knob and turned back toward him. "I won't soon forget this humiliation."

"Again, my apologies," he murmured, unable to think of another response. Bowing politely, Royce straightened to find the room empty. A slam of the front door announced Margaret's departure from the house.

Wincing at the sound, Royce sank down into his chair and wished he'd found a way to handle it better. But how? Even now, Royce couldn't think of a gentler manner to let Lady Margaret know she'd made a horrible mistake. Lord, the way she'd clung to him, he couldn't even imagine entertaining the thought of marrying her.

And yet, he thought, eyeing the settee along the wall, if it had been Laurel who'd come to call, the afternoon would have ended far differently.

"Pardon me, Lady Laurel, but a gentleman has come to call."

Accepting the card from the maid, Laurel couldn't suppress a groan as she read the name. Lord Archibald Devens.

Just wonderful.

"Please give Lord Devens my apologies and . . ."

"Come now, love, there's no need to offer your apologies," Archie murmured as he strolled into the room. "If you see me now, then there will be no need to get back to me."

Dismissing the maid with a nod, Laurel steeled herself to receive Archie. As soon as the door clicked shut, she asked calmly, "What can I do for you, Lord Devens?"

"Lord Devens?" Archie slanted a smile at her that once would have turned her heart. "My, how formal you've become. I used to be Archie."

"You used to be many things, Archie, but that was long ago." She affected a pleasant expression. "Now, what may I do for you, Lord Devens?"

Pressing a hand to his chest, Archie acted wounded. "You've grown cold over the years."

"No," she disagreed smoothly, "only smarter."

With a graceful sweep of his arm, Archie fell to one knee before her. "I throw myself on your mercy and beg you forgive me for breaking our engagement," he said, rounding every syllable. "In all of Europe I failed to find anyone quite like you, Laurel."

"I well believe that, my lord, for someone as naive as I once was must be rare indeed."

"It's not that at all, my dear Laurel, but rather your sweetness of nature, the charm of your personality, your very essence, which makes you unique."

Shaking her head over his verbose prose, Laurel would give him no ground. "Have you run through your funds already, Archie? I suppose you're again seeking an heiress. Why didn't you find one in Europe? Were the women too cagey for you? I imagine that since you'd had such luck with me, you might return to where you found such ripe pickings."

Archie's expression of wounded outrage was comical. "It hurts me greatly that you would believe such a thing of me."

"For that I'm sorry," she said blithely.

He ground the heel of his hand against his chest.

"A knife to the heart would be far more preferable to the pain you're inflicting upon me now."

Staring at him, Laurel was at a loss for words, so she did the only thing that came naturally.

She held her sides and laughed aloud at the absurdity of the man who very nearly became her husband. And then she thanked her lucky stars.

Lord Simmons strode toward the parlor door, determined to oust the bastard. The nerve of the man barging into their home without permission. Why, it positively enraged him.

The last person his daughter needed to pester her was a greedy wretch like Devens. Why couldn't the man have had the good grace to stay gone for good? No, instead the blackguard came prancing around his daughter the minute he returned to England. Well, this time, Lord Simmons was having none of it.

As he neared the parlor door, a sound captured his attention and brought his steps to a halt. Oh, dear God, it was the sound of Laurel's laughter. Laughter! Bloody hell, he'd rather hear her in tears than laughing with the wastrel.

A horrible thought struck him. What if his daughter was in danger of falling under Devens' spell yet again? While it seemed unlikely that his practical child could ever be deceived twice, he had no idea what Laurel would do if she believed herself in love. What if she had convinced herself that she'd never truly gotten over Devens? Would she take the scoundrel back into her life and her heart?

Slamming a fist into his hand, Lord Simmons decided he just could not stand back and watch his daughter flounder. No, he was going to have to take a more forceful stance and push Laurel in the right direction.

Straight into the arms of Royce Van Cleef.

His gentle nudges toward Van Cleef would now become full-fledged bumps until Laurel came to her senses and realized that Van Cleef was the perfect man for her.

But for now, he needed to attend to the matter at hand.

Thrusting open the parlor door, Lord Simmons strode in, only to see Devens on his knee in front of Laurel. With a strangled exclamation, Lord Simmons reached down and, grabbing hold of the back of Devens' jacket, hoisted the blackguard to his feet. "You, sir, are unwelcome in my home," Lord Simmons pronounced in a steely voice.

"But—"

"I do not wish for an explanation," he said, cutting off the younger man. "Now hie yourself off or I will be forced to call upon my footmen to accomplish the task."

"Father—"

"I'm sorry, Laurel, but this man has insulted this family enough for one lifetime. I will not afford him another opportunity."

Tugging down on the ends of his cravat, Archie cleared his throat. "Ah . . . perhaps it is time for me to take my leave."

"Past time, I'd say," Lord Simmons added.

"Laurel," Archie murmured, bowing toward her. "My lord."

Crossing his arms, Lord Simmons scowled at the preening dandy. "Begone."

Following Devens into the foyer, Lord Simmons waited until the bugger left, then returned to Laurel. As she opened her mouth to offer an explanation, he held up both of his hands to stave it off. "I consider myself a fair and decent man, Laurel, but in this matter I will not budge. That man grievously harmed you, and therefore he is never welcome in this house again. Understood?"

The wide-eyed gaze she turned upon him made Lord Simmons feel a twinge of guilt. He never dictated to his daughter, so he well understood her surprise. However, in this matter, he would not, could not, yield. "Do you understand?" he repeated firmly.

Her eyes sparkled as if she held a secret, making Lord Simmons suspicious, but an instant later, she dropped her gaze and murmured, "Yes, Father."

Snorting at the demure response that was so unlike his daughter, Lord Simmons nevertheless accepted her answer with a firm nod. "Very well, then. If you ever have a problem with that wastrel again, you let me know and I'll make certain he understands his status with this family."

"I believe you made that quite clear already, Father," Laurel said, amusement brightening her voice.

"True," he groused, "but with a man like that, I can't be certain if he'll heed my warning." Smoothing his hands down the front of his vest, Lord Simmons reassured his daughter. "If there is a next time, however, I will make the point a bit . . . clearer," he finished.

Satisfaction filled him as he bid his daughter farewell and left her to her thoughts. Indeed, there were times when a man just had to get aggressive in order to get the job done.

Seething, Margaret stormed through the door of her townhouse, humiliated to the core. How *dare* he refuse her!

"Ah, you're home, angel," her mother sang out from the front salon. "Where did you get off to?"

"I went to see Lord Van Cleef, if you must know," she replied sourly, walking into the room.

"By yourself?" Her mother's eyes widened.

"Yes, *by myself*," Margaret said snidely as she flopped down into a chair. "I thought I was the woman he'd chosen to marry. In fact, I was positive of it."

Lady St. John's eyes grew wider still.

"Stop popping your eyes out at me like that, Mother. It's most unattractive."

Blinking, Lady St. John adjusted her expression. "Sorry, dear, you simply caught me by surprise."

"That's what Royce said as well." Margaret wasn't about to go into detail over her horrid set-down.

While her mother's eyes flared once again at the use of Royce's Christian name, she didn't remark upon it. Instead, she murmured, "And I take it you were incorrect in your assumption that you were his intended bride."

"Isn't that obvious, Mother?" Margaret asked in a huff. "Do you think I'd be this upset if everything went perfectly and I was now engaged to Royce?"

Shaking her head, Lady St. John reached out to pat her daughter's knee. "There, there."

"Don't try to placate me, Mother," Margaret ground out, feeling a sweep of white-hot fury. "I'm certainly not about to allow Royce Van Cleef to utterly humiliate me and walk away unscathed. Oh, no. I'll find a way to make him sorry for his carelessness with my emotions." Clenching her hands, she vowed, "And once I discover who he *did* choose for his bride, I'll make her wish she'd never caught any man's attention."

"Oh, dear me," murmured Lady St. John, her hand fluttering against her chest.

But Margaret paid her mother no mind, for she was far too busy planning her revenge.

"I appreciate you coming along with me, Laurel," Lord Simmons said, cupping his daughter's elbow as he escorted her into the stable area at Tattersalls. "You always have a fine eye for prime horseflesh."

Laughing brightly, Laurel swatted lightly at her father. "Don't patronize me, Father. We both know I'm more likely to choose a horse for its fine color than for any other reason. You just wanted company and I was all there was available."

"Even if that were true, what type of gentleman would I be if I admitted to it?" Winking at her, Lord Simmons released her hand. "Now if you'll excuse me for a few minutes, I'll step into the back room and see how much the owner would like for the stallion."

Laurel glanced into the stall, admiring the handsome black horse. Nodding in approval, she agreed with her father's choice. "His coat gleams so nicely and you'd look quite dashing atop him."

Leaning closer to his daughter, he whispered, "I'll refrain from mentioning how dashing I'd look upon the stallion to the owner, because I'm certain that would drive the price up."

"Get along with you," Laurel said with a laugh.

Laurel watched her father disappear around the corner, then returned her attention to the stallion. As if her father truly needed her opinion on a horse, Laurel thought with an inward scoff. Ever since Archie's visit yesterday, her father had been hovering close to her. It was as if he were afraid that if he let her out of his sight, she'd once again fall prey to Archie's charm.

Oddly enough, she'd found Archie's charm tarnished and had easily seen beyond the phrases meant to delight her. Instead of finding him dashing, she'd found him, well, humorous. How could she have found anything attractive in a man who, after not seeing her for years, threw himself down on his knees before her and pledged his admiration? Utterly *ridiculous*.

Still, her father's concern touched her deeply, and though she'd tried to reassure him that his worries were groundless, he'd continued to stay close by her side. Knowing time would ease his mind, she had indulged him, even to the point of accompanying him here.

"I suppose if I assumed that smile was for me, I'd be incorrect, wouldn't I?" Royce's voice intruded on her thoughts.

"Quite right," Laurel agreed, once she'd gotten

over her surprise. "You have an uncanny knack, my lord, for turning up in all the wrong places."

"Now that, my lovely Laurel, depends upon one's viewpoint." Strolling forward, Royce rested his arms on the door to the stallion's stall. "From where I'm standing, I'd say my timing is perfect."

Laurel fought to keep from smiling. While Archie's flowery praise left her cold, Royce charmed her with only a few words . . . and that was saying a lot considering she knew exactly what he was up to.

Which made him all the more dangerous to her peace of mind.

"Whatever the case may be, I believe I shall go find my fath—"

"Laurel, wait," Royce urged, holding out a hand. "Please."

It was the *please* that reached her. Growing still, she looked at him. "Why?" she asked softly, not wanting to argue yet again. "We've already said everything that needs to be said."

"No, I don't believe that's true." He speared her with his gaze. "Why don't we discuss the wager?"

Gasping, Laurel was stunned by his question. "The wager?" she squeaked.

He nodded firmly. "After I spoke with Harriet, I realized that she knew about the wager . . . and if she knew, then chances were good that you did as well."

Laurel dropped all pretenses. "Now you know why I'm so determined to avoid you."

"Because of the wager?"

"Of course."

Studying her for a long moment, he asked, "Why does that bother you so?"

"I can't believe you even need to ask me that!"

"While I can hazard a guess, I'd prefer if you'd enlighten me."

Folding her arms across her chest, Laurel leaned back against the stall door. "I hardly wish to be involved with a man I can't trust."

"You *can* trust me!" he protested immediately.

"You've been dishonest with me from the very beginning, Royce, so why would I ever be so foolish as to trust you?"

Royce rubbed his hands across his face. "That blasted wager," he muttered, before dropping his arms to the side. "Must it always be this way between us?"

Though she wished she could answer differently, Laurel said softly, "Yes."

He leaned closer. "What if we started over? What if we begin anew right here, right now?"

Her heart leapt at the thought, but she squelched the spark of hope. "I don't see how that is possible. There can be no going back."

"Then let's not go back; let's go forward." Leaning into her, Royce shifted closer. "The more time I spend with you, the more time I *want* to spend with you. Just give me a chance to prove that we are meant to be together."

"I can't trust you," she whispered with a shake of her head. "You're far too much like Archie."

His head jerked back as if she'd slapped him. "How many times must I say it—I'm *nothing* like Devens."

"And yet you are, in many ways. Like him, you aren't above lying to accomplish your goals."

Closing his eyes, Royce took a deep breath before

meeting her gaze once more. "I promise you that if you let us start again, there will be nothing but complete honesty between us."

"But there is the very problem," she pointed out. "How do I know if you're telling me the truth if I can't trust you?"

"Right away you won't, but hopefully, after time, you'll learn that I'm being honest with you." Lifting one hand, he caressed her cheek with his fingertips. "What do you say, Laurel? Will you give us another chance?"

How could she forget all that had gone before? Just a few days ago, he'd tried yet again to trick her into marriage. It tormented her to realize that despite all the reasons not to agree to his plea, her heart cried for her to accept, to give them time to begin again without lies or trickery between them.

Torn, she shook her head. "I don't know," she whispered, wishing she could say yes. "I just don't know."

"Then you think about it," Royce urged, "and when you're considering my proposal, I want you to remember a few things."

Questioning him with her eyes, she waited for him to continue.

"Remember how I make you feel."

His hot breath rushed over her parted lips. Closing her eyes, Laurel awaited the touch of his mouth upon hers. Instead, she felt his lips skim across her brow, a tender touch speaking of emotions far deeper than passion.

"Remember that you make me feel more than I've ever felt before."

The words whispered across her temple as he moved along her brow, pausing to press a kiss upon each closed eyelid.

"Remember that whenever I'm with you I forget all about wagers or games."

Nipping gently at the curve of her cheek, Royce continued his seduction of her senses. Breathlessly, Laurel ached to feel his lips on hers, to taste the sweetness of his kiss, to experience once again the elation of desire.

"But most of all, Laurel, I need you to remember that when I'm with you, I *want* to be a better man."

Sweetly, he brushed his lips against hers. Lifting her lashes, Laurel met his heated gaze and felt her heart tighten. Slowly, Royce lowered his head toward her and she lifted onto her toes to greet him.

The sound of approaching voices broke the spell that had been cast around them, snapping Laurel from the fantasy Royce had so expertly woven. Looking up at him, she wondered if his entreaties had come from his heart or from his clever mind. Perhaps all the sweet phrases were simply another way for him to win his game. He'd told her that he didn't think of wagers or games when he was with her, but that didn't answer her troublesome question.

Could she believe him?

Waving to Laurel as she and her father rode off, Royce watched until they'd disappeared behind a line of carriages. Tucking his hands into his pocket, he felt the smoothness of Lord Simmons' missive tucked within. Royce had been stunned at the note, but he wasn't about to question his good fortune. He'd simply rescheduled his day so that he could stroll into Tattersalls a few minutes after Laurel had arrived with her father.

Fragments of his conversation with Laurel teased his mind, making his stomach roll. Laurel had accused him of withholding the truth to suit his needs, of behaving like Devens. Nonsense, Royce thought with a shrug.

And yet, Lord Simmons' note seemed to grow heavier with each passing second. It was then that the truth struck Royce. Even as he'd been promising her that he would move forward honestly, he'd neglected to tell her that her own father had arranged their meeting. Instead, he'd allowed her to believe that he'd happened into Tattersalls by chance.

But was that a lie? Would withholding the information be considered a lie or simply the most expedient way to convince Laurel of his intent? After all, nothing could have been served by telling Laurel about her father's minor deception. Indeed, she would have undoubtedly grown upset at her father if she'd discovered his interference, and upsetting Laurel would have accomplished nothing.

Trying to comfort himself with that thought did little to ease his conscience. Regardless of how he tried to justify his actions, Royce knew that his omission was, in essence, a lie. Laurel had just accused him of lying to her just as Devens had. The realization that he had indeed done just that didn't sit well with him.

God knew, he didn't ever want to remind Laurel of Devens.

Drawing a deep breath, Royce vowed that, starting tomorrow, he would be completely honest with Laurel.

Yes, tomorrow would end all the half-truths to Laurel.

Tomorrow.

Chapter

13

❦

"You failed me, Harris."

Elizabeth glared at the young man before her.

"I attempted to enter Lady Laurel's room, but your son chased me away."

Tapping her fingers against the arm of her chair, Elizabeth turned the events at Hammington's over in her mind. "I hadn't anticipated my son's actions," she murmured, more to herself than to the man she'd hired to disgrace the Simmons girl. "Because of your poor planning, my son ended up a laughingstock."

Harris nodded glumly. "At least some of the attention was directed toward Lord Morris as well," he pointed out.

"Don't be an idiot," Elizabeth snapped. "The reason people were laughing at my son was precisely because he was found *with* Steven."

"On the bed," Harris added.

Frowning at the dull-witted man, Elizabeth realized it was little wonder her plan went askew. Walking to her desk, she retrieved the pouch she'd placed there earlier. "Here is your payment. And remember," she said, lowering her voice, "if I ever hear a word of our arrangement I will hire someone to track you down and teach you the value of holding your tongue."

Gulping, Harris nodded wildly, eagerly grabbing the money. "I won't breathe a word of it," he promised as he headed out the door. "Not one."

"See that you don't." As the door shut behind him, Elizabeth resumed her seat in front of the fire and mulled over her problem.

Next time she wouldn't be so foolish as to hire such a dim-witted buffoon. And there *would* be a next time.

If both Royce and Lord Morris had felt free to call upon the Simmons girl at such a late hour, then she was correct to question the chit's moral fiber. She couldn't allow a strumpet to become the next Countess of Tewksbury.

Elizabeth straightened in her chair. No, she'd worked far too hard to rebuild the title to ever allow the Simmons girl to damage their name. Lord knew, before she'd married Royce's father, the Tewksbury legacy had consisted of empty coffers, spendthrift ways despite the lack of funds, and the Earl's reputation for womanizing.

But Elizabeth had soon changed the Tewksbury legacy. The moment Royce's father had slipped the ring upon her finger, she'd tightened the coffers, now filled with money she'd brought to the estate. After producing an heir, as was her duty, she'd banned her husband from her bed, ending all that messy business, and proceeded to raise their son to honor his family name.

Of course, things ran much smoother after her husband had the good grace to pass along. But now her son threatened the name with an unsuitable choice for his bride. Elizabeth knew she owed it to herself and to the Tewksbury legacy to keep the blood free from undesirables. The idea of him marrying someone like the Simmons chit, well, it just couldn't happen.

And she would do anything to ensure that.

Slowing her horse down to a walk, Laurel glanced at Steven, who rode beside her. "To tell you the truth, Steven, I don't know what to do about Royce anymore."

"Anymore?" He grinned at her. "When did you ever?"

"True enough," she agreed. "He can be a bit—"

"Exasperating?"

Sighing, Laurel nodded once. "Exactly."

"Ah, but that's not the real problem, is it?" Steven paused, before adding, "You could easily handle Royce if he was simply exasperating. However, my friend can also be charming, loyal, and amusing . . . to name a few of his finest qualities."

Another sigh escaped her, this one deeper than the last. "That is the crux of the problem."

"Hmmm," murmured Steven. "You have quite the dilemma."

A rustling sound in a nearby bush caught Laurel's attention. Ever since she'd left the house, she'd felt as if someone was watching her. "What was that?"

"I didn't hear anything." Steven peered around at the nearby bushes.

She shrugged away her apprehension as pure foolishness. "I was wondering if you thought—" She broke off as she heard another loud rustling, this time closer than the last. Before she knew what was happening, her horse bolted forward.

Terror lancing through her, Laurel clutched at the reins, trying desperately to regain control of her horse. The thundering hooves of her mount beat in furious rhythm with her heart as she raced through the park. Branches tore at her riding habit, ripping at the material, scratching the flesh beneath.

Wildly, she pulled back on the reins, hoping she could slow the mare's mad pace before she was thrown. Her arms ached as she tugged with all of her might until, finally, her horse began to calm. A few minutes later, she stopped him. Shaking with relief, Laurel slid off her mount, landing safely upon the ground where she collapsed, exhausted and frightened.

The sound of a horse charging down the narrow path caught her attention. Wearily, she lifted her head, expecting to see Steven charging forth, but she was wrong.

"*Laurel!*" Royce called as he leapt down from his horse and rushed to her side. Gathering her in his arms, he ran his gaze over her. "Are you hurt?"

Shaking her head, she settled against him, absorbing his comfort.

"Lord, I was so frightened," he admitted as he rubbed his cheek against the top of her head. "I was riding toward you and Steven when I saw your horse bolt."

Another horse raced down the path with Steven on its back. "Is she hurt?" he called out.

"I'm not certain." Royce's response vibrated in his chest. "Why don't you ride back and bring a carriage to the east path? I'll carry Laurel out of the woods and we'll meet you there."

"Right." Wheeling his horse around, Steven headed back the way he'd come.

Royce hugged her closer still. "Nothing is ever easy with you." Pressing a kiss upon the top of her head, he laughed softly.

"I like to keep you guessing," she murmured weakly.

Standing slowly, Royce lifted Laurel into his arms, carrying her gently as if she were cherished. "You succeed, my sweet Laurel," he said. "Most heartily."

Heading straight for Lord Simmons' sideboard, Royce poured himself a brandy before he was invited to do so. Formalities be damned; he was still shaking from the sight of Laurel atop a runaway horse. Emptying his snifter, he topped off his glass again.

"I believe I'll join you," Lord Simmons said as he moved into the room.

"As will I," Steven added, shutting the door behind him.

Stepping back, Royce waved the other two men forward. "Lord knows we deserve it," he said as he sank into one of the armchairs. "I vow it took years off my life to see Laurel in danger like that."

"Mine as well," Steven agreed, sitting across from Royce. "I'm just thankful that you came along when you did, Royce, or else I would have been forced to leave Laurel alone while I rode for help."

Royce's hand shook as he took a sip of his brandy.

"Royce stopped here this morning and I directed him toward the park," Lord Simmons said as he joined them. "I'd say it was good timing all around."

Swirling his brandy, Royce asked the question that preyed on all of their minds. "Was the noise Laurel heard simply an animal or was it a person intent on startling her mount?"

"I don't know," Steven said with a shake of his head. "I didn't see anything at all."

"It must have been an animal. Who would want to hurt my daughter?"

"I'm not certain, but we can't rule it out." Swiftly, Royce explained what had happened at the Hammingtons, beginning with the man he'd chased away. "This is the second time someone has tried to hurt Laurel."

"Do you really believe we can compare the two incidents? After all, one only threatened her reputation while this latest endangered her very life," Lord Simmons pointed out.

Leaning forward, Royce met the older man's gaze. "I don't see how we can dismiss what happened at the weekend party. What if the attempts to harm Laurel are intensifying?"

"Whoa," Steven said, holding up both his hands. "Aren't we getting a bit ahead of ourselves? For all we know, it could have been an animal that startled her horse."

"Perhaps it was," Royce conceded, "but what if it wasn't? What if someone is looking to harm Laurel for some reason beyond our comprehension? If we fail to consider every possibility, regardless of how far-fetched it might seem, then we might be endangering Laurel in the process."

Lord Simmons frowned, concern etching harsh lines upon his brow. "How should we proceed then?"

Propping his elbows on his knees, Royce clasped his hands to keep them still. "I suggest that we keep a closer eye on her."

"I was riding right beside her when this happened, Royce," Steven said dryly. "How much closer can we be?"

"Point well taken." Royce leaned back in his chair, trying to think of a suitable solution. After a moment, an idea began to form. "Lord Percy, would you consider placing your staff on alert? For instance, it would help if the next time Laurel went riding, a groom checked her saddle and bridle to ensure no one had tampered with it."

"Or if she received a package, it could come to you for inspection before being given to Laurel," Steven added, warming to the idea.

"Exactly." Tapping his fingers against the arm of his chair, Royce continued to expand upon his plan. "And whenever she decides to attend any social function, you can arrange for someone you trust to personally accompany her."

Pressing two fingers against his temple, Lord Simmons leaned his head back against his chair. "*All* of her social events?" He groaned softly. "I shall have to enlist the help of others for I can't even hope to keep up with Laurel's social obligations. I'm not as young as I used to be."

"Then call upon me," Steven offered without hesitation. "I'd be delighted to escort Lady Laurel wherever she wished to go."

"As would I," Royce added, shooting a glare at Steven.

Lord Simmons nodded in agreement. "I will most certainly call upon you both to aid me in protecting my daughter."

The slow smile that crept upon Lord Simmons' lips caught Royce's attention. "Why are you looking so satisfied?"

"It's nothing, really," Lord Simmons stated, affecting an air of nonchalance as he leaned back in his chair.

"Come now," Royce returned, a corner of his mouth quirking upward.

"Very well." Lord Simmons stretched out his legs. "It's just that I realized if the two of you are intent on dancing attendance on Laurel, then it will leave very little room for Devens to come around."

Royce grinned broadly, more than satisfied with that result. It would be bad enough for him to be tripping over Steven; the last person he wanted to deal with was that bastard Devens.

Margaret arrived at Lady Hamilton's soiree garbed in her finest attire, determined to show Royce that he hadn't affected her in the least.

Whipping open her fan, she joined a group of young ladies who were dowdy and plain and would make her appear even more sophisticated and beautiful. After making certain she was positioned where she could see the entire room, Margaret began scanning the crowd for Royce.

"I swear to you, Eleanor, I saw him carrying her through the park."

"Impossible."

"How scandalous."

"*I* thought it was romantic."

Margaret felt like hissing at the ninnies around her to be silent so she could concentrate. However, the handsome Lord Conover was smiling at her from across the room and she didn't want to appear anything less than the perfect lady.

"Personally, I thought it was the stuff of dreams," sighed the first speaker, Plain Ninny Number One.

"I still find it difficult to believe that he would carry her through the park in broad daylight . . . with everyone watching."

Plain Ninny Number Two, Margaret thought, her throat aching to shout at them to be quiet.

"It was most inappropriate."

Obviously Plain Ninny Number Three had spinster blood running through her veins, for Margaret had to agree with Plain Ninny Number One. Indeed, she would have found the gesture extremely romantic.

"Then I suppose she's the one he's chosen," sighed the last girl.

That phrase caught Margaret's attention. Spinning on her heel, she turned to face the unattractive quartet. "I couldn't help but overhearing," she began in her most pleasant voice, "and you've gotten me curious as to whom you're speaking about."

"Why, the Earl of Tewksbury, of course," supplied Plain Ninny Number Two.

Number Three sniffed at her. "I thought everyone who was anyone had heard the tale by now."

Sneering at the snaggle-toothed witch, Margaret snapped, "Obviously you were mistaken." She shifted her attention onto Number Two. "Are you certain it was the Earl of Tewksbury?"

She nodded her overly large head. "Sarah saw it with her own eyes."

Immediately, Margaret focused on the ninny named Sarah. "When did you see Lord Tewksbury?"

"Just today," stammered the young woman.

Margaret reeled backward. While she'd been planning her revenge and regretting exposing her vulnerability to Royce, he'd been traipsing through the park wooing a female for all to see. Shaking with the effort to suppress her anger, Margaret demanded, "Who was she?"

Sarah's eyes grew wide, apprehension darkening them. "Perhaps I shouldn't gossip about—"

Reaching out, Margaret clasped the ninny's wrist and dug her nails into the soft underside. "Tell me," she hissed in a low voice.

"It was Lady Laurel Simmons," the ninny stammered, tugging at her arm. "Now, *please* let me go."

Flinging away the girl's wrist, Margaret struggled to calm herself; she needed to decide how to handle this new bit of gossip. Oh, Royce was going to pay for his sins doubly now, for not only had he decided upon another woman, but he'd also as good as publicly declared his affections.

And she'd had to learn the truth from the Ninny Quartet.

Stumbling only once, Margaret made her way outside, hoping the fresh air would calm her.

After all, she had to be collected in order to plan her revenge against Royce and his unlucky bride-to-be, Lady Laurel Simmons.

The scrape of a heel alerted Margaret to the fact that she was no longer alone on the veranda, so she couldn't give in to her urge to scream in anger. Taking a deep breath, she smoothed out her expression before turning to see who had joined her.

The very moment she saw the man standing behind her, everything clicked into place. She had found her perfect accomplice.

"All of society is talking about it," Harriet said as she adjusted her sunbonnet. "How the dashing Lord Van Cleef came striding out of the woods with the once independent Lady Laurel draped across his chest . . . snuggled against him in a most *intimate* fashion," she finished in a mock whisper.

Groaning, Laurel laid her head against the chaise that her father had moved into the gardens at the rear of the house. "It was nothing like that at all," she explained. "I had just been startled to the point of weakness and Royce was carrying me to a carriage Steven had called for us."

"*I* know that, but you have to admit the gossips' version is far more romantic," Harriet said with a smile.

How could anything be more romantic than having Royce come to her rescue just when she so desperately needed him? Still, Laurel didn't want to admit to anyone, not even her best friend, how Royce had made her feel when he'd cradled her against him. What was it about him that made her start to tingle, yet melt at the same time, whenever she saw him? Whatever it was, Laurel knew it was best to avoid him until she was able to regain control of her emotions.

"Even I love to hear the story about your rescue," sighed Harriet, twirling a ribbon on her dress. "I'd love to have just *one* gentleman want me, but they all seem infatuated with you at the moment."

Frowning slightly, Laurel shook her head. "That's not true at all. What I am this season is the prize in a wager . . . which has nothing at all to do with infatuation."

"I'd settle for being the prize," Harriet disagreed. "The attention Royce gives you is far more than most women receive from gentlemen who claim to love them."

"At least those ladies know they possess the affections of their intended." Sobering, Laurel felt all of her doubts and fears well up inside of her. "Once Royce achieves his aim and claims me, then what happens? Will he tuck me in a house in the country where he will visit me only at his convenience?"

"I see your point," Harriet conceded, reaching out to help herself to a finger sandwich. "Then perhaps, Laurel, you should consider one of the other men who are interested in you."

"Other men?" Laurel scoffed with an indelicate snort. "What other men?"

"Come now, Laurel, don't tell me you haven't noticed." Laughing gaily, Harriet brushed the crumbs off her skirt. "You have quite a few suitors literally chasing after you. Just think of yesterday."

Waving a hand, Laurel dismissed her friend's claim. "Don't be ridiculous. They were only chasing after me because my horse turned wild."

"Ah, but Laurel, you're failing to notice that there were *two* men with you in the first place."

"Royce was joining us simply because he foolishly considers Steven a threat to winning his silly wager. You know that."

Rolling her eyes, Harriet reached for another treat. "And you were riding with Steven." She held up two fingers. "Two gentlemen."

"Steven only spends time with me because I asked for his help."

"Don't be naive, Laurel. No gentleman would spend so much time with a lady if he wasn't attracted to her." Harriet's expression turned decidedly smug. "Besides, I've seen how Steven looks at you when he doesn't think you notice. He is *most* interested in you."

"You must be wrong." But even as she said the words, memories filtered through her, memories of Steven smiling down at her as they danced, of his offering her his hand, of the way he always appeared by her side at social functions. Worry shifted through her. "I hope you're wrong, Harriet. I would hate to think that I'd encouraged him unintentionally in my efforts to best Royce." For if

Harriet was right, then Laurel was engaging in the very behavior that she herself abhorred. Why, she'd accused Royce of acting with only his own interests in mind, never once considering that in her quest to outwit him, she'd been doing the very same thing.

$\mathcal{E}$ntering his townhouse, Royce tossed his hat onto the sideboard. His visit to the Bow Street Runners had been exceedingly frustrating. They'd failed to uncover the identity of the man he'd accosted outside Laurel's door. For God's sake, there were enough people at Hammington's party. Surely *someone* had to have seen *something!*

Apparently not, if he was to believe the runner.

Raking a hand through his hair, Royce strode into his study, only to pull himself up short. The chaos that lay before him was shocking.

Bookshelves were overturned, papers ripped to shreds, and, worst of all, his business ledgers lay upon the fire that eagerly consumed the fragile papers. Grabbing a poker, Royce pulled the books from the blaze, but one glance told him he was too late. All of the figures, all of his work, had been burned in a matter of minutes.

"Giles!" he bellowed.

The butler ran into the room. "Dear Lord!"

Giles's exclamation echoed Royce's sentiments exactly. "Who did this?"

"I . . . I . . . don't know, sir," stuttered the butler. "No one has been in here since you left."

"It's quite obvious, Giles, that *someone* was indeed in my study." He turned toward his butler. "Call the servants together. We shall question everyone."

"Immediately, my lord," replied the butler as he hurried from the room.

Looking down at his books, Royce knew it would take him a long time to re-create them. The tremendous amount of work before him only made Royce more determined to discover who had committed this heinous act.

Tightening his jaw, Royce strode out of the room to find some answers.

"My lady!"

Her maid's shout brought Laurel's head up sharply. "In here, Mildred," she called out from the library, where she'd been enjoying a fine book of poems.

Running into the room, Mildred skidded to a halt. "Your clothes, milady!"

Laurel glanced down at her attire. Granted, she was wearing an older, slightly faded gown, but certainly nothing to cause alarm. "Yes?"

"Upstairs," the maid gasped, "upstairs your clothes are . . . are . . . ruined."

"Ruined?" Laurel asked.

"Completely ruined."

Closing her book, Laurel rose to her feet. "Why don't we go upstairs so you can show me what you mean."

The maid trailed along behind Laurel as she mounted the stairs. "I went to your chamber to prepare your clothes for the evening—just like I always do—when I stumbled upon the mess."

The explanation hastened Laurel's step. Hopefully, the maid was exaggerating.

"Dear Lord!" Laurel exclaimed as she entered her room.

"I told you," mumbled the maid from behind her.

But Laurel paid her no heed, for she was too stunned to speak. Dresses, shoes, shawls, undergarments, were all strewn about her room, each one torn or soiled. Not a stitch of clothing remained in her armoire. Reaching out a shaking hand, Laurel fingered the destroyed silk from one of her favorite gowns. "How did this happen?" she whispered, the hoarseness in her voice betraying the depth of her shock.

"I don't know, milady," cried the maid as she stood wringing her hands.

Laurel shook her head as she tried to gather her thoughts. "I'll round up the servants and find out if anyone knows what happened here today."

"What shall I do with the gowns?"

Closing her eyes briefly, Laurel took a deep breath and opened them again, steeling herself. "Since they're beyond repair, I suppose they're best suited for rags now."

Still shaken by the destruction of her wardrobe,

Laurel headed downstairs to find her father. Knocking on his study door, she waited for a moment before entering. "Good evening, Father," she said, moving to press a kiss upon his cheek.

"This is a pleasant surprise," murmured Lord Simmons, setting down his quill. "It's not often that—" He broke off his words as soon as he glanced up at her. "You're looking a bit peaked. Are you feeling poorly?"

Laurel offered her father a tremulous smile. "I was feeling fine until a few minutes ago."

Lord Simmons frowned. "What's happened?"

"Someone went into my room and destroyed all my clothes."

"What?" bellowed Lord Simmons, thrusting to his feet.

Somehow her father's anger calmed her shaky nerves. "Nothing appears to have been taken, but all my garments were utterly ruined."

"Have the servants been questioned?" Lord Simmons asked as he rounded his desk.

Laurel shook her head. "I was going to do that after I spoke to you."

"Then what are we waiting for," said Lord Simmons as he stormed from the room. Pausing at the door, he glanced back. "Are you coming?"

"Yes." As always, they would do it together.

"I can't believe that no one saw anything," Lord Simmons grumbled as he walked back into his study.

"It surprises me as well," conceded Laurel as she sank into a chair. "I just don't understand why anyone would come into our home simply to destroy my things."

Her father paled. "Sweet Lord, Royce was right."

"What do you mean he was right? About what?"

Sitting down, her father appeared deeply shaken. "He was convinced that you were in danger."

Laurel opened her mouth to dismiss Royce's concerns, but the image of her clothes lying in ruined heaps stopped her. "He told me that someone was trying to enter my room at Hammingtons' weekend party, but I didn't believe him," she murmured as she lifted her gaze to her father. "I wonder now if he was indeed telling the truth."

"He undoubtedly was," Lord Simmons said. "He also believes that your accident the other day was, well, no accident. He'd speculated that perhaps someone had been hiding in the bushes, waiting to startle your horse . . . which explains the sound you heard before your horse bolted."

Swallowing, Laurel struggled to accept all of what her father was telling her. "But who would want to hurt me?"

"That's what we need to discover." Rising, Lord Simmons headed toward his desk. "I'm going to send a missive to Royce and invite him to dine with us this evening. I believe we should bring him up to speed on the latest turn of events."

Glancing down at her old and stained gown, Laurel squelched the instinctive feminine urge to preen for him. Perhaps one look at her in this attire and he would soon abandon his wager. Laurel didn't like the pang caused by that thought.

Determined to prove herself unaffected by Royce, she nodded her head. "I believe that is a fine idea, Father. Perhaps Royce might have some insight into the situation that we're overlooking."

There, she thought smugly, that sounded level-headed and calm . . . but was completely at odds with the nerves jumping in the pit of her stomach.

Rubbing a hand across his bleary eyes, Royce waited for the Simmons' butler to open the door. For the better portion of the day, Royce had been tallying receipts and trying to rebuild his books from memory. Receiving the invitation to dine with the Simmonses, Royce had decided he deserved a break from all the tedious business of rebuilding his financial records.

Following the butler into the salon, Royce sketched a bow to Lord Simmons and his daughter. "I appreciate your kind invitation."

"It is our pleasure," Lord Simmons replied, slapping a hand upon Royce's shoulder. "May I offer you a drink?"

Accepting, Royce looked at Laurel and was somewhat surprised by her appearance. She'd never looked less than perfectly put together. Yet this evening, she looked, well, like she'd been cleaning all day. However, even rumpled and dusty, Laurel was a sight for sore eyes.

And he should know, Royce thought with a smile.

Blinking to ease the ache in his reddened eyes, Royce took the drink from Laurel's father, then sat in one of the chairs.

"Are you feeling all right?" Laurel asked, peering at him closely.

"Yes, I'm fine," he said. "With the exception of a pounding headache and bleary eyes."

"What's wrong? Are you ill?"

Just thinking on the events that had occurred earlier today infuriated him. "No, nothing as simple as that. Someone broke into my home today and destroyed all of my financial papers."

Laurel's eyes widened. "Really? Someone broke into our house and destroyed all of my clothes," she said. "Well, all but this old thing," she added, lifting the edge of her skirt.

"Having both of our houses broken into on the same day is *not* a coincidence," Royce murmured, thinking out loud. "But why would someone want to harm us?"

Shaking her head, Laurel answered, "I have no idea."

"If we put all the incidents together—"

"*Incidents?*"

"A strange man who seems to have disappeared off the face of the earth tries to enter your room," he said, holding up one finger. "Then your horse is startled and you are almost seriously injured." He held up a second finger. "Lastly, your clothes are destroyed." Holding up three fingers, Royce drove the point home. "It is obvious, my dear Laurel, that someone is out to harm you."

Laurel paled, visibly shaken.

"I agree," Lord Simmons murmured. The silence in the room seemed deafening. Finally, Laurel's father asked, "What did you mean that the stranger had disappeared off the face of the earth?"

"I set a Bow Street Runner on the case, but he was unable to give me even one possible suspect," Royce explained. "Yet, the man happened upon Laurel's room in nothing but his nightclothes, leading me to believe he was a guest of Lord Hammington's."

"A guest or a servant," Laurel added quietly.

Her observation caught his attention. "A servant," he murmured. "I never considered that possibility. I shall have to send around a note to the Runner in the morning and have him expand his search to include the staff."

"Along with any personal servants of the guests," Laurel concluded.

Admiration filled Royce. "I've never appreciated your intelligence quite so much."

Widening her eyes, Laurel let loose a laugh. "Oh, so you thought me a dullard?"

"Of course not," he quickly corrected, "but such a keen sense of cunning—"

"—befitting of a fox," she returned.

"Indeed," he agreed, not missing a beat. "You possess a fox's keen sense of cunning."

"Which is precisely why your plan to *entrap* me failed so miserably," Laurel pointed out. "Only the most clever hunter can possibly hope to outwit a fox."

For the first time, his wager lay between them as a joke, rather than a source of conflict. "Ah, but that's just the point, Laurel." Leaning forward, Royce met her gaze. "I happen to be the best hunter amongst the ton."

She leaned forward as well. "If you are the finest example of a hunter, then I pity the rest of the gentlemen for their horrible lack of skill."

Lord Simmons' roar of laughter caught Royce off guard. He'd been so intent upon Laurel that he'd forgotten they weren't alone. "Ah, the two of you will provide me with spirited grandbabies," Lord Simmons said brightly.

"*Father!*" gasped Laurel.

Royce only grinned. "I shall do my best, sir."

"While I'm enjoying your courting, I'm afraid we really should focus upon the matter at hand."

"The threat," Royce replied to Lord Simmons. "You're quite right. It's most intriguing that whoever is behind the threat to Laurel has also turned their attention to me."

"The fact that your study was destroyed soon after society connected you with my daughter should not be dismissed," Lord Simmons said, rubbing his chin. "Though the main target still appears to be Laurel."

"And my connection to Laurel is the only reason my study was ransacked."

"That *does* make sense," Laurel agreed. "But who would want to harm me?"

Shaking his head, Lord Simmons murmured, "I don't know, but we need to uncover the culprit before the attacks escalate."

"I agree. At this point it would be best if we began to work together." Royce nodded to Lord Simmons. "Any information I uncover, I will share with you."

"Likewise," Lord Simmons replied.

"And what would you like me to do . . . other than act as bait?" Laurel asked a bit too sweetly.

"That will be quite enough, Laurel," Royce returned.

Pressing a hand to her chest, Laurel sighed deeply. "Ah, so wonderful to feel useful."

He couldn't hold back his laughter. "Isn't it?"

Climbing into his carriage, Royce leaned his head back against the cushion and mulled over the evening. Despite the confirmation that someone was indeed out to harm Laurel, he'd had a wonderful evening. Laurel's wit and practical suggestions in the face of such adversity were remarkable. Still, he couldn't allow his romantic interest in her to distract him from uncovering who was behind the threats.

After all, Laurel might be in real danger.

The thought made his stomach clench and he vowed to increase his efforts. First, he would look toward Margaret St. John. He wouldn't put much past that spoiled snippet. Besides, it would suit her needs to force him to spend time apart from Laurel. Destroying his personal ledgers would certainly occupy the bulk of his time, just as it would take Laurel a good many days to replace her wardrobe.

Yet, try as he did, Royce found it difficult to imagine her behind Laurel's riding accident. It seemed too vindictive, even for someone as shallow as Margaret. Regardless, Royce decided to begin his investigation first thing in the morning.

* * *

Standing on the edge of the dance floor in the Hammingtons' town house, Laurel kept her gaze upon Archie. After giving the matter much thought while being fitted for gown after gown, her ex-fiancé was the only person she could put on her list of suspects. He'd come back from Europe expecting to apologize and have her fall at his feet. Only she'd disappointed him by refusing to see him, much less marry him. Naturally, if he perceived Royce as a rival for her hand, Archie would be tempted to vent his frustrations upon Royce as well. Still, she doubted if he'd try to physically harm her by star-tling her horse.

Suddenly, Laurel saw Archie approach from the opposite side of the room. Bracing herself, Laurel shifted her expression to one of bland disinterest.

"Good evening," Archie murmured as he bowed before her.

"Archie," she returned shortly, unable to bring herself to wish him a good evening. Lifting onto her tiptoes, Laurel searched for her father who had just gone to fetch a cup of punch.

Giving her a fawning smile, Archie slid his hand beneath her elbow. "I was wondering if you might give me a moment of your time."

Yet instead of allowing her to respond, he simply drew her toward a darkened corridor. Not wanting to cause yet another scene, Laurel allowed herself to be dragged along, certain her father would search her out.

"Ah, this is perfect," Archie pronounced as he pulled her into the deserted morning room.

Yanking her arm free, Laurel marched into the

room, then spun around to face him. "Perfect for what, Archie?"

"I've been waiting for the opportunity to have a word with you in private."

The purring quality to Archie's voice grated upon her ears. Deciding not to give Archie the upper hand, she went on the offensive. "Did you send someone to destroy my things last night?"

"*What?*"

His response disappointed Laurel for it was too genuine for even a liar like Archie to manufacture. Boldly, Laurel moved toward the door.

"Hold up a moment," he said, grabbing hold of her arm. "We haven't had a chance to speak to each other yet."

"I've found out everything I wanted to know."

"Well, I haven't," he said, his expression hardening. "I *need* to speak with you."

Laurel suppressed the shiver of fear that shot down her spine. It was only Archie; he wouldn't harm her. "Very well," she said finally, unwilling to let him see he'd frightened her. "What did you wish to say to me?"

"That I missed you," he murmured.

Laurel snorted at his statement. "Perhaps you missed my money or my naiveté, but me?" Shaking her head, Laurel met his gaze head-on. "You never even knew *me.*"

Anger shimmered in his eyes. "That's not true," he said roughly, before softening his tone. "Memories of your kiss keep me awake at night."

Alarm raced through her as Archie pulled her against him. Struggling to break free, Laurel pressed her hands on his chest. "Release me this instant," she demanded, annoyed to hear the quiver of fear in her voice.

"Not before I remind you of what we once had," he said, lowering his head.

Fighting against him, Laurel opened her mouth to scream, but the sound was swallowed by Archie as he ground his lips against hers.

Chapter
15

❧

*S*omething was wrong. He felt it in his bones.

Looking around the crowded room, Royce tried to find a cause for his unease.

"Good evening, my lord."

Suppressing a groan, Royce turned to face Margaret St. John. Here was the source of his discomfort. "Lady Margaret," he said warily, remembering their less than amicable parting and his suspicions.

She beamed up at him, tilting her head at a pretty angle. "The dancers look quite entertained."

Her less than subtle hint didn't escape him, but he wasn't about to indulge her. "Indeed they do."

The intensity of her smile dimmed a bit. "I vow my feet are itching to dance," she said with a forced brightness.

Her charming manner set off alarms within him. Where was the Lady Margaret that practically spat at him when she'd last seen him? It was as if she were trying to distract him . . .

Immediately, Royce scanned the room, searching for Laurel. Just a few moments ago, she'd been standing with her father near the punch bowl, but now she was nowhere to be found.

"Looking for someone?"

The snide tone in Lady Margaret's question caught his attention. Twisting around to face her, Royce demanded, "Where is she?"

Margaret's pleasant expression stayed firmly in place, but her eyes were frozen chips of blue ice. "Where is who?"

Suddenly, somehow, he knew Laurel was in danger again . . . most likely at the hands of this vicious creature before him. Turning from her in disgust, Royce strode across the room.

"Excuse me, Lady Pennson," he said, addressing a matron he'd last seen standing next to Laurel. "I was wondering if you knew where Lady Laurel had gotten off to."

Lady Pennson's gaze shifted away. "I believe I saw her step away with a gentleman."

His nerves quivered in alarm. "Do you know *which* gentleman, by chance?" At her hesitation, Royce hastened to reassure her. "Lord Simmons asked me to keep an eye on his daughter and I fear I've been most neglectful in my duties." Smiling pleasantly, he forced himself to be patient when all he wanted to do was shake the answer out of her.

"Lord Simmons is over at the punch bowl," she said, gesturing with her fan. "Why don't you ask him?"

"Because if he was fetching punch for his daughter, it would be highly unlikely that he observed who she went off with, wouldn't it?" Royce asked as politely as he could manage through his gritted teeth.

Pressing her lips together, Lady Pennson looked highly displeased with his questions. After a moment, she finally nodded once. Leaning closer, Lady Pennson looked both ways before whispering, "I saw her go down that corridor with Lord Devens." She shook her head, a disapproving set to her mouth. "It is most unwise of Laurel to spend time in that man's company. I fear it will only bring her sadness again."

"Don't concern yourself," Royce said as he began to move away. "I shall never allow that to happen."

Fighting Archie off, Laurel reached up to yank at his hair, at his ears, at anything she could, trying to dislodge his mouth from hers. But nothing she did seemed to affect him.

Keeping one arm firmly latched around her, Archie roamed her body with his free hand, palming her breast, caressing her buttocks, squeezing her hip. Humiliation mingled with anger as she tried to devise a way to break free.

Suddenly, her wish was granted.

Laurel grabbed hold of a chair to keep from falling to the ground as she was pushed aside. Dragging air into her lungs, Laurel saw Royce standing over Archie like an avenging god taking out his wrath upon a lesser soul.

She'd never seen a more beautiful sight in her life.

Dark fury colored Royce's features. "Are you all right?" he rasped in a low voice.

Beginning to shake from relief, Laurel nodded once. "Yes," she whispered.

Royce's entire body vibrated with ill-suppressed emotions. "Shall I tear him apart for you?"

Though she wanted to say yes, Laurel forced herself to shake her head. "Please don't, Royce. He's not worth the effort."

For a moment she didn't think he'd honor her request, but after a long hesitation, Royce stepped back from where Archie lay upon the floor, cradling his jaw.

"If that's what you want . . ." Royce finally said, still glaring down at Archie.

Laurel could see the fury still flowing strong within him, yet he held it back because she'd asked it of him. "Thank you, Royce," she whispered.

"Go find your father, so we can decide what to do with this piece of offal." Royce nudged Archie none-too-gently with the toe of his boot.

Walking toward the door, Laurel paused with her hand on the knob. "I'll be back in a moment."

Royce glanced over his shoulder. "We're not going anywhere," he said wryly.

"I think you—Royce!"

Shouting his name, Laurel watched in horror as Archie kicked out with his foot, catching the inside of Royce's thigh, sending him crashing to the floor. Grimacing, Royce pushed himself up until he sat on top of Archie. Pulling back his hand, he let loose a punch, hitting Archie square in the jaw and sending his head knocking against the floor.

About to rush over to Royce, Laurel felt the door push open, but before she could move out of the way, she was shoved against the wall, completely hidden from view.

"Good God!" exclaimed Lord Hammington. "This is getting to be a habit for you, isn't it Van Cleef?"

"I hope you're not annoyed at me for staying out of sight," Laurel said to Royce as they slipped out the side door, heading toward the carriages.

"Not at all," he reassured her. "I wanted you to stay out of sight. In fact, I even positioned myself in front of the open door to ensure that you stayed hidden."

"Lord Hammington was scandalized enough; I can't imagine his response if he'd realized I was in the room as well," Laurel said, stepping into Royce's carriage.

"That's true." Royce followed her into the conveyance, taking a seat next to her. "However, instead of being on a bed with another man, I was sitting atop him this time."

She couldn't help but smile. "I can picture it quite vividly."

"I vow, Laurel, the members of the ton are going to think I'm a bit . . . odd if this continues to happen." Gently, he stroked her hair away from her face. "I'm just glad that your name wasn't associated with that scene."

"It was really very gallant of you to protect me like that. And I appreciate you braving the ballroom to explain to my father what had happened."

"I will admit that the looks I received told me that everyone had heard of my latest foible," Royce admitted. "Thankfully, your father understood what had really transpired."

"I imagine he was as grateful as I," Laurel said, laying a hand upon Royce's leg. "Did Archie injure you?"

"Not at all," he replied, his voice tight. Clearing his throat, Royce reached for her hand and, removing it from his leg, held it within his. "I think you should know that once again Lord Hammington received a missive requesting his presence in the morning room."

"Just like at his country party," Laurel said with a gasp.

"Yes, and you would have been discovered kissing Devens."

"Not by choice," she corrected, wiping at her mouth. "I can't fathom that someone would go to all the trouble of arranging for someone to make improper advances, then ensuring that the act is witnessed—" She broke off as the reality of the situation hit her. "Good Heavens, there really *was* someone at my door that night in the country, wasn't there?"

"Now you believe me?" Royce replied with a laugh. "And all it took was being kissed against your will and getting knocked behind a door."

"Some of us are harder to convince than others," Laurel agreed, shrugging lightly. Placing her hand against his chest, she gazed up at him. "I'm sorry I ever doubted you."

Gently, Royce leaned down and placed a sweet, tender kiss upon her swollen mouth, his touch erasing the awful memory of Archie's embrace. "You had reason."

Wanting to tumble into Royce's arms, Laurel forced herself to straighten, pulling slightly away from him. "Do you believe Archie sent the missive?"

"No," Royce replied, shaking his head. "I think it was Margaret St. John."

"Why would she wish to harm my reputation?"

"Because she believed she was the woman I'd wagered on capturing as my bride and proceeded to throw herself at me, thoroughly embarrassing herself in the process." Royce's jaw tightened. "I can only assume that she hoped I'd lose interest in you if your reputation were marred."

"Hmm . . . I never tried that approach."

"And you never will."

Tilting her head, Laurel arched an eyebrow at Royce. "Are you telling me how to behave again?"

"Absolutely," he said without hesitation. "Do you expect anything less from me?"

Laughing at his unapologetic arrogance, Laurel rested her head against the seat. "Foolish me." Sighing deeply, she turned to look at Royce. "That weekend at Hammington's must have been a difficult one for you. First you are hounded by Margaret, then found with Steven, followed by an argument with me."

Royce shook his head. "Margaret didn't confront me until *after* the party."

"Then why would she arrange for someone to come to my room?"

"Bloody hell," Royce whispered, rubbing a finger against his temple. "She can't be the one who sent the first missive, because she didn't know about you. In fact, she believed that I was looking for her that night."

"Does this mean that we have more than one person trying to torment us?"

"It would appear that way," Royce said, looking down at her.

"Well," Laurel returned briskly, "I must say that I far prefer it when people actually like me."

Her attempt at levity made Royce chuckle and, placing his arm around her, he anchored her against him. "So do I, Laurel." Slanting a look down at her, he asked, "Do *you* like *me?*"

Laurel felt her heart race at the simple question. The response that rose to her lips frightened her far more than Archie ever could. Royce had rescued her tonight, then honored her wishes, but the painful memories of past injuries made it impossible to give him the response that echoed in her heart. Still, she needed to gift him in return.

One corner of her mouth tilted upward as Laurel slowly nodded. "Oh, yes, Royce. I do indeed."

His mother arrived in a whirlwind of fury.

"This is twice that you've been discovered in an appalling situation," she charged, slamming her reticule onto his desk. "You told that idiot Hammington that you were *wrestling* with Lord Devens. Are you a fool, Royce? What were you thinking? While there was no mention of that Simmons chit, I'm positive she's involved in this fiasco some way."

"As I've said before, Lady Laurel Simmons is not open to discussion," Royce said, leaning back in his chair. "However, if you paid me a visit to discuss some other matter, I'd be more than happy to entertain you."

"Don't be ridiculous, Royce. You know as well as I that we need to discuss this problem."

"No, Mother, I don't see where this is a problem at all." Rising from his chair, Royce went to his sideboard and poured himself a drink. "I handled everything last night."

"If *handling* it means that you played the fool for public fodder, then you did that quite nicely," she returned tartly. "And even if you won't admit it, I *know* that Simmons girl was involved."

"Her name is Laurel," he said slowly.

"Do you hear yourself?" Making a noise of disgust, Elizabeth pointed a finger at him. "Even *now* you defend her."

Sighing, Royce realized he could no longer even carry on a conversation with his mother without it disintegrating into her condemning everything in his life. "If you've only come to chastise me about Laurel, then this visit is at an end," Royce said wearily, putting down his drink and crossing his arms.

Regally, his mother rose from her seat, her chin lifted high in the air. "I will not allow you to disgrace our family name."

"I'm not trying to disgrace our name, Mother," Royce murmured. "I'm simply trying to live my life in a manner that makes me happy."

"You are the Earl of Tewksbury. Your personal happiness comes second to the duties to that title."

The sad thing was his mother truly believed that, Royce knew, for he'd never known her to be happy. "I'm sorry you feel that way, Mother." He reached for her, only to let his hand drop back to his side. "I'm afraid I disagree with you. Naturally I shall honor the family name, but *not* at the expense of my happiness."

Disapproval radiated from her in unceasing waves. "I thought I'd raised you better," she informed him coldly, then, turning on her heel, she marched from the room.

Retrieving his drink, Royce lifted it in a salute. "Good-bye, Mother," he said to his now empty study, before draining his glass.

Nothing was happening as he'd planned, Archie thought sourly. Taking a sip of his brandy, he looked around his rented townhouse. Lord knew, his family holdings had been sold off long ago to pay debtors. The fortune he'd inherited had come from his mother's uncle, a miserly old coot who'd hoarded every penny he'd earned. Of course the man had been in trade, but that little fact was a blot on his family history that he preferred to ignore.

However, his trouble with Laurel wasn't quite as easy to forget. Her suspicions that he'd run through his funds were, of course, well-founded, but he didn't understand what that had to do with anything. He'd still make a solid husband for her. And if he married her, then they'd both be getting something out of the bargain.

If only that interfering Van Cleef weren't underfoot all the time, Archie knew that Laurel would have long ago fallen back into his arms. But it seemed as if every time he tried to convince Laurel that she should take him back, Van Cleef managed to spoil everything.

Thinking about last night, Archie was positive that Laurel was just about to twine her arms around his neck and return his kiss. The plan the St. John chit had devised had been sound and he'd been reaping the benefits . . . until Van Cleef interrupted them. Instead of winning Laurel's hand, all he'd ended up with was a sore jaw and a blackened eye.

Indeed, only Van Cleef stood between him and his fortune, Archie thought with a smile. Well, he'd just have to take care of Van Cleef once and for all.

The maid held out a silver platter with a snowy white card resting upon it. Hesitating only for a moment, Laurel reached out and picked up the card.

Royce Van Cleef, the Earl of Tewksbury.

Sighing, she laid the card back down. "Please show him in to the morning room." She watched the maid leave the study, all the while wanting to call her back, to ask her to tell Lord Van Cleef that she wasn't at home.

Guilt bit into her, making her feel absolutely horrid for thinking such thoughts, but she couldn't help it. Lately, Royce had been wonderful to her, even coming to her rescue several times, but deep inside she wondered if his actions were prompted out of true concern for her or because he wished to step into her good graces. The thought had plagued her all last evening, disturbing her sleep and stealing her appetite. Laurel heartily wished Royce hadn't called upon her today; it was far easier to deny her feelings when he wasn't around.

It was critically important that she guard herself against him for she'd gone and done a terribly foolish thing. She'd fallen in love with him and left herself open to heartache . . . yet again.

But she'd never reveal that secret to Royce and

hand him the power to devastate her. Instead, she'd treat him as a friend, allowing him into her heart with fondness, but locking away any deeper emotions.

It was the safest course.

Satisfied that she'd made the right decision, Laurel rose from her desk, leaving the week's dinner menu undone. When she arrived at the morning room, Laurel greeted Royce, who was surveying the glass birds upon the mantel. "This is an unexpected surprise."

"I hope it's not an unpleasant one."

"Of course not," she rushed to assure him. "Having rescued me from Archie earns you the right to call upon me anytime."

"I'll remember that," he returned with a grin.

Laurel could have kicked herself for offering him open access to her home. Having Royce constantly underfoot was the last thing she needed in her life.

"Would you care for some refreshments?"

Shaking his head, Royce politely declined her offer. "I'm unable to stay long, but I did want to discuss my plan with you."

"*Plan?*" she asked, uncertain what Royce meant. "I thought we'd simply continue on as we have been."

"Let me remind you, Laurel, that in the past few days you've had someone try to sneak into your room," he began, ticking off each point with his fingers, "you've nearly been injured by a runaway horse, your wardrobe had been destroyed, and you were accosted by your ex-fiancé at a party." He leaned against the mantel. "From where I'm standing, it doesn't look like your current plan has been working."

Flushing, Laurel accepted his comments as truth. "Well, if you put it that way—"

Royce shook his head. "Trust me, Laurel. There is no other way to phrase the threat you face to make it more palatable. No matter how you look at it, the entire situation is hazardous to your health."

Dropping down into a chair, she gazed up at him. "Very well, then, what would you suggest we do?"

"First and foremost, you never, ever go off with Devens."

She waved a hand at him. "That goes unspoken."

"I thought as much, but I prefer to be certain." Heading for a chair, Royce favored his right leg, wincing slightly as he gingerly lowered himself into the chair.

"You *are* hurt." Laurel rushed to his side, dropping to her knees before him. "You should have told me immediately."

"It will pass," he said matter-of-factly. "My leg is a bit bruised and I must be favoring it more than I realized."

He was obviously chagrined to have shown her any weakness, yet instead of making her believe him less manly, the knowledge that he'd been injured while defending her made her want to wrap her arms around him and hold him until the pain went away. Now where did *that* thought come from?

Swallowing her gasp, she jerked backward, almost falling onto her behind before she managed to steady herself and retake her seat. "What shall we do going forth?"

"I believe the first thing I'm going to do is to pay visits to Lady Margaret St. John and Devens."

"To convince them to cease in their nasty games," Laurel concluded.

Nodding once, Royce rubbed the muscle in his thigh. "Precisely. Hopefully they'll be smart enough to heed the warning."

"And if they're not?"

Royce's features hardened. "Then we'll have to do a stronger job of convincing them."

Shivering at his ominous tone, Laurel said, "With those two out of the way, perhaps things can return to normal for us."

"I'm not certain of that," Royce admitted, scraping his hand along his jaw. "We've already concluded that Margaret wouldn't have arranged for someone to enter your suite at the Hammingtons' party."

"And Archie hadn't yet returned to England," Laurel supplied.

"Indeed." Frowning, Royce continued, "But I don't know who would have tried to enter your room that night. If not for the note to Hammington, I would assume that the fellow simply stumbled upon the wrong room." He shook his head. "What really baffles me is that missive. We can't connect either Devens or Lady Margaret with the first incident, yet they used the exact ploy last night."

"It seems to be too much of a coincidence," Laurel agreed.

"Quite."

Toying with the fabric in her skirt, Laurel shook

her head. "I find it hard to believe that we have so many people opposed to the idea of you and me together—not that we are," she hastened to add.

One side of his mouth quirked upward. "Not yet."

The soft promise reverberating in those two words made Laurel shift in her chair. Choosing to ignore his vow, she continued, "How shall we discover who else is seeking to discredit us?"

"After we remove Margaret and Devens, then we can keep a close vigil to see if the problems stop. If they do, then we know who was behind all of the pranks. If not, then we'll have to go on from there."

"But what if Margaret and Archie continue to wreak havoc?"

Groaning, Royce leaned his head against his chair. "You do realize, Laurel, that there is one very easy, simple way to end all of this, don't you?"

Shaking her head, Laurel gazed at him quizzically. "What?"

He leaned forward. "Marry me."

Her breath caught in her throat.

Seeing her reaction, Royce pressed onward. "If you marry me, it is certain to foil whatever plans Margaret and Devens might cook up."

"I hardly consider that a reason for marriage," Laurel whispered.

"Come now, Laurel, you know very well that my reasons go far deeper." Royce reached out and placed his hand over hers. "You know I've wanted to claim you for my wife from the very beginning."

"You only wanted to claim me to win your wager," she countered. "And that doesn't count for much."

"Things have changed," he replied vehemently.

"So you say."

"Indeed I do," he insisted. "And you should trust me."

"Trust is earned, not given."

She expected anger at her retort, but instead Royce released her hand and sat back in his chair. "Very well."

His reaction threw her off balance. "What do you mean 'very well'?"

"I mean that time is my ally and you will come to realize that I am trustworthy." Crooking one arm across the high back of the chair, Royce seemed completely unaffected by her rejection. "In the meantime, I shall content myself with ending the threat to you."

Laurel looked at Royce, every nerve ending on alert.

She sensed a ploy.

Chapter

16

❦

"*I* wasn't certain if you would want to come riding with me this morning," Steven said as Laurel caught up to him.

"After what happened last time, I must say it gave me pause, but I decided the risk was worth taking," Laurel replied, leaning forward to pat her horse on the neck.

"I'm not certain if Royce would agree."

Laughing softly, Laurel smiled at her friend. "Then I'm lucky that I don't need his approval."

Steven lifted a brow at her. "Are you certain? After all, Royce believes it's a man's right to monitor his fiancée's actions."

"Any intelligent woman would fight that dictate," Laurel assured him. "And since we're not affianced, there really is no issue."

Pulling his horse to a stop, Steven gave Laurel his full attention. "You're not engaged?"

"No, we are not," she said firmly. "What on

earth would make you believe—" Laurel paused. "Royce."

Steven nodded in agreement. "He referred to you as his fiancée just the other day."

"How dare he make an announcement that is so blatantly untrue," she exclaimed, outraged at Royce's arrogance.

Shrugging, Steven nudged his horse forward once more. "Perhaps he considers your acceptance of his proposal a foregone conclusion."

"Then he is sorely mistaken," she replied, fuming. "That man needs to be taught a lesson."

"And you're the one to do it?"

"Exactly."

For a long moment, silence reigned between them. "I hope you realize that you have other options," Steven murmured softly.

"Options? What do you mean?" asked Laurel.

Keeping his eyes fixed firmly on the path before them, Steven said, "Only that Royce isn't the only man who would take you for his wife." Suddenly, Steven pinned her with his gaze.

Flustered, Laurel struggled to find a graceful way out of the conversation. "I am extremely flattered, Steven," she began carefully.

"But you wish for us to remain friends," he finished for her.

Wincing at the bitterness she heard in his voice, Laurel wished she could have fallen in love with this kind, gentle man. "I don't know what to say," she murmured, feeling helpless against the guilt riding through her. "I wish things could be different."

"But you're in love with Royce."

Laurel hastened to deny her feelings. *"No,* of course not."

"The vehemence of your reply contradicts your words." The grin Steven wore couldn't hide the glimmer of pain in his eyes. "Once again, Royce wins." Steven shook his head.

"He hasn't 'won' anything," Laurel replied swiftly.

"I suppose being your friend is better than nothing," Steven said, his voice injected with forced lightness. "After all, if I didn't get to watch you and Royce try to outdo one another, my life would turn horribly dull."

"And we wouldn't want that, would we, my friend?" Laurel said, relieved that their conversation had returned to safer ground.

Steven hesitated for a moment before slanting her a grin. "No, indeed we would not . . . my friend."

Regretting the awkwardness between them, Laurel kept her smile firmly in place. "Race you," she said brightly before kicking her horse into a gallop.

Royce headed into his study, determined to get through more of his investment papers. Things were falling into place nicely with Laurel. He'd undermine her wall of resistance toward him by burrowing in as her friend, using their closeness to convince her to marry him. And then, oh, then, he could take her in his arms and feel her soft curves pressed against him until he . . .

Royce drew in a deep breath. Damn, but the woman plagued his thoughts. He couldn't wait until he was happily married and could resume his life without the distraction of courtship. Shaking his head, he strode over to his desk and took his seat.

Glancing down, Royce noticed a note sitting atop his newly redone ledgers. Retrieving it, he began to read:

> *My dear Lord Van Cleef,*
> *I have taken the liberty of informing your in-*
> *tended, Lady Laurel Simmons, about your past indis-*
> *cretions. I've made certain to include the* ménage à
> trois *and the wager you made while grouse hunting*
> *in Scotland about how many local maidens you could*
> *bed. I'm certain she will find it fascinating reading.*
> *Your devoted servant*

Dear God! Royce crumpled the paper in an odd combination of frustration and fear. Right at this very moment, Laurel could be reading about his foolish, misspent youth. Tossing aside the missive, he strode from the house, too impatient to wait for his carriage. Hell, he could walk the distance to Laurel's house in the same amount of time.

The need to see Laurel pulsated through him, along with the fear that she would be so disgusted by his youthful indiscretions that she'd refuse to see him.

Busy pruning the rosebushes in the greenhouse, Laurel had her hands buried in dirt when she heard the maid call. "My lady, are you in here?"

Wiping her hands on her apron, Laurel turned as the maid rounded the corner, holding out a letter.

"This just arrived for you, my lady. The messenger said it was urgent."

Thanking the maid, Laurel accepted the note and waited until the girl had left before she opened it. The first line jumped out at her.

For your own well-being, I felt you should know what type of man you've been seeing . . .

Her curiosity piqued, she quickly read the entire letter . . . and then read it again.

"Ho, Royce," William hailed as Royce approached him from the opposite direction. "I haven't seen you at White's in quite a while."

"I've been rather busy," he returned, not pausing in his steps.

"With courting the lovely Laurel?" called James in a decidedly laughing voice.

"Sorry, but I can't talk now," Royce said, passing the two men. "This matter is most urgent."

William's eyes widened as he watched Royce disappear down the street. "Good Lord, I can't ever remember seeing Van Cleef so disheveled or preoccupied."

"Nor I," James agreed, rocking back on his heels. "But, if you notice, he's heading toward the Simmons' townhouse. So something tells me there's a woman behind his present state."

Nodding slowly, William remained quiet for a few moments, before he glanced up at James. "Well, bully for him."

"It's about time," James concurred.

Grinning broadly, William said, "I don't believe I've ever seen him look better."

"I know precisely what you mean, my friend. Van Cleef looked positively . . . human," James replied with a laugh. Clamping an arm around William's shoulder, he asked, "How about if we head to White's and drink a toast to our once unflappable friend?"

"Splendid idea."

Laurel had begun to repot her lilies when Royce burst into the greenhouse. Seeing his distress, she guessed at its source. "Did you receive a missive as well?" she asked, dusting the dirt off her hands and turning to face him.

"Yes," he rasped, out of breath and obviously anxious. Reaching out a hand, Royce stepped forward. "Laurel, we need to talk about what the note said."

"Why don't you read it first?" she offered, holding it out.

She watched Royce's face drain of all color as he read the contents. Swallowing hard, he looked up and met her gaze. The stoic light in his eyes told her he was prepared for the worst.

"I wish I could tell you that these are all lies," he began in a low voice, "but I can't. Everything in this letter is true." A shiver vibrated through him. "However, these events happened in the past. I used to be a bit wild—"

"Apparently so," Laurel interjected.

Royce blanched some more, but he continued with his explanation. ". . . and I would accept all sorts of crazy wagers—"

"Like the one you made about me."

Crumpling the note, Royce glared at her. "You're not making it very easy for me to explain my actions."

"I'm sorry," she said in mock innocence. "Is that what you wanted? For me to make this *easy?*"

"Laurel," Royce ground out in frustration. "Please allow me to explain."

"Why?" she asked calmly. "You're my friend, Royce. There is no need to justify your actions, past or present, to me." She shrugged lightly. "It honestly makes no difference to me," she finished, hiding the jumble of nerves that welled inside her. She didn't want to even hint at the emotions she'd felt when she'd read all about Royce's exploits, knowing all the while that she was simply another wager in a long line of wild bets.

She'd been smart to never express her love for him.

Thrusting a hand through his hair, Royce almost vibrated with his frustration. "Even if we are just friends," he spat out the last word, "I would like to tell you that I no longer make a habit of accepting wagers."

"Royce, we met because you accepted a challenge from your friends."

"Yes, but that was a logical wager," he protested. "It was time that I marry and you—" He cut off his explanation as if he realized that he'd revealed too much.

But Laurel had heard enough. Allowing a measure of anger to show, she finished for him. "I fit your profile for the perfect wife."

"True," he acknowledged, "but I've already told you that you've become more to me."

"Indeed I have." Laurel lifted her chin. "I've become your friend."

"You know very well I didn't mean that, Laurel," Royce returned quickly. Releasing his breath in a huff, he shook his head at her. "You're not going to let me explain, are you?"

"Actually," she drawled slowly, "there is something I'm most curious about."

Immediately Royce straightened. "Yes?"

"Is it truly possible to do what the letter mentioned against a fence post with two women at once?"

Frowning deeply, he thrust the letter back at her. "I can see you're not going to be serious about this, so I believe it might be best if I leave now."

Shrugging, Laurel carefully folded the missive. "If you wish," she replied, "but I would dearly love an explanation." She tilted her head to the side. "I wonder if such a thing could be physically possible."

"Hell will freeze over before I *ever* describe it to you," Royce mumbled as he turned on his heel and walked from the greenhouse.

The moment the door shut behind him, Laurel sank onto a nearby bench, exhausted by the confrontation. The entire time she'd been speaking to Royce, images of him frolicking with other women taunted her. Yet, at the same time, she couldn't help but wonder how it would feel to have Royce touch her intimately. But those erotic images were blotted out with one thought.

If she were intimate with Royce, she would simply become another wager he'd won.

How could Laurel be so cool? The accusations in the missive were shocking, albeit true. The only way she could remain so unaffected would be if she truly felt nothing but friendship for him.

Doubt twisted at him, making him wonder if he had only imagined the response, the desire, in her kiss. After he'd knocked Devens on the floor, she'd given him such a look of admiration, he'd been certain her feelings went far deeper than she claimed.

But what if he'd been wrong? After all, she'd made it clear that she didn't trust him . . . and with good reason, he admitted reluctantly. Having her learn that she was the last in a long line of wagers hardly helped convince her that she could trust him. How could he make her believe in him again?

Surely he was clever enough to devise a strategy that would make Laurel realize that he wanted to marry her for far better reasons than to win the wager. What he needed to do was come up with another solution, a better strategy, one that would ease her fears.

After all, he was an intelligent fellow. Like most things in life, if you take time to plan and strategize, everything will fall into place.

Including wary brides-to-be.

Chapter
17

"I believe the best way to proceed is to make a list," Laurel said briskly to Harriet. "If I approach this logically, perhaps the pattern will emerge."

Harriet scooted forward on her chair, discarding her tea without a second glance. "Excellent idea. Now where do we begin?"

Retrieving a piece of notepaper from her father's desk, Laurel began to write.

1. *My horse bolting in the park after I felt as if someone were watching me.*

"I thought the incident at the Hammingtons' country party was first," Harriet said, frowning slightly. "If you're going to truly understand what is happening, you will want to consider all the possibilities."

Agreeing with her friend, Laurel scratched out the number one and replaced it with a two, before writing about the man Royce saw trying to enter her room and making that top her list.

3. *My clothes were destroyed; Royce's ledgers were destroyed as well.*

"Who could have wanted to do that?" Laurel still couldn't imagine anyone wanting to hurt her. Not even Archie or Margaret.

"Let's finish listing everything that's happened, then we'll try to create a list of people who might be behind each one."

Considering Harriet's suggestion an excellent one, Laurel continued.

4. *Lord Hammington receives yet another note and if Royce hadn't intervened, I would have been found in Archie's embrace.*

Or worse, she thought to herself, unable to suppress a little shiver. Archie had been so aggressive, so threatening; she'd never seen him like that before. Pushing the thoughts from her mind, she added the last item to the list.

5. *Note regarding Royce's past.*

"That's all of them," she told Harriet, turning the paper so they could both read it at the same time.

"Do you have any idea who could have arranged to have you discovered with a strange man in your room?" Harriet asked, pointing to number one.

"No." Shaking her head, Laurel explained, "While

I would have suspected Margaret St. John, Royce told me she believed he had made the wager about her. So, if she thought Royce went to the room to find her, she wouldn't have arranged for someone else to come—"

"Also, if she believed Royce was interested in her, she'd have no reason to try to discredit you," concluded Harriet.

Pointing to the second notation on their list, Laurel again didn't have any idea who could have wanted to startle her horse.

"Let's move on to number three," Harriet suggested finally.

Laurel shook her head. "Perhaps this is a waste of time. We aren't coming up with any answers."

"Look at this next one," Harriet insisted. "Margaret could certainly be responsible for destroying your clothes and Royce's ledgers."

"And Archie as well." Bending forward, Laurel wrote the two names down, feeling better to have a few suspects. "We can definitely add them to the fourth item as well. After all, Archie was the one who dragged me off at the Hammingtons' ball and it is possible that Margaret arranged for the note to be sent."

"Yes, add them both," Harried agreed with a nod. "From what you said, Royce was convinced that Margaret sent the second note to Lord Hammington."

"He also felt that Archie had begun to work with Margaret to discredit me."

"There's a discomforting thought."

"Indeed," Laurel agreed softly. "I must admit that it is upsetting to realize there are people who wish to harm me."

Reaching out, Harriet placed a hand upon Laurel's shoulder. "At least you know who they are and can now be extra careful whenever you are around them."

"I won't put anything past either of them," she murmured, before forcing herself to let the upsetting thought go. It would do her little good to bemoan something she couldn't change. "And as for the note about Royce's past, I believe that can be laid upon Margaret's door as well," Laurel added, tapping her fingernail on the parchment.

Leaning back in her chair, Harriet gave Laurel a steady look. "It would appear that dear Margaret has done more than her share of mischief. Now only one question remains." Harriet paused, before she asked, "What are you going to do about her?"

"It's very simple, really," Laurel said firmly. "I'll disarm her with a powerful tool that very few choose to employ." Giving Harriet a pointed look, she finished, "I'll tell her the truth."

Royce saw Laurel enter the room in her evening finery and shadowed her movements. Having come up with a new strategy, one certain to disarm Laurel, all he had to do was wait for an opportunity to speak with her privately. As soon as she moved near a vacant alcove, he stepped forward, gently guiding her into the darkened corner with him.

Placing his fingertips against her lips, he silenced her protest before she had an opportunity to speak. Immediately, he launched into his rehearsed explanation. "I've recently come to regret many things in my past, Laurel, but I won't apologize for any of

them . . . nor would I change them if I could."
Slowly, he removed his hand from her mouth, allowing his fingers to stroke her cheek in a gentle caress. "I know that it offends you to have been a prize in a silly game, but I can't regret making the wager because it brought me to you."

Her eyes widened, and the look encouraged him.

"I like to believe that I would have met you and become enamored of you without any wager, but there's no way of turning back time." He smoothed his fingertip along her arched brow. "It's true that I wish you'd never learned the truth about my wild youth, but, in a way, my impetuous nature is the very reason I met you." Leaning forward, he met her gaze steadily. "Now how could I ever regret that?"

Brushing a soft kiss against her mouth, Royce fought the urge to deepen the touch, contenting himself instead on the astonished look upon Laurel's face. Without another word, he turned and left her standing, wide-eyed, in the alcove.

It took Laurel a full minute to regain hold of her composure. Dear Lord, that man knew how to send her into a spin. Time after time, he could destroy her resolve with a few carefully chosen words. Feeling flushed and light-headed, Laurel wound her way toward the ladies' retiring room.

As soon as the door shut behind her, she sank into a nearby chair. How would she ever resist—

"I would like a word with you."

With a start, Laurel stood and faced Royce's mother. "Of course, my lady."

"I want you to stay away from my son," Lady

Van Cleef snapped, looking at Laurel as if she were a nasty bug that had snuck into her tea. "I saw you out in the dining hall with my son, kissing him, no less." Lifting her chin, she looked down her nose at Laurel. "I always knew you were unfit."

Caught off guard, Laurel floundered for a response. "I fear you've mistaken me for someone who—"

"I have not," pronounced Lady Van Cleef, straightening her shoulders. "For some inexplicable reason, my son has decided upon you, despite my instructions to the contrary. At every turn, you've provided me with ample proof that you would bring disgrace to the Tewksbury title."

"I beg to differ," Laurel murmured, refusing to argue the point. "However, it is of little consequence as I have no intention of ever becoming the Countess of Tewksbury."

"My son believes differently."

"True, and while I have no control over his actions, I do have control over mine," Laurel pointed out. "And if I do not wish to marry your son, then you have nothing to fear."

Stepping forward, Lady Van Cleef glared down at Laurel. "How do I know I can trust you?"

Laurel stood firm beneath the harsh stare. "I suppose you don't," she admitted.

Anger shifted into Lady Van Cleef's expression. "Do you truly believe for one moment that I will trust you? I've worked far too long to bring honor to this family to let it all hang on the *possibility* that you might honor your word." She patted her chest. "I taught my child day after day to respect his obligation, to fulfill his duty, and what does he do?" A sneer curled her lips upward. "He settles upon someone like you."

Shaking her head, Laurel couldn't help but feel sorry for Royce's mother, a woman so obviously trapped within her own confines of propriety. "I'm sorry that I can't do more to ease your mind," Laurel said softly.

Lady Van Cleef's head snapped back, making Laurel wonder if Royce's mother had been expecting anger instead of empathy. "Just stay away from my son," Lady Van Cleef muttered, turning toward the mirror, effectively dismissing Laurel.

Pausing by the door, Laurel glanced back at Lady Van Cleef. Poor Royce, she thought as she closed the door behind her, what life must have been like with a mother like that.

Flushed from her distasteful confrontation, Elizabeth Van Cleef patted her cheeks, angry that she'd been forced into such unpleasantness.

"Excuse me, my lady."

Glancing to her right, Elizabeth was surprised to see the corner seat occupied. Humiliation flooded her as she realized this young girl had witnessed her unladylike confrontation.

Immediately on the defense, Elizabeth glared at the girl. "It is impolite to listen in on private conversations," she said, condescension dripping off every word.

The sly smile upon the girl's face caught Elizabeth's attention. "I believe we can help each other." Rising, the girl dipped into a slight curtsey. "Allow me to introduce myself. I am Margaret St. John."

Elizabeth didn't know why, but something about the girl's manner caught her interest. Perhaps it was the malicious sparkle in her wide blue eyes. "Go on," Elizabeth commanded.

"I am in love with your son," Margaret pronounced.

About to dismiss the statement out of hand, Elizabeth paused. Perhaps this girl was the answer to her problems. Of course, Elizabeth would need to check into the girl's background before she could sanction a match with her son. Yet, even if Margaret St. John proved unsuitable, she would still be useful in getting rid of the Simmons girl.

Elizabeth waved the girl into a seat. Joining her, she encouraged, "Now tell me how you came to love my son." Naturally, she cared not a whit for Margaret's response. No, she was merely seeking a way to rid herself of that pesky Simmons chit.

Someone tapped him on the shoulder. Glancing behind him, Royce was startled to find Laurel. Immediately, he turned toward her.

"Might I have a moment of your time?" she whispered, glancing around him at the two gentlemen with whom he'd been conversing.

"Certainly," Royce replied immediately, unwilling to let this opportunity pass him by. Murmuring his excuses to his friends, Royce cupped Laurel's elbow and steered her down a hallway.

Looking into room after room, Royce searched for an empty one and, finding one, escorted Laurel into Lady Ellsworth's parlor.

"Oh, my," Laurel murmured as she looked around the room.

Taking in the pink and lavender decor, Royce could easily understand her reaction. "No wonder this room was empty."

"Indeed," she returned with a chuckle.

Leaning back against the door, Royce gazed at Laurel. "Why did you wish to speak with me?"

"Because I needed to tell you of my conversation with your mother."

"My *mother*?" he asked warily.

Nodding, Laurel hastened to explain. "She came into the ladies' retiring room and asked . . . well, *told* me to not see you again."

Anger choked him. "She did?"

Again, Laurel nodded. "I only wanted to tell you because I thought it far better that you hear about my conversation with her from me."

"Trust me, my mother wouldn't have uttered a word," Royce replied. Drawing in a deep breath, he looked at Laurel. "I can only apologize for her actions and assure you that it won't happen again in the future."

Her soft smile caught him off guard. "Can you really promise that, Royce? Surely you can't possibly hope to control anyone else's actions?" Shaking her head, Laurel continued, "You can only alter how you *react* to an unpleasant confrontation. I simply wanted to tell you that I understand how upsetting she can be."

The generosity of her spirit overwhelmed Royce. Her sympathetic response humbled him. Still, if he could enhance her reaction, then perhaps—

He broke off his thoughts as the disgracefulness of his behavior hit him. Dear God! Here Laurel had been offering him comfort and instead of thanking her, he stood wondering how he could use this to his advantage.

He grew appalled at his coarse behavior. Straightening away from the door, Royce vowed to abandon any future ploys or strategies to win Laurel. If he was going to claim her for his bride, then he would do it through honesty, trust, and . . . love.

Swallowing instinctively, Royce nonetheless recognized how well the word fit. He stepped forward, reaching out to stroke Laurel's arm. "Thank you for being so understanding."

She ducked her head, shifting away from his touch. "You're welcome," she returned. "I'm only sorry your mother is feeling so . . . threatened by something she has no need to worry about."

"Hasn't she?" he murmured.

Her head jerked upward, her gaze catching his. "No," Laurel finally said, her voice shaking. "No, she doesn't."

"Laurel," he began, "do you remember the question I asked you in Tattersalls?"

"If we could begin again?"

Slowly, he nodded. "Have you given it any more thought?"

"N-n-n-o," she stammered.

"Would you reconsider my offer?"

"I . . . I . . . no, Royce. I'm sorry, but I can't." She shook her head. "I just can't."

He remained silent for a long moment. "I'll ask again," he finally said.

"I can't say if my answer will change."

Shrugging lightly, Royce smiled at her. "That won't make any difference in how often I ask."

"Fair enough," Laurel replied.

"I think so."

Looking ill-at-ease, Laurel gestured toward the door. "I'd better return to the ballroom before anyone notices I'm missing," she said, giving him one last shaky smile before she left.

Her refusal to give him another chance didn't matter, because for the first time, Royce felt as if he'd stumbled upon the way to truly win Laurel's heart.

With love.

Toss in a little trust, time, and honesty and she would soon be his.

As she hurried down the corridor, Laurel pressed her gloved hands against her flaming cheeks. She'd needed to get away from Royce, away from the temptation to give in to his charm. Glimpsing into his childhood had explained so much to Laurel, making her realize that all of his wildness had simply been in reaction to his environment.

Who wouldn't have rebelled against such strictness?

Still, understanding didn't necessarily lead to forgiveness. She wouldn't easily forget that she was simply a pawn in his game, nor would she allow herself to trust him with her emotions. Not yet anyway.

Taking a deep breath, Laurel stepped into the crowded ballroom, hoping no one had noticed her brief absence. She'd already caused enough gossip lately; the last thing she wanted to do was cause more by hieing off with Royce every chance she got.

Glancing back down the hallway, Laurel thought of Royce . . . and wondered if she should have accepted his offer, after all.

No, her choice was the far safer course.

But was it the best one?

Chapter
18

Dismissing her maid, Laurel studied her reflection in the mirror, wondering if she'd made the right decision last night. Earlier today, Royce had sent her an invitation to the Opera and from the moment she'd held the card in her hand, Laurel had felt a tingle of excitement—certainly not the reaction of one friend for another.

But could she begin again? Could she truly forget all that had gone between them and learn to trust him once more?

She didn't know; but one thing was clear, she *wanted* to give him another chance. Allowing her fear of being hurt to keep her from happiness seemed a cowardly way to live. Perhaps she was making a mistake in starting anew, but, in her heart, she knew she couldn't make any other choice.

Squaring her shoulders, Laurel made her way downstairs. As she passed the second landing, her father stepped into the foyer and stopped when he saw her. "You look lovely, darling."

"Thank you, Father," Laurel said, pressing a kiss onto his cheek.

"Just like your mother." Lord Simmons cleared his throat. "Would you care to join me for a glass of sherry before Royce arrives to escort you to the Opera?"

"Certainly," Laurel accepted, linking her arm through her father's and walking with him into the study.

"I admit that it pleases me to see you spending time with Van Cleef." Handing her a glass, he assisted her into a chair before taking a seat himself. "He strikes me as a fine gentleman."

Sipping at the sherry, Laurel looked at her father. "I would have thought his reputation might bother you."

"Not at all." Lord Simmons shook his head. "Personally, I believe a gentleman is far better suited to settle down into the role of husband if he's sown his wild oats." Pressing a hand against his chest, he leaned forward to admit, "In my youth, I was a bit of a rake, but once I met your mother, I changed my ways and became the boring old curmudgeon you know and love."

"You're very seldom boring," she replied with a laugh, warmed by her father's sentiments, growing more certain she had made the right choice. Tonight at the Opera, she would tell Royce that she accepted his proposal to begin their relationship anew.

Her father scowled at her with mock ferocity. "What do you mean by very seldom?"

Widening her eyes, Laurel gave her father a look of bewilderment. "Did I say that?"

Lord Simmons laughed aloud, the sound bringing a smile to Laurel's lips as well.

"Come now, Lord Simmons. How am I ever supposed to entertain your daughter half as well as you do?" Royce asked as he strolled into the study unannounced.

"Laurel was simply laughing at my shortcomings. I'm quite confident, sir, that you can easily entertain my daughter." Lord Simmons stood and offered Royce a sherry.

"No, thank you, my lord," Royce declined. "I believe we should be off if we wish to catch the opening aria." Turning to face Laurel, he held out his hand. "Shall we, my lady?"

Her cheeks warmed as she placed her hand within his.

Stepping forward, her father pressed a kiss to her forehead. "Enjoy yourself, darling."

"Thank you," Laurel replied, hugging her father.

Royce led her into the foyer where he retrieved her wrap and placed it around her shoulders. His solicitous behavior made her feel cherished. She was certain now that she was right to let go of her lingering fear and to give this man a second chance.

An odd tension filled the air as both Royce and Laurel sat quietly within the confines of the carriage. After they'd gone quite a distance, Royce finally observed, "You have been terribly quiet this evening. Is something amiss?"

"No," she returned, meeting his gaze and praying she wasn't blushing.

Tugging on his cravat, Royce took a breath before saying, "I want to tell you something before we arrive at the Opera."

Eagerly, Laurel leaned forward. "Yes?"

"If you wish to remain solely friends, that is fine with me." Reaching out, Royce placed his hand upon hers. "I enjoy your company far too much to give it up."

His consideration touched her as nothing else could have, erasing any lingering doubts. "Royce," she said softly. "I had something I wished to tell you as well."

He remained silent, waiting for her to continue.

Feeling oddly shy, Laurel struggled for a way to begin. "Last night you—"

Before she could finish, the carriage rocked to a stop. As the footman opened the door, Royce stepped down and, reaching back, offered Laurel his hand. On the sidewalk, he tucked her hand into his arm and asked, "You were saying?"

Glancing at the people milling about, Laurel shook her head. "I'll tell you after the performance."

He squeezed her fingers. "Very well then," he said as he escorted her into the Opera hall.

Feeling light-of-heart, Laurel tucked her hand into Royce's elbow as they made their way through the lobby. Just as they were about to head up the main staircase, Steven stepped in front of them.

"Van Cleef," he said in greeting, before turning to her. "Laurel."

The single word was tinged with disappointment and sadness. "Steven," she returned lightly. "How delightful to see you."

He held her steady within his gaze. "I wasn't expecting to see you here."

With Royce. The implied words were unspoken, but Laurel was quite certain that they echoed in all of their thoughts.

Clearing his throat, Royce shifted until he was slightly in front of her. "Lady Laurel graciously accepted my invitation just this morning," Royce said smoothly. "I consider myself most fortunate."

Steven's mouth tightened. "Indeed you are, Royce," he replied stiffly. Bowing slightly, he murmured, "Enjoy the performance."

Laurel wanted to call him back as he moved away, to do something to ease his pain, but knew in her heart that nothing she said could accomplish that. Guilt bore down upon her.

Lifting her chin with one finger, Royce gazed into her eyes. "Didn't you tell me just last night that you can't control another person's actions, only your reaction?"

Indeed she had. Like Steven, she'd been hurt when her love had been rejected, but she'd not only survived, she'd come to realize she'd been mistaken all along. Her feelings for Archie were mere shadows of those she felt for Royce. Hopefully, Steven would soon find the woman of his heart, a woman who would heal his ache.

"Thank you," she whispered.

"Always my pleasure," Royce returned before escorting her up the stairs.

As soon as they reached his family's box, Royce pulled back the curtain, allowing Laurel to enter before him. Following her, he bumped into her back as she came to an abrupt halt.

"I didn't realize you would be attending this evening, Royce."

Stiffening, Royce looked at his mother, who sat rigidly upon her chair like a queen holding court. Holding back a sigh, he responded pleasantly, "Nor I you. Mother," he continued smoothly, "I'd like to introduce you to—"

"We've met," Elizabeth interrupted with a chill in her voice.

"So I heard."

Arching a brow at him, his mother asked, "Surely you don't expect me to share our family's box, do you?"

"Lady Laurel is my *guest*," Royce said firmly.

"Perhaps," his mother said, rising to her feet. "But she is not *mine*."

Royce watched his mother march out, humiliated by her actions. Glancing at Laurel, he tried to gauge her reaction, expecting abject embarrassment. Instead, she greeted his hesitant look with twitching lips and sparkling eyes.

"If I were the sensitive type, I might believe your mother doesn't care much for me."

Relief flooded him as he reached out, lifting her hand to press a kiss upon the back of it. "You, my dear Laurel, demonstrate the traits of a true lady."

"Oh, I don't know about that," she protested with a laugh. "I'm far too outspoken to ever be mistaken for a paragon of ladylike virtue."

Looking at her, Royce wondered if she honestly didn't know how appealing she was to him. "In all the ways that truly matter, you are a sterling example."

Her eyes glowed with pleasure as he assisted her into the chair his mother had recently vacated. Some of his contentment faded as he took in the glances being shot their way from people in nearby boxes, partially hidden behind hands or fans. Obviously, they'd observed his mother's direct snub of Laurel. Three boxes down, his mother sat, her mouth moving at a rapid pace, spouting nothing but complaints, Royce was quite certain.

Bloody hell, he thought, glancing at Laurel. He'd wanted to begin a courtship in earnest, not to cause her to become fodder for gossips.

"Everyone appears most interested in us, my lord," Laurel murmured calmly. "I've always found it fascinating that such a small thing as a snub could cause such a stir."

Stunned, Royce turned toward her. Only Laurel would react in such a manner, turning the displeasure of others into a source of amusement for herself.

Smiling at him, she said, "My goodness, I do hope Lady Pennson is careful. If she doesn't stop craning her neck like that, I fear she might hurt herself."

"You are amazing," he murmured, ignoring the eyes trained upon them to lightly trail his hand down her arm. "And here I was worried that you might be upset."

"Many things have been known to upset me, Royce, but having the ton gossip about me isn't one of them."

Every time he thought he understood Laurel, she turned him on his heel, surprising him with her reactions. Lord knew, his mother lived and breathed for the opinion of society, as did almost every other woman he knew.

It would appear that his final wager on Laurel had indeed been his best.

Following Laurel's example, he ignored the gossips and instead focused upon enjoying his evening.

Slowly fanning herself, Laurel waited for Royce to return with their refreshments since their steward seemed to have disappeared. Despite the rocky start, their evening was progressing nicely. If she ignored the people staring at them, forgot about her insecurities about his sincerity, and dismissed his mother's antipathy toward her, then she could almost believe that she might have a future with Royce.

With that thought, she realized she could either laugh or cry. She chose the former.

"Ah, the sound of an angel."

Her amusement dried up instantly as she turned to face Archie. "You are *not* welcome here," she said firmly.

Stepping forward, Archie announced loudly, "I couldn't resist you either, my love."

His response made no sense. "What on earth are you talking about?"

"I'm tired of fighting it as well." Again, he projected his voice, capturing the attention of those seated in the boxes closest to them.

Feeling the weight of the stares, Laurel stood slowly. "Please leave *now*, my lord."

Her demand was met with another bold announcement. "I know you never stopped loving me." Pressing both of his hands against his chest, he pledged his love to her. "Nor I you."

Reaching out, Archie grabbed hold of her shoulders and began to tug her closer to him. Memories of his unwanted kiss propelled Laurel into action. Raising her arm, she struck Archie across the face with her fan, causing a red welt to form on his cheek and his expression to harden into an angry mask. The loud report of gasps told Laurel that many people were watching the drama being played out in the Van Cleef box.

Archie's fingers dug painfully into her shoulders as he tried to pull her closer still. Bracing both of her arms against his chest, Laurel used every ounce of strength to hold him off. As she lifted her foot to kick him in the shin, Laurel lost her balance, tumbling against him.

The unexpected movement sent Archie stumbling backward. Releasing her shoulders, he flailed his arms to find his balance, but failed. Archie fell backward and crashed into a chair. Sitting in a crumpled heap, rubbing his head, Archie looked pathetic, but Laurel wasn't about to linger and offer him assistance.

Without a backward glance, she darted from the box in search of Royce.

On his way back to his seat, Royce spotted Margaret St. John lurking near the entrance to his box. He ducked behind a column, hoping she hadn't seen him. The last thing he wanted this evening was to engage in a conversation with Margaret. So until she moved, he would remain hidden.

Setting his drinks on a nearby table, Royce

looked up as Lord Hammington rounded the corner from the corridor that led toward the lobby. Hammington stopped when he caught sight of Royce. "Ho there, young man," he greeted with a short wave.

"Shhhh," Royce hissed, pressing a finger to his lips.

Frowning, Lord Hammington glanced around. "Have you arranged an . . . intimate meeting?" he asked with a puzzled frown, glancing around. "Though I must say you picked a poor spot for it."

Wishing Lord Hammington would simply move on, Royce shook his head. Perhaps if he didn't encourage the man, he'd leave.

"I say." Lord Hammington drew himself upward, scowling at Royce. "You're not meeting another gent, are you?"

Royce groaned softly.

"It's bloody peculiar is what it is," Lord Hammington said firmly. "Enough of that or people are going to talk."

For some reason that comment struck him as funny. "As a dear friend recently told me, people are always going to talk, sir. I am merely lending them a hand."

"Deuced odd, if you ask me," mumbled Lord Hammington as he rolled his eyes and continued down the hallway, straight toward Margaret. Pausing in front of her, he held out a warning finger. "You take care now, young lady." Lord Hammington glanced back over his shoulder and caught Royce peering out from behind the column. Shaking his head, he mumbled, "Damn peculiar fellows hanging about."

Royce heard Lord Hammington's complaint half-way down the hall. So much for discretion. The lights flickered, indicating the end of intermission, but Margaret still hovered outside his box. He'd give her a few more minutes to leave on her own before he left his hiding spot to confront her.

When it became clear that she wasn't leaving any time soon, Royce took a deep breath and stepped out into the hallway, just as Laurel came barreling out from behind the curtains. She careened into Margaret, knocking her against the wall, before spinning away and racing down the hallway. Immediately, Margaret entered the Van Cleef box, alarming him even more.

Rushing forward, he peered in through the curtains to see Margaret kneeling next to Devens, who was lying on the floor. It was all too easy for him to guess what had transpired.

Panic pulsed through him as he raced after Laurel, needing to find her more than he needed to punish Devens. He caught up to her as she reached the bottom of the stairs. Cupping her elbow in his hand, he steered her through a small door to the right of the staircase.

As soon as they were alone, Laurel fell against him. As much as he wanted to demand an explanation, he gave her a few minutes to recover.

Enfolding her close, Royce fought off his anger. Twice now Devens had terrified Laurel. While Royce had backed away once, he wouldn't do so again. No, this time, Devens would learn to stay away.

"Laurel," he whispered, brushing a kiss across her brow. "Are you hurt?"

Shaking her head, Laurel pushed back from Royce. "I'm fine." Swiftly, she explained all that had taken place while he'd been fetching their refreshments. Royce struggled to remain calm. She'd needed him and he'd been busy avoiding Margaret. Shame filled Royce as he listened to Laurel tell him about her fear.

When she fell silent, he tried to step away, but she held onto his arm. "Where are you going?"

"I have to find him," Royce ground out roughly.

"No, please," she whispered, tightening her grip. "No more tonight."

Looking down at her, Royce felt torn. He so badly wanted to find Devens and rip him apart. Yet this woman, who had stood so bravely before the gossips, laughed at his mother's venomous insults, and handled an unrequited suitor looked as if she were about to collapse. How could he leave her when she needed him?

Royce promised himself he'd pay a visit to Devens first thing in the morning . . . and convince him of his mistake. Now, however, he'd give Laurel what she needed.

Folding his hand over hers, he smiled gently at her. "Let me take you home."

"Please," Laurel murmured, sagging against him.

With an arm wrapped firmly around her, Royce escorted Laurel through the empty lobby and into the cool night air, all the while devising a plan to rid himself of Devens and Margaret for good.

Chapter
19

⁓

*A*rmed with information he'd only just uncovered, Royce demanded entrance to Devens' townhouse. During the night, his rage had cooled into a frozen determination to make this problem go away once and for all. Pounding on the door, he waited for someone to answer.

After a few moments, an elderly woman cracked open the door. "It's a mite early for a call," she grumbled.

"I don't plan on being polite," Royce muttered, pushing the door open wider before stepping inside.

"You can't come in 'ere!"

Royce didn't even pause at the maid's protest as he shut the door behind him. "Where is Devens?"

" 'E's still abed," replied the maid. As Royce headed for the stairs, she shouted after him. "You can't go up there."

Taking the stairs two at a time, he ignored her cries as he began to open door after door, looking for

Devens' bedroom. Four doors down, he found a darkened room. Stepping in, Royce looked at the bed and saw a large lump beneath the covers. With one swipe, he'd yanked the covers back, exposing Devens' nightshirt-clad body to the chill morning air.

"What the devil?" blustered Devens as he roused himself.

"The devil is right, for I'm mad as Hades." Royce slapped a hand against the bedpost. "Wake up, Devens."

Pushing into a sitting position, Devens had the intelligence to look apprehensive. "How dare you barge into my home like this?"

"You have no idea how much I'll dare," Royce returned, placing a booted foot upon the bed. "But I promise you'll be enlightened before I leave here today."

Devens held a pillow in front of himself. "I presume you're here to discuss Laurel."

"How perceptive of you," Royce drawled as he leaned forward. "Your comprehension surprises me, Archie old boy, because you haven't demonstrated a wealth of intelligence to date."

An affronted expression twisted Devens' features. "You break into my house and insult me when you have no understanding of the situation?"

"Oh, I understand perfectly," Royce replied, lowering his voice. "I know all about why you've returned and why you're pursuing Laurel."

"I missed her," Devens retorted.

Shaking his head, Royce corrected him. "You missed her *money*, Devens."

"That's not true," he protested. "I missed the way she—"

"Let's not play games," Royce interrupted, allowing the full measure of his anger to show. "I know about the creditors hounding you, about the debts to quite a large number of gentlemen, about the poor investments." He narrowed his eyes. "I know about it all."

Flushing, Devens cleared his throat. "That shall all be cleared up shortly."

"If you thought to do it with Laurel's funds, think again." Remembering his promise to Laurel, Royce took a step back, afraid that if he went any closer he'd do physical harm to Devens. "Consider this fair warning, Devens, if you so much as approach Laurel, no, if you so much as *look* at her, I'll ruin you," Royce vowed, his voice vibrating with the intensity of his feelings.

"And just how would you do that?" Devens demanded.

Smiling slowly, Royce explained, "Most of the gentlemen to whom you owe large amounts of money are friends of mine. I could easily ask them to call in the debts immediately."

Devens froze. "You couldn't do that," he whispered.

"Ah, but I could, Devens," Royce countered. "Very easily, in fact." He crossed his arms and continued hammering his point home. "Then I could go one step further. What do you think would happen if I told all of the establishments where you had overdue accounts that I would no longer bring my business to them if they didn't call in your debts?"

Reaching out a hand, Devens steadied himself against the headboard.

"And we haven't even discussed how a magistrate would react if complaints were brought against you." Smiling pleasantly, Royce asked, "Have you ever seen the inside of debtor's gaol? I assure you it isn't a pretty sight."

"I . . . I . . . I have investments that are just about to pay out," Devens sputtered.

"I assume you're speaking of the ship due in from America," Royce guessed. At Devens' nod, Royce shook his head. "I fear you won't receive any profits from that investment either, Devens. You see, I decided you needed a small sampling of what would come if you didn't leave Laurel alone."

Before Devens could demand an explanation, a loud banging sounded on the front door.

"I believe that will be your solicitor to tell you that your last hope—that ship coming from the Americas—well, she arrived in port early this morning . . . with empty cargo holds."

Disbelief darkened his expression. "Impossible."

Enjoying the sweetness of revenge, Royce grinned broadly. "Oh, it's quite possible. I assure you it is." He rocked back on his heels. "You see, as I own the ship, I'm always the first to be informed of her losses."

"You had them dump the cargo?"

Royce lifted his brows. "Perhaps I did underestimate you, Devens. That's twice now that you've figured things out all on your own."

"But dumping the cargo would cost you a fortune as well," Devens rasped.

Grabbing hold of the bedpost once more, Royce

leaned in closer. "Yes, but the difference between us, Devens, is that *I* can afford to lose a fortune. Can you?"

Satisfaction filled Royce at the raw fury blazing across Devens' face. Heading for the door, he tossed one last warning over his shoulder. "Remember, if you go near her again, I *will* destroy you."

Devens' rage-filled roar sounded like sweet music indeed.

Royce shut the door behind him. Now it was time for Margaret St. John to learn a lesson of her very own.

"My lord," Margaret exclaimed in a breathy voice. "What an unexpected pleasure."

Not for long, Royce thought to himself. "We need to speak about last night."

If he hadn't been watching carefully, he would have missed the flare of alarm in her eyes. As swiftly as it appeared, it was gone, replaced by a look of innocence. "The Opera?" She fluttered her lashes at him. "I did so love the performance, didn't you?"

"Hmmm," he murmured, "especially the one that occurred in my private box."

"Excuse me?"

Her voice dripped sweetness and light, but Royce saw beyond the façade. "Certainly you remember standing guard for your friend, Archie Devens."

Even Margaret wasn't a good enough actress to mask her reaction. "You saw me?" she whispered, before catching herself. "I was waiting for *you*, of course."

"Of course," he returned dryly, "which is why

you didn't even notice me behind you as you rushed to Devens' aid."

Her mouth opened and closed.

"Don't go to the trouble of thinking up an excuse, Margaret." Royce grabbed her chin between his thumb and forefinger. "I've already seen beneath your façade, Margaret . . . and what lay beneath isn't appealing."

Jerking herself free, Margaret glared at him. "You don't know me at all."

"True, but the little I do know hasn't encouraged me to look further." Taking a step forward, Royce issued his warning. "Think twice before you scheme up any other tricks, Margaret, or I'll forget I'm a gentleman."

"What will you do, my lord? Challenge me to a duel?"

"Come now, Margaret. Nothing as crass as all that." He folded his arms. "I prefer to arm myself with the truth."

Lifting her nose, Margaret sneered at him. "The *truth?* What a foolish threat," she said with a laugh.

"Don't discount it, Margaret. I can be most . . . inventive, if properly motivated." A chill swept over him. "And when you threaten Lady Laurel Simmons, it inspires me as nothing else could."

Margaret waved her arm. "You must treat me to some of these wondrous tales you'd tell."

"Not *tales*, Margaret. The truth," he reminded her. "With the right incentive . . . or should I say the right amount of coin . . . even the most loyal of servants would turn against their employer."

"What the devil are you talking about?"

Royce tilted her chin up. "What I'm speaking about, Margaret, is this scandalous story I just paid a pretty penny for . . . one about you and a young footman exchanging intimacies in the pantry."

The color drained from her face. "Who told you that?"

"Does it truly matter?" Dropping his hand to his side, Royce moved away. "But never fear, Margaret, I would never spread such a vile tale." He speared her with his gaze. "However, if you do not stay far away from Lady Laurel, I would not hesitate to let everyone know about your family's shaky finances. My sense of gentlemanly honor doesn't extend quite that far."

"You're vile," Margaret spat, her features twisting in disgust and fury.

Shrugging off her anger, Royce continued. "Look at the bright side, Margaret. If the truth were to come out, you wouldn't be troubled with fortune hunters any longer."

A small shriek of fury escaped her.

Satisfied he'd made his point, Royce wanted nothing more than to leave her soiled presence. "So heed my advice, Margaret, and stay away from Lady Laurel or pay the consequences."

Shaking with anger, Margaret fisted her hands. "No one would believe you."

"Oh, but they would," Royce corrected her. "I am a respected member of society." Tilting his head to the side, he asked her, "Now who do you think would be bold enough to call me a liar?"

"I don't believe you would actually spread any tales at all. You're too much of a gentleman," Margaret announced boldly, allowing her hands to drop to her sides.

Shaking his head, Royce glared at Margaret. "Don't force me to carry through on my threats, because I *will* expose your family finances, Margaret." Heading toward the door, Royce paused with his hand on the knob. "Just try me," he vowed again, before slipping out into the fine morning sun.

All in all, it had been a productive day . . . and it was early still.

". . . so you see, I left Devens with little choice," Royce finished as he sat back in his chair.

Nodding, Laurel took a sip of tea, digesting the information Royce had just given her. "Quite clever of you," she murmured.

"Not really," he demurred. "I merely applied a common strategy to rid us of that pest."

"Ah, one of your infamous strategies."

Stiffening, Royce looked at her. "It worked, didn't it?"

"Indeed, it did," Laurel acknowledged softly. "As do most things when you apply your stratagems to them."

"That's true," he replied, relaxing once more. "Life is infinitely more enjoyable when you approach it logically."

And what neat slot did she fit into? Laurel wondered. Taking a sip of her tea, Laurel couldn't understand what had come over her this morning. Last night had been so traumatic, so overwhelming, she'd woken up in a pensive mood.

Still, Royce's blunt statements bothered her even

though she tried to think of them calmly. Suddenly she was glad that she hadn't had the opportunity to speak to Royce about giving their relationship a second chance.

Holding in a sigh, Laurel looked at Royce. "I appreciate all you've done for me," she said, meaning every word. Regardless of what the future might hold for them, she would always appreciate his efforts.

Royce gave her a crooked smile. "When you say it like that, it sounds as if you're bidding me farewell."

"Of course not," Laurel replied, keeping her reservations to herself.

Mollified, Royce reached for his tea. "Might I escort you to Lord Cummings' party this evening?"

Considering his offer, Laurel nodded slowly. "I believe I will attend. After all, Margaret is almost certain to be in attendance and I need to speak with her."

"*Speak with Margaret?*" Royce exclaimed, sending tea sloshing over the edge of his cup before he set it down with a crash. "Why would you want to do that?"

"Because I need to show both Margaret and Archie that they don't frighten me."

"Don't be ridiculous, Laurel," Royce said, thrusting to his feet. "You don't need to prove anything to those two."

"Perhaps you're right," she conceded, lifting her eyes to his. "Perhaps I need to prove it to myself."

Taking another sip of tea, Laurel watched as Royce exploded into motion. Striding around the room, he vibrated with frustration. "Of all the silly—"

"Pardon me, my lord," Laurel interrupted, rising as well. "But I wasn't asking for your approval."

"I believe it is my right as your—"

"As my what? My friend?" Laurel asked.

Narrowing his eyes, Royce stepped closer. "As someone who only wants what is best for you."

"I appreciate your concern, Royce, but I believe I am fit to judge what is best for me," Laurel replied quietly.

"Of course you are, Laurel—"

"If you could try to sound a bit less condescending, Royce, it might help me to believe you really mean what you say," she said wryly.

Royce's exasperation became clear as he sighed loudly. "Let's not play this game, Laurel." Giving her a level look, he said, "I am asking you to stay at home this evening and not confront Margaret or Devens."

Laurel shook her head. "I won't promise you anything."

"Very well," Royce said firmly, moving toward the door. "Then I shall return this evening."

"To make certain I remain at home?"

He offered her a polite smile. "Of course not," he said blandly. "I simply enjoy your company."

"He's threatened to destroy me financially," Archie explained as he paced across the room. "He must be stopped."

Watching Archie strut to and fro was making Margaret dizzy. "Do sit down, Archie," she snapped, pressing a hand to her temple. "I can't concentrate with you pacing about like a mad bull."

"A mad bull?" retorted Archie, coming to an abrupt halt. "Well, pardon me! My welfare, *my future*, has just been threatened, so I'm entitled to pace if I bloody well feel like it."

The anger in Archie's voice brought a smile to Margaret's face. "Ah, men, what predictable creatures you all are."

"I beg to differ," he said stiffly. "Just last night I devised a clever plan to—"

"What you did was sheer stupidity," Margaret corrected him harshly, "and I was more the fool for agreeing to help you!" She shook her head. "All your plan succeeded in doing was casting aspersions upon your name while putting Laurel Simmons in the roll of victim."

"That's not true," Archie protested.

"Oh, but it is." Drumming her fingers against the arm of her chair, Margaret tried to focus on what needed to be done. "You need to destroy *her* good name, not your own!"

Archie glared down at her. "Which is precisely what I was doing! If she hadn't tripped and knocked me down, I would have kissed her in front of everyone. Now what do you think *that* would have done to her reputation?"

"Absolutely nothing," Margaret pointed out. "It was quite apparent to all last evening that Laurel was an unwilling partner in the embrace. Your goal should have been to make everyone believe that she is so enamored of you that she'd ignore propriety and kiss you passionately in public."

Understanding eased the angry lines on Archie's

face. "Ahhh," he murmured, grinning broadly at her. "So even if she doesn't wish to spend time with me, if I can give the illusion that she does, then the gossips will feast upon her."

"Precisely." Margaret smiled up at Archie. "Now, do sit down, so we might devise a plan."

Chapter
20

⌒

"*I* can't tell you how much it pleases me that you've come to your senses, Laurel," Royce said as he eased himself into a chair in the Simmons' parlor. "You seemed so determined to confront Margaret St. John."

"I did, didn't I?" Laurel murmured with a soft smile.

Her response made him wary. Despite the delicate image she portrayed in her stunning evening gown, Laurel was seldom, if ever, submissive . . . a fact that captivated him. "What made you change your mind about seeking Margaret out this evening?" he asked, allowing suspicion to creep into his voice.

"Why, your compelling arguments, of course. What else could have done it?"

Her eyes widened as she beamed innocently at him, yet he didn't believe her for a moment. However, before he could remark upon his suspicions, Laurel stood gracefully.

"I'm parched," she announced. "I shall ring for tea."

"More tea?"

"One can never have too much," she replied airily. Moving toward the door, Laurel pulled the cord to summon a servant.

The gentle sway of her skirts captured his attention. "You are dressed quite formally for an evening at home," he remarked softly.

"This?" she asked with a laugh, holding out the lace edged skirt. "Don't be silly." Once again, she tugged upon the cord.

Leaning back in his chair, Royce studied her even closer. "It looks like a new gown."

"Of course it is," Laurel chided, shaking her head. "All of my other clothes were destroyed, remember?"

Chagrined, Royce nodded. "Of course. I forgot," he murmured.

"What is keeping those servants?" Laurel muttered, giving the cord another tug. "Pardon me for a moment, Royce, while I order the tea."

Without another word, Laurel slipped from the room, shutting the door behind her.

Relaxing in his chair, Royce allowed his thoughts to drift while he awaited Laurel's return. All in all, things had turned quite handily in his favor. Just look how she'd taken his advice about Margaret.

When the clock struck on the hour, Royce suddenly became aware of just how much time had passed; Laurel had been gone close to half an hour. Wondering what had happened to her, he wandered over to the pull cord, intent on summoning a servant to inquire about Laurel's whereabouts. He pulled on the cord and immediately realized something was awry.

Glancing up, Royce froze, before leaning in to get a closer look. "Why, that little—"

He broke off with a soft curse that turned into a quick chuckle. Shaking his head, Royce silently berated himself for not foreseeing her next move.

His clever vixen had tampered with the pull cord, rendering it useless.

Heading toward the kitchens, it didn't take Royce long to discover that Laurel had slipped out of the house. Her reason for deceiving him seemed obvious; she was going to confront Margaret.

Stepping into the ballroom, Laurel immediately searched for Margaret. She knew it wouldn't be long before Royce figured out that she'd tricked him. Her plan had worked beautifully and she reveled in the thrill of outsmarting Royce.

It had alarmed her to realize just how much she'd been leaning upon him recently, so it felt wonderful to be striking out on her own once again. Suddenly, a blond head whirled by, capturing her attention. Margaret.

Breaking off her thoughts, Laurel began to maneuver closer to her quarry. When the music ended, Margaret curtsied to her partner and allowed him to lead her to the edge of the dance floor. Seeing her opportunity, Laurel followed Margaret as she retired into the ladies' chamber.

The room was crowded with women repairing their attire, but Laurel ignored them, focusing all of her attention upon Margaret. Taking a seat next to

Margret, Laurel patted her hair, adopting an air of innocence. "My," she said, releasing her breath in a soft huff. "It certainly is warm this evening."

Alarm flared briefly in Margaret's eyes. "Indeed," she agreed warily.

Margaret's reaction proved to Laurel that Royce's intervention had been successful. Still, this was her battle to fight. "Perhaps it might be best if I sit out a few dances," Laurel murmured. "After all, it would hardly do to start tongues wagging." Widening her eyes, Laurel affected an innocent expression. "We both know how quickly a few bits of gossip, true or not, spread throughout the ton."

Margaret narrowed her eyes, glaring at Laurel. "While that is true, I suspect no true lady would sink to such levels."

"I don't know," Laurel continued. "I wouldn't underestimate anyone." Leaning forward, she added, "Some ladies can be most . . . *vindictive.*"

Margaret's expression darkened. "Are you referring to anyone in particular, Lady Laurel?"

There was no missing the suspicious note in Margaret's voice. "Not at all," Laurel said in an offhanded manner. "Why, most anyone could be moved to seek revenge." She looked fully at the other woman. "Even me, for instance."

Margaret slapped her fan onto the table before her and turned to face Laurel. "Let's cease this cat and mouse game, shall we?" Glancing around to ensure no one was close enough to overhear her, Margaret hissed. "Are you threatening me?"

"Threatening you?" Laurel asked, forcing surprise into her question. "Whatever makes you think that?" She shook her head. "I was merely commenting on how anyone, even me, could be moved to seek revenge if properly motivated." Raising one finger, Laurel acted as if a thought had just struck her. "For instance, if someone, oh, let's say you, had harmed me or arranged for another to harm me, then even I might be tempted to inform others of your actions, thus creating a nasty bit of gossip that would irreparably damage your reputation."

Margaret's gasp spoke volumes.

Laurel smiled brightly at Margaret. "Luckily, I know I'll never be forced to participate in such unpleasantness." Rising, Laurel brushed at her skirts. "It was lovely having this chat with you."

Lunging forward, Margaret grabbed hold of Laurel's wrist, curling her nails inward. "I know a threat when I hear one."

Bending down, Laurel peeled Margaret's fingers away from her skin. "How very clever you are," she murmured dryly, before releasing Margaret's fingers.

Laurel spun on her heel and walked from the room, pleased at the outcome of her little tête-à-tête. Threats, when properly applied, were oh, so satisfying.

Pleased with Margaret's response, Laurel stepped back into the ballroom and, glancing across the room, saw Archie standing near the gaming room. A frisson of anxiety slid down her spine, but Laurel forced it away.

Gathering her courage, Laurel stepped briskly toward him.

"Archie," she said by way of greeting, her voice a chill rasp.

Surprise flashed upon his face, a brief glimpse before his features smoothed out into a practiced smile of welcome. "Laurel," he murmured. "What an unexpected surprise."

"I'll wager it is," she agreed. "Might I have a word with you?"

His smile dripped with smug pleasure. "Certainly." Holding out his hand, he gestured down the hallway. "Shall we?"

Remembering all too clearly what had occurred the last time they were alone in a room, Laurel shook her head. "I would prefer the terrace."

His mouth pinched into a frown. "But—"

"The terrace, Archie," Laurel interrupted firmly.

"Very well." Grasping her elbow, Archie escorted her outside.

The moment they entered the cool night air, Laurel broke off the contact, shaking her arm free from his clasp.

"I'm so pleased you sought me out," Archie murmured, his voice low and intimate.

Laughing softly, Laurel shook her head. "I imagine you are." How could she have been afraid of this man even for a moment?

His brows drew together. "I don't believe that is a compliment," he grumbled.

"No, I don't believe it is," Laurel agreed. Waving her hand, Laurel decided to get to the point. "I wished to tell you that if you ever touch me or threaten me again, I shall be forced to take drastic measures."

An ugly expression twisted his handsome features. "Drastic measures? Such as . . . what?"

"Oh, I don't know," she murmured, "There are so many different methods to choose from."

"I find that difficult to believe," he smirked, crossing his arms. "What could *you* possibly do to *me*?"

Laurel played her high card. "If I smeared your name, then you would find it impossible to find yourself another heiress." She smiled at him, satisfaction warming her. "And remember that you told everyone that I cried off when our engagement was broken, so what do you think would happen if I explained my reasons behind calling off our engagement? What do you believe the mamas and their wealthy daughters would say if they knew how quickly you run through fortunes?"

Vibrating with anger, Archie hissed, "You . . . you . . ."

Lifting her chin, Laurel dismissed his anger without thought. "Whatever insulting name you settle upon, I assure you, my dear Lord Devens, that I shall accept it as a compliment."

"Why, you little . . ." he began, reaching for her.

As if dancing, Laurel stepped aside, ready for his move. "Ah, ah, ah, Archie. You wouldn't want to upset me."

His gaze burned into hers. "You'll be sorry."

"I highly doubt it," she retorted swiftly.

A low growl escaped Archie as he pushed past her, heading back into the ballroom. After Archie presented her with his back, she giggled once, delighted at her success.

"Please tell me that your elation has nothing to

do with Devens' obvious displeasure." Leaning against the stone pillar on the porch, Royce waited for her response.

Smiling gaily at him, Laurel tilted her head to look up at him. "And if it does?"

"Then you leave me no choice but to be extremely annoyed with you." He crossed his arms. "And, my darling Laurel, considering the fact that you snuck out on me to track down Margaret and Devens, I assure you I'm already quite perturbed."

"Should your disapproval bother me?" she asked lightly.

"Feisty this evening, aren't you?"

"Indeed," she agreed as she lifted her skirts to walk up the short flight of stairs. "I've been feeling out-of-sorts for a few days, but I'm back to my usual self now."

"Lord help me," Royce murmured.

"I believe He already has. After all, you found me, didn't you?" She paused beside Royce on the top step. "How *did* you find me so quickly?"

Leaning closer, he gazed into her eyes. "Since you'd mentioned approaching Margaret at the Cummings' affair, it wasn't too difficult to figure out where you'd gone. Besides," he continued, "I know how you think, Laurel."

His response couldn't have pleased her more. "You know me," she whispered.

"Of course," he replied, straightening. "Remember, I studied you."

The bubble of pleasure burst. "How could I forget?" Pushing aside the prick of pain, Laurel turned on her heel and headed for the house. "I should be getting back before anyone remarks upon my absence."

"Not so fast," Royce said, catching hold of her elbow and bringing her to a stop. "You can't leave a gentleman waiting for tea, disappear without a word, and expect to escape without repercussions."

"Ah, but there is one thing you're forgetting." Laurel smiled at Royce, before spinning away, breaking his hold. "First, you need to catch me."

Chapter
21

❦

*I*t took a full minute for Laurel's taunt to sink in. Torn between laughter and annoyance, Royce couldn't decide how to react. His vixen had returned in full force, leaving the tearful woman behind. Royce grinned at the realization. Yet, oddly enough, even though he enjoyed seeing Laurel in her bold glory, he couldn't forget the feel of her in his arms, soft and vulnerable. As much as she tried to deny it, he knew she needed him.

Without further hesitation, Royce stepped into the ballroom to search for Laurel. As always, the moment the eager mothers caught sight of him, they hurried over, each one singing the praises of her little angel.

"Lord Van Cleef! How wonderful it is to see you," gushed Lady Rotham.

Glancing down at one of the biggest gossips in the ton, Royce forced a smile onto his face. "The pleasure is all mine."

Lady Rotham twittered at his polite rejoinder. "I fear I must naysay you, my lord, for you see I have been eager to speak with you." Leaning closer, she flipped open her fan, hiding behind the ivory depths. "What is this delicious news I hear that you've settled upon one special young lady?"

At that moment, Royce caught sight of Laurel standing on the opposite side of the dance floor.

She'd turned the mamas and their eager daughters loose on him again, just when he thought they'd tired of chasing after him. What would she do if he turned the tables on her?"

Turning up the intensity of his smile, Royce leaned down toward Lady Rotham. "It's true," he confided in a whisper. "Though you know, I'm sure, that I've remained silent as to the lady's identity."

Lady Rotham's eyes widened, eagerness shimmering in their gray depths, looking like a hungry cat preparing to pounce upon a fat, juicy mouse. "Oh, do tell, Lord Van Cleef." Pressing a hand against her chest, she assured him, "I will keep your confidence."

"Of course you will," he returned, pausing a moment in mock hesitation. Finally, he bent closer still. "The lady I plan to marry is none other than the beautiful Lady Laurel Simmons."

The expression on Lady Rotham's face reflected her delight at having learned the ultimate bit of gossip. Royce was certain his tidbit would spread like wildfire throughout the ton, thereby boxing Laurel into his snare. While he had promised himself he'd put aside the game and approach Laurel with noth-

ing but honesty in his heart, desperate times called
for desperate measures.

Straightening, he nodded slowly. "I trust I can
hold you to confidence."

"Oh, most certainly," returned Lady Rotham. "I
wouldn't tell another soul."

And he was the bloody Prince Regent. Bowing,
Royce excused himself. "If you will pardon me, I believe the lady of my intentions is seeking a dance
partner."

Walking away, Royce didn't have to glance behind him to know that Lady Rotham was undoubtedly spreading his confession across the room.

Splendid.

Just as he'd done the night they first met, Royce
strode boldly across the dance floor, keeping his
gaze firmly fixed upon Laurel.

Instead of backing away, Laurel stood her
ground, waiting for him with a smile playing upon
her lips.

Without a word, he clasped her hand and pulled
her onto the dance floor, swinging her into his
arms.

"This is becoming a habit for you, isn't it?" she
asked after a moment.

"I found it far too delightful the first time around
to give it up."

"At least you are speaking this time."

Grinning at her, Royce lifted a brow. "Only because I wish to rail at you for abandoning me, not to
mention chide you for your foolishness in con-
fronting Devens."

"Ah," she murmured, her eyes alight with mischief, "then perhaps I'd be better served to refrain from telling you about my conversation with Margaret St. John."

He sighed lustily. "Is there no stopping you?"

"I've yet to meet someone who could."

Her challenge sounded a responding chord within him. "Then I shall have to see what I can do to change that," he returned briskly.

"As we've already discussed, my lord, I am perfectly capable of deciding what is best for me."

"So you've said," Royce agreed, aware of the numerous eyes trained upon them. "You've made it perfectly clear that you feel I have no claim upon you."

"So you *do* sometimes hear what I'm saying?" She shook her head. "Amazing."

Her dry wit amused him. "I try my best to impress."

"Of course you do," she returned, her tone slow and deliberate as if she were speaking to a child.

"In fact, I've just done something which I believe you'll find most impressive," he said lightly. "After all, it's a trick you've used on me."

In an instant, she grew wary. "Which one?"

"There are so many . . ." he replied, trailing off his words just to see her irritation peak.

"Royce!" she hissed, glancing around the room. "Stop teasing me so . . ." Again, she looked around her, this time taking in the scene developing around them. "Why is everyone staring at us?"

"Undoubtedly because of something I told them."

She narrowed her eyes. "Which was what?"

"As I said, I took a page from your book." Smiling

pleasantly at her, he continued, "I told Lady Rotham that you were the woman upon whom I'd settled my intentions."

Closing her eyes, Laurel groaned softly. "How *could* you?"

"How could I what? Add to the rumor *you* started?" He laughed under his breath. "I assure you, Laurel. It was exceedingly easy."

"To force my hand?"

"No more than you forced mine," he responded, dipping into a bow as the music ended.

The shimmer of tears in her gaze caught him off guard. "Laurel?"

Lifting her chin, she blinked back her tears. "You haven't bested me yet."

Before he could utter another word, before he could discover what he'd done to upset her so, Laurel spun on her heel and left him standing alone in the middle of the dance floor.

"Everyone is taking wagers on when you and Royce will wed," Steven informed Laurel the moment he entered her morning room.

Groaning, Laurel slumped in her chair. "I suspected as much."

"The odds are favoring an imminent announcement."

"Wonderful," observed Laurel, rubbing two fingers against her temple.

Steven relaxed his shoulders. "So what are you going to do about the rumors?"

Lord, she wished she knew. Rising to her feet, Laurel moved to the window, gazing out onto the lawn. How could Royce have put her in this position? His actions only underscored the knowledge that she was simply a commodity to him . . . a prize in his blasted wager.

Drawing in a deep breath, she turned to face Steven, aware that his proposal, and her rejection, sat between them. "However I decide to handle this problem, I promise you I'll not ask for your assistance."

"I'm more than happy to help," Steven replied, rising as well.

"I know that," Laurel murmured, "but it's unfair of me to continue to ask. It is far past time that I begin to outwit Royce on my own."

"You have been outwitting him on your own," Steven argued, coming to stand next to her. "All the plans were your design. I was simply your accomplice."

"True, but it was unconscionable of me to have used you for my own purposes."

Reaching out, he tugged lightly upon one of the ribbons woven in her sleeve. "No foul was committed, because I was more than willing to assist you."

And ended up offering her his name. Laurel smiled up at Steven before shifting away from his touch. "For that, I thank you, but I need to handle Royce on my own this time."

An expression of resignation settled upon Steven's face. "Very well."

"Thank you for understanding," Laurel murmured, wishing for all the world that she knew what to do about Royce's latest tactic.

* * *

"I want him destroyed."

Royce could see that his bald statement shocked his man of business, Henry Atherby, but the man's reaction was of little consequence. Devens had made a huge mistake when he'd stepped into the garden with Laurel. He'd obviously not taken Royce's threat seriously, and Royce feared it was only a matter of time before Devens forced his attentions upon Laurel again.

"I'm afraid it won't be as simple as it once was," Atherby replied, gripping his quill nervously. "After looking into Lord Devens' affairs again this morning, I discovered unanticipated changes in his financial wherewithal."

The news stunned Royce. "Details, Atherby. I want details."

"Unfortunately, my lord, I have none to offer. All I know is that a substantial influx of cash flooded his accounts yesterday." Before Royce had a chance to comment, Atherby raised a finger. "Along with most of his debts being settled."

Slapping a hand on his desk, Royce struggled to restrain his anger. "How did he do it?"

"As I said, Lord Van Cleef, I'm not quite certain."

Royce eyed the older man. "Then find out."

"That might be difficult to—"

"I'm not asking you if it will be difficult or not; I'm asking you to trace the money." Grimly, Royce nodded. "Money always leaves a trail."

Gulping, Atherby nodded once. "Very well, my lord. I shall get right on the matter."

"Excellent," Royce murmured. "As soon as we

know where he got it from, we can set about taking it all away again."

"You succeeded most admirably last evening," Margaret commented to Archie. "By escorting Laurel outside, everyone began to speculate whether or not you were about to reconcile."

"But then Van Cleef had to come along and spoil everything by announcing he intended to marry her," Archie complained.

"Simply because Royce chose to spoil our plans doesn't detract from the fact that you executed your plan perfectly." Margaret absently twirled a stray curl. "Still, Royce's announcement forces us to redirect our plans."

"What shall we do?" asked Archie. "Do you want me to continue to court Laurel? While her tongue has grown sharp over the past few years, she *is* still quite the looker."

Waving her hand, Margaret dismissed the idea. "No, the time for subtlety has ended. We must now take bold action if we are to succeed in keeping them apart."

"We *have* been taking 'bold action'," Archie sniveled.

"Not bold enough." Margaret shot him a look of impatience. "You want to marry Laurel in order to obtain an heiress, isn't that correct?"

Archie nodded briskly. "Absolutely."

"And I wish to capture Royce's interest," Margaret said. Then she'd teach Royce a lesson for humiliating her. Yes, she'd have him groveling at her feet before she publicly tossed him aside.

"Then the solution is obvious." Archie leaned forward conspiratorially. "We need help."

A multitude of schemes twisted in Laurel's head as she tried to devise a way to put Royce in his place. The problem was that her heart wasn't in it.

Sighing, Laurel watched the sun sink below the horizon. Her morose mood did her little good and if she spent one more minute alone with her thoughts, she would certainly go crazy.

What she needed was a distraction. Like Harriet. Just the thought of her cheerful friend lightened Laurel's mood. Swiftly, Laurel retrieved her reticule and left a quick note for her father before heading outside. Since Harriet lived only two short blocks away, Laurel decided to walk the distance, not bothering with a chaperon.

Slowing her pace so that she could take in the pleasantness of the evening, Laurel breathed in deeply, inhaling the fresh night air.

Suddenly, a heavy cloak flowed around her, enveloping her within the shadowy folds. Before she could scream, a cloak-enfolded hand pressed against her mouth, silencing her protests. Though she struggled, she was no match for the strength of her abductor as he easily led her toward the street.

Stepping up into a carriage that he'd obviously had waiting for him, her assailant dragged her into the conveyance behind him. The moment her skirts cleared the door, it was slammed shut and the carriage rocked to a start. Frantic to get free, Laurel slammed her elbow into her assailant's ribs, bringing a shout of pain from him. His arms loosened enough for Laurel to scramble out from beneath the cloak.

Pressing against the back of the carriage, Laurel got her first look at her attacker.

Archie.

Anger burst within her. "You imbecile! You frightened me terribly."

Shrugging lightly, he dismissed her protest. "It seemed necessary. After all, I highly doubt if you would have come willingly, now would you?"

"Of course not!"

"See?" He nodded once. "I thought as much."

"Why you—" Breaking off her protest, Laurel struggled to control her rage. She needed a cool head to get out of this muddle. "Where are you taking me?" she demanded.

"My, my," drawled Archie, tossing aside the cloak. "Now is that any way to talk to your future husband?"

"My future *husband?*" she retorted. "Hardly."

"We'll see," he murmured. Slanting her a look, Archie dusted off his jacket. "You were always such a submissive young miss when we were engaged. When did you become so . . . so . . . arrogant?"

"I prefer the term independent, Archie, and I received my first lesson at your hands."

"Ah, yes," he murmured, tugging at the sleeves of his coat. "I remember how distressed you were at the thought of losing me."

"Don't flatter yourself," she returned coldly. "I was far more upset with how your actions would damage my reputation."

"It's amusing that you should mention reputation," Archie began, one side of his mouth shifting upward. "For after our little jaunt, your reputation will be secure."

His cocky attitude disturbed her. "What are you talking about?"

Reaching out, Archie patted her on the arm. "Don't fret, Laurel. I have only honorable intentions toward you." He smiled down at her. "Now sit back and relax. I've heard the ride to Gretna Green is quite lovely at this time of year."

His words made her catch her breath. Gretna Green. The small town over the Scottish border where one could marry without license.

Immediately, she launched herself at the door, struggling to undo the latch, willing to risk injury rather than be dragged along on Archie's plan.

"Locked," Archie pointed out brightly.

Laurel tried to squelch the fear clawing at her, but failed miserably. "I shall scream," she rasped, sinking back onto her cushion.

"Be my guest," he invited, spreading his arms wide. "In an enclosed carriage clattering its way across cobblestones, I doubt if anyone would hear you."

He was right. Dear God in Heaven. She was trapped.

Chapter
22

The sun had just set when Atherby was shown into Royce's study. "Did you learn anything?" Royce asked immediately, gesturing for Atherby to take a chair.

"Indeed, my lord," he murmured, sounding most reluctant.

Royce urged him onward. "What is it then?"

Shifting in his chair, Atherby seemed agitated.

"Out with it," ordered Royce, growing more wary with each passing moment.

"You were quite right, Lord Van Cleef. I was able to trace the money back to its source."

"Excellent," Royce pronounced, eager to end the threat toward Laurel. "How did he come by the money?"

"It appears that he got it from . . ." Atherby paused, glancing away, ". . . your mother."

His heart tightened. "Impossible," he whispered. "Even for her."

"Oh, but I assure you it's not. In fact, I checked

with more than one source to verify the information." Atherby's eyes darkened with compassion. "I wish I were wrong."

Royce didn't know how to respond. Dear Lord, his *mother* had given Devens money. It was all too easy for him to connect the pieces that had eluded him for so long. She'd shown up unexpectedly at the Hammingtons' weekend party, so perhaps she'd sent the note to Hammington in the hopes that Laurel would have been found in a delicate position.

His mother could have easily orchestrated the rest of the incidents, bringing Margaret and Archie together. She could have done it all . . . in order to protect her precious family name.

Pressing as far back into the corner of the carriage as possible, Laurel searched for a way to escape. She needed to break free and return to London before anyone noticed she was gone. A night with Archie would thoroughly destroy her reputation.

She wouldn't, couldn't, allow that to happen.

"We've arrived at our first stop on this lovely trip of ours," Archie announced as the carriage pulled to a halt.

As the door opened, Laurel spotted an inn with lights blazing. Seeing her only opportunity, Laurel leapt from the carriage.

"Stop her!"

With Archie's shout ringing in her ears, she stumbled onto the ground, slamming her hands against the hard dirt road. Ignoring the pain, Laurel struggled to regain her balance, but just as she found her footing, one of the coachmen reached out to grab hold of her arm.

Tugging with all of her might, Laurel desperately sought to escape him. "Let me go," she pleaded, unable to hide her fear, though she knew at a glance that the coachman wouldn't be moved by her entreaty. "Please."

Much to her surprise, however, the servant's expression tightened in concern.

With a spark of hope, she continued, "I only wish to return to my father. Please help me."

Before the coachman could say a word, Archie scrambled down from the carriage and enfolded her within his cloak again. "That will be all, Headley," he said, dismissing the servant.

"Begging your pardon, my lord, but it don't appear that—"

Archie's body stiffened. "Since when do I pay you to express your opinion?"

Laurel lost hope of any intervention when the coachman pulled himself up, once more becoming an expressionless servant.

"Come along, my bride, our wedding bower awaits us." Chuckling, Archie tugged her along beside him.

Pushing against him, Laurel still fought to break free, despite the hopelessness of the situation.

"Come now, love. I understand you might be apprehensive about our wedding night, but I assure you . . . I'm a *most* spectacular lover." Leaning down, he nipped at her ear. "I promise I'll make it good for you."

Laurel's stomach rolled. Waiting until they'd

crossed the threshold, Laurel began to shout for help. "Please help me! This man is—"

Her words were cut off as Archie spun her into his arms and slammed his mouth against hers, drowning out her protests. Breaking off the kiss, Archie pressed Laurel's head into his neck, creating a loving pose. No one would notice that his hand covered her mouth because of the large cloak.

Laurel tried to raise her head, but he kept her firmly against him, conveying the appearance of eager lovers seeking the nearest bed. "Lord Archibald Devens and my bride, Lady Devens," he lied smoothly to the innkeeper.

"Pleasure to have you. Roger Everly at your service," greeted the man. "Still, it don't appear as if you'd like to spend the night jawing with me."

Archie's smooth laugh vibrated in his chest. "You have the right of it, my good man."

His affable tone made Laurel cringe. What sort of man could act so congenial while planning to force a wedding night on her? Laurel began to struggle again, but Archie simply pressed her tighter into his body until she felt faint from lack of air.

"Here we are," announced the innkeeper after Archie had dragged her up the stairs.

"Very good." Twisting to his side, he pushed her into the room. "My . . . wife is a bit shy and nervous about her wedding night." Laurel heard the jingling sound of coins changing hands. "That's a little something to make it worth your while if you leave us be, regardless of what you might hear."

"I'll be as deaf as a door," promised Everly.

Bidding the innkeeper a good evening, Archie shut the door firmly.

Gasping for air, Laurel backed away from Archie, bumping into a table that rested against the far wall.

"Alone at last," Archie murmured. "I can't tell you how much I'm looking forward to this evening."

"*No*," Laurel whispered frantically, shaking her head.

"Shhhh, love." Shrugging out of his jacket, Archie then began to tug on his cravat. "It's only natural that you're a bit frightened, but I promise you one thing." A sensual expression twisted his lips. "You'll thank me in the morning."

Lord help her.

"Why did you give Devens money?"

Panic flashed in his mother's eyes before the expression was cloaked with confusion. "Devens? Who on earth is that?"

She could play innocent all she liked, but Royce had seen her initial reaction. "Why?" he repeated again, his voice low and controlled.

Elizabeth sunk into a chair, her demeanor as regal as any queen. "Because she was unfit," she replied smoothly, dropping all pretense.

Her admission staggered Royce. He hadn't realized that he'd been hoping that somehow Atherby had been wrong and his mother hadn't been involved. Grabbing hold of a chair, Royce steadied himself. "Did you arrange for a man to enter Laurel's room at Hammingtons' country party?"

"And if I did?" Elizabeth retorted. "It wasn't as if she were innocent."

"How can you say that? The only reason she would have been discovered with a gentleman in her room was because you'd arranged it."

"I didn't arrange for *you* to go to her room," his mother pointed out.

Conceding that fact, Royce moved on. "Were you also responsible for destroying Laurel's clothes and my ledgers?"

"Don't be ridiculous," Elizabeth sniffed. "I would never sink to that level."

Still stunned by his mother's duplicity, Royce couldn't believe her denial. "And what of Laurel's horse bolting? Did you arrange for that as well?"

"You are wasting my time with this nonsense."

He dug his fingers into the cushion. "Don't you dare dismiss my concerns, Mother. When you admitted threatening Laurel's reputation, you lost your right to protest any questions I place before you." He took a deep breath. "Now answer my questions."

Glaring at him, his mother lifted her chin. "No, I did not make an arrangement to startle her horse."

"The problem I'm faced with now, Mother, is whether I can believe one word you say."

"Don't be naive, Royce," his mother snapped, anger flashing in her eyes. "I am not the only person who would like to see you and the Simmons chit kept apart."

"Margaret St. John," he said softly, watching his mother's reaction closely.

"I did everything for you," she remarked, tapping her fingers upon the arm of her chair. "If only you hadn't insisted upon someone so obviously unfit, then I wouldn't have been forced to go to such extravagant measures."

Ignoring his mother's last comment, he probed her for more answers. "Did Margaret arrange to have Laurel's clothes destroyed?"

His mother smiled. "Ask yourself that question, keeping in mind that the objective would be to keep you and the Simmons girl apart."

"Laurel was occupied with replacing her wardrobe while I was absorbed with replacing my books." More of the puzzle straightened into place. Margaret could have sent the note about his past to Laurel and also arranged to have Hammington discover her with Archie.

"I must point out that her plan was hardly effective. After all, the two of you managed to attend a function the very next evening."

His mother's statement caught his attention. "You seem to know quite a bit of detail about her plans."

Startled, Elizabeth tried to cover her mistake. "I'm merely observant."

"I don't believe you, Mother." Releasing his hold on the chair, Royce stepped closer. "No, I think you might have planned the entire incident."

Shaking her head, Elizabeth slowly rose. "I didn't plan *everything,*" she stated firmly. "If I had been in charge then, I would not have arranged for Lord Devens to go to our family box. Dear heavens, Royce, I've done all of this to *protect* our name."

"*Then?*" Royce asked, pouncing upon the one word. "Are you saying that you're in charge now?"

Silence reigned as Royce stared his mother down. Finally, Elizabeth answered, "Since it is far too late for you to do anything now, I might as well inform you of our final plan."

Royce's gut tightened as he waited for his mother to continue.

"At this very moment, your Lady Laurel Simmons is racing toward the Scottish border with Archibald Devens."

"The Scottish bord . . ." Royce cut off his question as he realized where his mother meant. "Gretna Green."

"Precisely. By tomorrow, she will no longer be a threat to the title of Tewksbury." His mother reached out for him . . . only to let her hand drop back to her side. "I did what I felt was best for *you*, Royce."

"No, Mother," he said, backing away. "You did this for *yourself*. Not me. None of this has been about me."

Turning away, Royce ran from the room . . . praying with every step that he wouldn't be too late.

As Archie advanced toward her, Laurel felt behind her, searching for something, anything, that would aid in keeping him away.

"Are you ready for a spot of fun now, love?" Archie asked, giving her a reassuring smile.

"Please don't do this," Laurel rasped, backing into a table.

"It's not something to fear," Archie cajoled, stretching out his hand. "Come here now, Laurel, and let me show you."

"Stay away." Pushing against the table, Laurel flailed her arm backward, seeking balance. She knocked over a lamp, shattering the glass globe.

Steadying herself, Laurel flinched as a piece of glass cut deeply into her palm.

"Now you've gone and hurt yourself," Archie chastised. Setting the key to the room on the small table near the door, he moved closer, holding out his hand. "Let me see the cut. I'll bandage it up before we seek our pleasure."

Cradling her hand against her chest, Laurel shook her head, sidling out of the way, edging closer to the fireplace.

"It's foolish to be so stubborn, Laurel. You're bleeding all over your—"

"Archie!" Loud knocking accompanied the call. "Open up."

With a muttered oath, Archie opened the door to admit Margaret St. John.

With one glance, she took in Laurel's blood-stained gown. "My, it looks as if you were having some sport," she mocked.

"Shut your gob," snapped Archie, thrusting a hand through his hair. "This entire business is not going as I'd planned, so I'd very much appreciate it if you'd just tell me what you want and be on your way."

"What I *want*, Archie, is to know what took you so long." Margaret placed her hands on her hips. "I've been waiting here, wondering if you'd managed to snare her or if you'd mishandled everything again."

Laurel's hand throbbed, but she pushed the pain aside, concentrating on their exchange, hoping an opportunity to escape would present itself.

"If this is all you've come for, then you can just get out now." Archie pointed a finger toward the door. "Laurel's gone and cut herself . . . and cleaning it up won't exactly put me in a romantic mood," he complained.

Stepping closer, Margaret laughed at him. "Getting testy, aren't you?" she asked.

As Margaret moved farther into the room, Laurel saw her opportunity. Lunging forward, she knocked into Margaret, sending her sprawling forward into Archie. The two of them fell to the floor in a tangle of arms and legs. Without hesitation, Laurel snatched up the key and ran from the room, slamming the door behind her. Shaking in relief, Laurel twisted the key, locking Margaret and Archie in the room together.

Stumbling across the hall, Laurel sank down onto the floor, trembling in relief. She ripped a piece of her petticoat off and wrapped it around her cut hand. Archie began to bang upon the door, demanding to be let out, but, as Archie himself had directed, the innkeeper ignored the sounds.

For once, it appeared Archie had done her a favor. Fatigue weighed heavily upon her, but Laurel fought it off until her lids closed on their own volition. She'd only rest for a short moment, she promised herself. Only a short . . .

The pounding of his horse's hooves echoed a frantic beat within him as Royce pushed the stallion harder than he'd ever pushed before. He'd already stopped at two inns along the road toward Gretna Green with no sign of Laurel or Archie. Dawn was fast approaching, heralding the end of any hope of returning Laurel to London.

Royce spurred his horse onward when another

inn came into sight. Please God, let me be in time, he prayed.

Vaulting off his horse, Royce rushed into the inn, calling for the keep. When the older man came out scratching his belly, Royce began to question him.

"My pardon for waking you at this early hour, but it is imperative I find a certain young lady. Has anyone checked in this evening?"

"Indeed, but this is a private inn," the keep pronounced. "I'll not be giving out the names of my guests."

Royce didn't have the time to politely ask the man to reconsider. Instead he grabbed hold of the man's registration book and scanned the names. There, bold as could be, was an entry for Lord and Lady Devens.

Tossing the book down, Royce mounted the stairs, taking them two at a time, bringing a shout of protest from the innkeeper. The sight that greeted him in the upstairs hallway made his heart stop.

There, crumpled against the wall, lay Laurel in a bloodstained dress.

Rushing forward, he pressed two fingers against her neck, checking her pulse.

At his touch, she roused, her lashes lifting. "Royce?" she murmured, disbelief mingling with hope. "Is it really you?"

"Yes, darling," he returned, gathering her into his arms. Pressing her close, he savored the feel of her against him. "Are you all right?"

She nodded against his neck. "I've locked Archie and Margaret in that room," she told him, pointing one finger toward the door across the hall.

"The blood, Laurel," he asked, his voice cracking. "Where did it come from?"

Lifting her hand, she showed him the cut. "I hurt my hand when I broke a lamp by accident."

Relief flooded him. While the cut had bled quite a bit, it didn't look too deep. "Everything will be just fine now, Laurel," he murmured, pressing a kiss against her forehead. "Let's find an empty room where you can rest while I fetch a doctor to stitch up your hand."

Resting her head against him, Laurel murmured sleepily. "I'm so glad you came for me, Royce."

Without haste, Royce found another open room at the end of the hall. Judging from the monogrammed bags, he assumed it belonged to Margaret. Gently, Royce laid Laurel upon the bed, tucking her into the covers. Unwrapping her makeshift bandage, Royce dipped a cloth into the water pitcher and began to clean off the blood, revealing a shallow cut on the palm of her hand.

Reaching over, he loosened the fingers on her other hand, releasing her grip on a key. It could only be to the room where she'd locked up Archie and Margaret. Tucking the key into his pocket, he made his way downstairs to order the innkeeper to fetch a doctor.

When the physician finally arrived, Royce left his post at Laurel's bedside.

"This is Doctor Wilks," the innkeeper announced, stepping aside to allow a gaunt fellow to enter.

"My lord," the doctor murmured, taking the seat Royce had just abandoned.

"My wife cut her hand," Royce explained, gesturing toward the bandage wrapped around Laurel's palm.

"*Your* wife?" exclaimed the innkeeper, peering closely at Laurel. "I thought she was married to the other fellow."

Coldness settled into Royce's gut. "I assure you, this lady belongs to me."

Frowning, the man shook his head. "My apologies, my lord. I meant no offense. It's just I could have sworn this young lady checked in with another gentleman who claimed her as *his* wife."

Royce lifted one brow at the keep. "Are you suggesting that I don't know my own wife?"

"No, no," hastened the innkeeper as he backed out of the room, mumbling about the oddities of the gentry.

Turning toward the doctor, Royce pointed out her cut hand. "A piece of glass sliced into her palm, Dr. Wilks. I cleaned it as best I could, but I believe she will need stitches."

"I believe you're right," the doctor agreed, before setting down his bag and attending to the cut. Working in silence, the doctor quickly cleansed, closed, and redressed the wound. Laurel thanked the doctor before drifting off to sleep once more.

"Thank you," Royce said to Dr. Wilks as he pressed some coins into his hand.

"Change the bandages on that cut frequently for the next few days. If a fever develops, you'd be smart to consult a surgeon." Heading for the door, Dr. Wilks paused with his hand on the knob. "By the way, my lord, your claim that the lady is your wife might be accepted if you placed a ring upon her finger."

Flushing, Royce stood his ground. "The lack of a ceremony at the present time makes no difference to me. I claim her for my own."

"Then do right by the girl," advised the doctor.

"I intend to."

With a nod, the doctor left them alone. Gazing down at Laurel, Royce knew he had another duty to attend to before he could focus all of his attention upon his bride-to-be.

First he needed to rid them of a pair of vermin.

Cold fury settled in him as he strode down the hall.

Chapter
23
❦

$\mathscr{A}$s soon as Royce walked into the room, he headed straight toward Archie and plowed his fist into the other man's face. The sharp ache in his hand felt incredibly satisfying, assuaging a bit of the rage churning inside of him. "Stand up, you bastard, so I can do it again."

Archie fingered his jaw. "I'd prefer to remain on the floor."

"Coward," Royce sneered. A movement on the other side of the room caught his eye. Jerking his head, he saw Margaret trying to ease her way toward the door. Taking one step back, he slammed the door closed, effectively cutting off her path of escape. "Not before we come to an understanding, Margaret."

"I did nothing," she protested.

"The simple fact that you are locked here in the room with this piece of filth says otherwise." Royce calmed himself, focusing on the quickest way to rid himself of these two menaces so he could return to Laurel.

Archie lifted his hand to ward off Royce as he moved closer. Grasping Archie's fingers, Royce tugged off the Devens' family crest and slipped it into his pocket. "For security measures," he informed Archie.

"What the devil are you talking about?" Archie demanded, though his prone position eliminated any threat to Royce. "Give me back my ring."

"No," Royce said bluntly. "Listen carefully, both of you. You are both going to visit Scotland for a long, long while and as of this moment, the two of you ran away to Gretna Green to wed."

"*What?*" shrieked Margaret. "I will never agree to such a demand."

"Ah, but you will," Royce countered, "or I shall be forced to inform the magistrate that you were responsible for startling Laurel's horse and endangering her very life." He tilted his head to the side. "Somehow I don't believe prison would agree with you, Margaret."

"You could never prove it."

"Yes, I could." Stepping forward, he grasped her monogrammed locket and snapped it off her neck. "You see, your locket got caught in the nearby bushes and carelessly you didn't notice it was missing."

Worry flashed in her eyes, before she shook her head. "That still would not be proof."

"I am the Earl of Tewksbury, Margaret," he reminded her coldly. "Most of my friends are very influential personages. Do you honestly believe they would doubt my word?"

Her eyes narrowed in anger. "Damn you," she hissed.

"I believe it will be the other way around." Royce tucked her necklace into his pocket. "The same goes for you, Devens. If you return to England, I will have you brought up on charges."

"How could you bring us up on charges and not your own mother?" crowed Margaret, tossing back her head. "I'll wager you didn't know about her helping us."

"You'd lose that bet, Margaret." Royce crossed his arms. "Who do you think told me about this little adventure?"

"She wouldn't have told you," Archie denied. "If she had, she would have incriminated herself."

"My mother admitted everything." Returning his gaze to Margaret, he shook his head. "Don't believe for one moment that threatening to expose my mother will save you."

"Your mother is obsessed with keeping your precious family name free of smears," Margaret said, confidence ringing in her voice. "All of society would be shocked to learn how far she'd go to protect the title."

"You're wrong," Royce informed her. "No one would believe it." He smiled coldly. "Remember that my mother has devoted her life to being the epitome of a countess. Who would believe that the quintessential lady would sink so low?"

"Bloody hell," Archie groaned, closing his eyes. "How long must we remain out of the country?"

"Oh, only twenty years or so," Royce retorted. "If I even hear a rumor that either one of you has returned, I will bring my evidence to the magistrate and file charges." He opened the door, revealing three burly stable hands outside. "I've hired these gentlemen to escort you to the border. You will leave immediately." Stepping out into the hall, he paused to give one last direction. "If either one of them attempts to escape, you have orders to shoot them."

Standing back with his arms folded across his chest, Royce watched while the three men dragged Archie and Margaret from the room . . . and out of his life.

Consciousness came to her slowly. Lifting her lashes, Laurel gazed around the room, trying to remember where she was. Memory came flooding back and with it, alarm. Curling her fingers around the bandage on her hand, Laurel struggled from the bed, driven to put as much distance between her and Archie as possible.

She didn't know how she'd ended up in this room wearing only her chemise, but she wasn't going to waste time sorting it all out. Tossing back the blankets, she'd just swung her feet onto the floor when the door opened.

Gasping, Laurel reached for the candlestick resting on the night table, ready to defend herself.

"It's only me," Royce said quickly. "Now please put that down before you open your stitches."

Sagging against her pillows, she returned the candlestick to the table. "How did you get here?"

"I followed you."

She shook her head. "I meant how did you know where I was?"

Pulling a chair close to the bed, Royce sat down, his hands clasped between his knees, his head down. "My mother told me."

How had his mother known? Before Laurel could voice the question, Royce lifted his head, meeting her gaze.

"She was behind the entire scheme," he told her quietly.

Hearing the soft echo of pain in his voice, she reached out a hand to him.

A sound of disbelief rippled from him. "I tell you it was my mother who did this to you and you offer me comfort?" He shook his head. "I've never known anyone like you, Laurel."

"If Margaret St. John is an example of the ladies you've known in the past, I shall take that as a great compliment," she quipped.

"I look forward to never again laying eyes upon *that* particular lady," Royce told her of how he'd taken care of Archie and Margaret. "I toyed with the idea of dragging them both back to London and bringing them up on charges, but it would only prolong this unpleasantness for us. As it is, we need to deal with my mother when we return."

Squeezing Royce's fingers, she offered him silent support.

Clasping her hand between his, he grew solemn. "You realize that there will be repercussions to this night's events. By now, someone will have noticed you were missing all night. With the way servants talk, I doubt if it can be kept quiet."

Her throat tightened. "Yes, I know," she whispered, "but I won't marry Archie just to make them go away."

"No," Royce agreed. "You'll marry me."

" 'Tis very early," Laurel said, looking out the window of their hired carriage. "Perhaps we should wait until later to be wed."

"No, weddings are always morning affairs," Royce reminded her.

Sitting back against the cushions, she bit back a sigh. Her apprehension had increased the closer they'd gotten to Gretna Green.

Was she really doing the right thing?

The carriage pulled to a stop in front of the inn. Cautiously, Laurel stepped from the conveyance, looking around the small town.

Cupping his hand on her elbow, Royce escorted her toward the small chapel that stood at the far end of the street. In the garden edging the chapel stood a robust woman tending the flowers.

"Excuse me, madam," Royce said, offering her a smile. "I was wondering if the clergyman was about this fine morning."

"Och, yer lookin' ta wed then?" asked the woman. Beaming at them, she wiped her hands on her apron before gesturing back down the street. "The parish clerk and the pastor are out for a spell, but ye can get the job done at the smithy's shop."

Blinking once, Royce asked, "Pardon me?"

"The blacksmith," she repeated, slower this time.

"I understand *what* you're saying; I just don't know why you're saying it."

Looking at him as if he were daft, she explained,

" 'ere in Scotland, we do things a wee bit differently than you fancy gents south of us. 'Ere all you need do is pledge yourself to 'er in front of another respectable fellow and that does the trick."

"That's all it takes?" Laurel asked incredulously.

"Indeed it is," confirmed the woman with a nod.

"I always knew I loved Scotland." Royce held out his hand. "After you, my dear."

Laurel dug in her heels. "I am *not* about to be wed by a blacksmith!"

"You heard the lady. It's all very simple."

"Regardless, I prefer we wait for the clergyman."

"Laurel . . ."

Leaning closer, she lowered her voice. "No, Royce. I won't pledge myself to you amidst the smoke from the smithy's fire and the sound of hammers hitting steel." She shook her head. "I won't do it."

Sighing, Royce gave in. "Very well," he agreed. Turning back to the lady, he asked, "We've decided to wait for the clergy and his clerk to return. Might we wait in the chapel?"

"The door's always open," the lady invited, waving them forward. "There's lovely benches in the vestibule. You may wait there."

Thanking her, Royce escorted Laurel into the small entryway and glanced down at the benches. "They're made of stone," he observed.

Laurel laughed; she couldn't help herself. "At least we have a place to sit."

He arched a brow at her. "For you to make a statement like that, it is obvious that you have never sat upon cold, hard stone benches for very long."

"No, I haven't," she admitted. "Perhaps they make them so uncomfortable so that couples can't relax and, instead, reflect on whether or not they're doing the right thing." The moments the words of doubt left her mouth Laurel wished them back. "What I meant to say was—"

"You aren't certain if you're doing the right thing by marrying me," Royce finished for her. Grasping her by the shoulders, he slowly pulled her closer. "Why do you have doubts?"

"You wish to protect me," she whispered, before baring her soul, "but do you wish to love me as well?"

His smile was one of the most beautiful things she'd ever seen. "Of course I do."

Her heart expanded beneath his reassurance. "I love you, Royce."

"I know."

His arrogant response made her laugh. Poking him in the ribs, she teased, "I shall make you regret—"

"Well, now, I understand the two of ye are lookin' ta wed."

Both Royce and Laurel turned to face a tall, gray-haired man who wore a broad smile. "Indeed, sir," Royce answered, holding out his hand. "We would be pleased if you would do the honor."

"Indeed I would," the pastor agreed. "I'm Parson McHugh and I'll wed ye right up if ye'll step inside now." The clergyman shooed them toward the altar. "Now then, I'll be havin' yer names and then— Pardon me fer a moment," Parson McHugh asked. Lifting his head, he bellowed, "Rob! Step lively, lad.

We've got a pair needing to exchange their pledges."

A thin, wiry man hustled into the church. "This 'ere's Rob. 'E's the parish clerk and 'e's got the ledger."

"Ledger?" Laurel asked tentatively.

"Och, ain't ye 'eard of tha *ledger?*" asked Rob, his eyes wide. "It be where ye place yer names all legal like."

"The parish register," Royce whispered. "Normally it's kept in the vestry, but I suspect they do things *a wee bit differently* up north."

Pressing a hand to her mouth, Laurel held back a giggle.

"Do ye—" Parson McHugh paused, looking expectantly at Royce. "Yer name, sir?"

"Oh, yes," Royce replied with a chuckle. "I'm Royce Edward Van Cleef, the Earl of—"

"Up, up," interrupted Parson McHugh. "We don' go in for those fancy English titles up 'ere. Yer Christian name will do." Clearing his throat, the clergyman began again. "Do ye, Royce Edward Van Cleef take . . ."

"Laurel Eleanor Simmons," supplied Laurel at the pause, earning a nod of approval from Parson McHugh.

". . . take Laurel Eleanor Simmons fer yer own?"

"Don't you mean for his bride?" Laurel asked.

Rolling his eyes, Parson McHugh held his hands heavenward. "Are ye the parson or am I?"

Before Laurel could answer, Royce said, "Yes, I take her for my *own* . . . bride."

She grinned at Royce. "And I take him for my own husband."

"These English . . . always in a rush," mumbled Parson McHugh. "Very well then, give 'er the ring."

For a moment, Royce looked disconcerted, until his expression cleared and he slipped his signet ring off his own finger. "With this ring, I thee wed," he murmured as he slid it onto her ring finger, lifting her hand to press a kiss there.

"Fine, then. Go on, sir, and kiss the bonny lass."

Royce didn't need to hear that direction twice. Cupping her face between his hands, he leaned down and gifted her with a tender pledge of his devotion. The sweetness of his kiss brought tears to her eyes.

As Royce began to lower his head again, Parson McHugh placed a hand upon his shoulder. "Ah, ah, ah. Non' a that now. Once is plenty for the pledge. It's time ta sign the ledger and then we'll be off for the bridal feast."

"Bridal feast?" Royce asked.

"Ay, we need to break the fast with ye . . . in order to bless the marriage," explained Rob. "Follow me and we'll sign my ledger right up."

Bemused, Laurel followed Royce into the vestry where she signed her name with a flourish. Putting down the quill, she looked up at her new husband.

"I'm sorry the ceremony was a bit . . . unorthodox," Royce murmured. "I hope you aren't upset."

"Of course not," Laurel assured him. "I look at it this way—it was undoubtedly more than we would have received in a blacksmith's shop."

Royce's laughter accompanied them out into the sunshine.

* * *

Upon their return to London, Royce called upon his mother one last time. Not waiting to be announced, he found her in the parlor, reading a book of poems.

"Royce," she said, setting the book aside. "From the look of you, I'd wager that you went after Lady Laurel." Sighing deeply, she shrugged. "I'm quite certain you're furious at me, Royce, but I assure you once you've distanced yourself from the situation, you'll agree that she was completely unsuitable and I only acted in your best interest."

"Laurel and I were married yesterday."

His mother lost all color.

"Yes, Mother, that's right. I caught up with Laurel, Devens, and Margaret St. John at an inn where Laurel had managed to outsmart them both." He clasped his hands behind his back. "Naturally, I sent the two of them packing with strict orders to stay out of England for a very long time."

"I see." Rising gracefully, his mother faced him. "And have you now come to send me packing?" She tried to smile at him, but the gesture seemed too much for her. "Shall I take an extended tour of the Continent?"

"It might be best," Royce agreed, wishing his answer could have been different.

"Very well." Obviously shaken, his mother walked toward the door.

As he watched her leave, Royce couldn't keep from asking, "Why did you do it?"

Turning to face him, Elizabeth shook her head. "I only wanted to do what was best for you, Royce."

"No, Mother," he replied, rejecting her pronouncement. "You did what you felt was best for the family name."

Sadness colored her expression. "Don't you realize that you *are* the family name?"

Slowly, he shook his head. "No, Mother, I am much more than the title and I hope that one day you will be able to accept that."

His mother gazed at him for a long time. "Perhaps in time," she said finally, gathering her pride about her like a mantle and walking from the room.

His wedding night.

Instead of staying a night in Scotland, he and Laurel returned home immediately. They'd slept most of the long ride back to London.

His wedding night.

Again, the thought pulsated through Royce as he took the stairs two at a time. They'd stopped to visit Lord Simmons upon their return and he'd been overjoyed to hear their news. Then he'd left Laurel in his townhouse while he visited his mother. But now it was *their* time.

Entering his bedchamber, Royce tried to squelch the disappointment that raced through him when he didn't find Laurel in the room. He'd change into his dressing gown and seek her out in her chamber, then he'd—

"Welcome home, Royce."

Raw need crashed through him at the sight of her tucked beneath the covers. Tugging at his cravat, he felt clumsy and untried in his eagerness. "Laurel, you're . . . you're . . . here," he stuttered.

"Of course I am," she said with a laugh. "Where else did you think I'd be?"

Where else indeed. Not his bold Laurel. She'd never shy away from anything, rather she'd meet it head-on. The fastenings on his shirt popped off as he tugged at them impatiently. Bare-chested, he sat upon the edge of the bed to tug off his boots and nearly came out of his skin when he felt her cool hands slide across his back.

"Are you all right?"

All right? No, at the moment, he was far better than all right. It took him a minute to realize that she was talking about his confrontation with his mother. Tossing aside one boot, he glanced over his shoulder at her. "Oddly enough I am," he murmured.

"I'm glad," she said, laying a gentle hand upon his shoulder. "But I'd prefer if we'd discuss the details of your conversation with your mother later. I believe this bed is only big enough for two."

He knew precisely what she was doing by injecting humor into their discussion . . . and he loved her all the more for it. The realization settled into his heart and felt right. He'd tried to deny his love for this woman, preferring to believe he wanted her only because she would "suit" him. Instead, she *completed* him.

Groaning, Royce reached for his wife.

The soft nightgown she wore flowed around him, brushing against his flesh as he gathered her close. Kneeling upon the bed, Royce pressed her against him, knee to chest, rejoicing in the soft curves. His fingers tangled in the length of her nightgown as he gathered it up and, sitting back upon his heels, tugged it over her head.

A deep flush tinted her cheeks as she knelt before him in naked splendor, but she made no move to cover herself. His hands shook as he reached out to trace her body, feathering the tips of his fingers across her shoulders, down her arms, then back up again, swirling over the generous breasts, dipping into the curve of her waist, and onto the flow of her hips.

Laurel's breath rushed from her in little gasps as he explored her with his eyes and fingertips. Unable to torment himself any longer, Royce slid his arms around her waist, bending her back to feast upon the nape of her neck. A moan escaped Laurel as he pressed against her, flesh against aching flesh.

Bending her back farther, he moved his mouth onto her breasts, tasting first one, then the other, as Laurel slid her fingers into his hair, urging him closer. Slowly, he retraced his path up to her neck to capture her mouth with his. Dipping his tongue inward, he consumed her desire, offering her his as he rubbed the moistened tips of her breasts against the soft hair on his chest.

He deepened their kiss, passion driving him forward as he satisfied the hunger raging within him. Needing to feel her softness against every part of him, Royce gently laid his wife back upon the bed, watching as she whispered his name, reaching for him. Love intensified his desire as he rushed to strip his breeches off, leaving himself open to her gaze.

Praying she wouldn't be alarmed by the flesh boldly jutting outward, Royce remained still beneath her wandering eyes. He sucked in his breath as she lightly stroked down his chest, scraping her nails along the sensitive flesh, until she reached the sculpted muscles in his thighs. Her hand paused over his manhood, hovering, until Royce thought he'd go mad and shifted to touch her fingers to his hardness.

Instinctively, she closed her hand around him, squeezing gently, bringing a curse to his lips. Holding still as she explored him proved too great a task. Angling toward her, Royce claimed her lips again. Laurel eagerly greeted him, winding her arms around his neck, arching into him with silent entreaty.

His hand boldly stroked down her and he followed with his mouth. Cupping his fingers against her womanhood, he brought his leg between hers, opening her to his touch. As he curved his finger inward, dipping into her moisture, Laurel moaned softly, making him crave more. Sliding downward, he shifted his entire body until he lay between her thighs.

Slowly, he traced his way up her legs, dipping his tongue into the hollow behind her knee, laving the sensitive flesh along her inner thigh, moving inexorably closer to her pouting moans. A shocked gasp broke from Laurel as he kissed her womanhood, but her taste was too wondrous to resist. Deepening the caress, he smiled against her when she clutched his hair, encouraging him to continue.

And continue he did.

Feasting upon her, he drove her higher and higher, reveling in the feel of her body as she arched against him. A cry of delight broke from her when she crashed over the edge, shivering in his arms.

Swiftly, he moved upward, positioning himself at her entrance. "My wife," he rasped hoarsely.

Her soft smile gripped at his heart. "My husband," she returned, resting her fingertips against his hips and opening herself further.

With a groan, he pressed forward, stretching Laurel, filling her, until he was completely surrounded by her heat. Overwhelming sensations bombarded him, making him lose all control. He groaned again as he pulled out, then returned into her warmth once more.

Slowly, he moved within her, picking up the rhythm as she joined him, her legs wrapping about his hips in wanton abandon. Hunger to fill himself with this woman pulsed through him and he lost himself within her. Faster, faster, he drove them, racing toward a pinnacle of pleasure far greater than he'd ever experienced.

White-hot sparks exploded through him as he buried himself into her one last time, gifting her with his essence as her flesh clung to his in ecstasy.

Collapsing onto her, he rolled to his side, gathering her close until she lay upon him. Stroking her hair, he murmured, "Making that wager was the best thing I've ever done in my life."

For a moment, she stopped breathing, then she lifted her head to look at him. "The wager." Pain darkened her gaze. "We just shared something so beautiful, yet the first words out of your mouth are about the *wager*."

"Damn me for being an idiot," Royce said,

silently chastising himself for his careless mistake. "I meant to tell you I love you."

After a long while, Laurel just smiled at him, an odd sadness lurking within the depths of her gaze. "It's all right, Royce," she said, pressing a kiss upon his chest. "I appreciate your efforts, but I'd prefer if we were honest with each other."

"What are you talking about?" he asked with a shake of his head.

"You don't need to profess love for me. I know you only said it in the church because I needed to hear it," she said, her breath catching. "But you don't need to say it anymore."

"Of course I do," he protested. "I *do* love you, so it is only right that I tell you."

"Royce," she sighed. "You are wonderful for wanting to give me everything I desire, but I am well aware of why you married me."

Lifting a brow, he tried to understand what she was getting at. "Would you mind telling me?"

"For the very reasons you made your wager in the first place. I meet all the requirements you want in a wife . . . and I now come with an added bonus because I love you." She laid her head back against his shoulder. "Besides, you wished to save my reputation."

He laughed. He couldn't help it. "Trust me, Laurel. If I hadn't wanted to marry you, I wouldn't have—not even to save your reputation."

"Please, Royce, you can hardly expect me to believe that you truly love me when the first words out of your mouth after we make love are about that *silly* wager!"

Rolling his eyes, Royce couldn't believe the dilemma he now faced. He'd finally fallen in love with the woman, but he couldn't convince her of that fact. Knowing he could profess his love until he had no breath left and she'd still doubt his word, Royce decided he had to find a way to prove his love.

After all, strategies had always come easily to him.

When Laurel slid her leg onto his, he decided in an instant that he could strategize tomorrow. Tonight belonged to passion.

Chapter
24

⌇⌇

"It's a wonderfully romantic tale," sighed Harriet. "I hope someday I have one of my own to tell."

"I'm certain you will," Laurel assured her.

"You're truly happy then?"

Smiling at her friend, Laurel nodded, ignoring the prick of doubt she still felt. Oh, he'd told her often enough in the past two days since their wedding, but part of her couldn't believe him. What if she allowed herself to believe that he was as vulnerable to her as she was to him, only to discover that she'd been mistaken? Her heart would surely break in two.

"I'm surprised to see you this evening." Harriet glanced around the crowded ballroom. "I thought for certain that the two of you would remain secluded for at least a few weeks."

Shrugging, Laurel explained, "Royce insisted we come this evening." She hid her smile at the thought that they very nearly hadn't made it at all. He'd come upon her in her chemise and it had been all she could do to get dressed in time after he'd seduced her in her dressing room. Her life was more than she ever dreamed possible and Royce had proved to be an incredible husband.

If she could finally overcome her nagging doubts, her life would be perfect.

Loud clapping brought her from her thoughts.

"Might I have everyone's attention?"

It was Royce. Curious to see what he was up to, Laurel lifted onto her tiptoes to see him standing on the riser for the string quartet. Immediately the room quieted for the man who had provided them with so much delicious gossip.

"What is he doing?" Harriet asked, leaning close.

Laurel shook her head. "I don't have any idea."

Lifting both his hands, Royce smiled at everyone. "I appreciate your allowing me this opportunity to speak, for I have something very important I'd like to share with everyone."

As his gaze met hers, his smile grew intimate. "As you know, I have recently wed, but I'm not certain if everyone knows all that led up to the wedding. You see, I arrogantly believed that marriage was a simple, straightforward matter. If a man chose his mate wisely and researched the habits and interests of his chosen lady, he could easily claim her for his own." Laughing, Royce shook his head. "What a fool I was."

Laurel couldn't believe her ears. Royce, her Royce, was admitting he'd been mistaken in public? The action was so out-of-character for him that Laurel was certain she'd heard him wrong.

Yet when he continued, it was more of the same. "I was so certain that my theory would work that I accepted a wager . . . even going so far as to allow others to chose my future bride. Luckily for me, they choose well, for I couldn't ask for better than Lady Laurel Simmons." He raised both of his hands again as a loud murmur rose in the room. "I know that most of you must be thinking that my theory was proven correct, especially since I just married the lady in question." His hands dropped to his sides and he met Laurel's gaze once again. "But you'd be dead wrong . . . for my clever plan failed miserably."

Why was Royce exposing himself like this? she wondered again. Ignoring the curious gazes trained upon her, she concentrated upon Royce.

"The lady was far too clever to be caught in my trap. By evading me, she forced me to take a closer look at my strategy. It was only then that I realized the truth about love." His smile touched her across the expanse of the room. "Love isn't a neat concept you can tuck into an allotted place and only think about when you wish to secure an heir. No, love is a twisting, living thing that demands more from you than you know you have to give, yet somehow love, true love, brings out the best in you."

Shifting on his feet, Royce cleared his throat. "Laurel," he began, speaking to her from his heart, "you made me into a far better man than I ever knew I could be and I shall thank God every day that I accepted that wager."

The entire room seemed transfixed by the scene playing out before them, but Laurel only had eyes for Royce.

One corner of his mouth quirked upward. "I love you, Laurel Van Cleef."

Dear God, he'd done this for her. He'd exposed his innermost emotions to the ton in order to convince her that his love was true. Heaven knew, he didn't have to do it, not now, not when he had everything already. She was wed, bedded, and fitted into his life, but he wanted more.

He wanted her to know he truly loved her.

Pure happiness burst within her as Laurel took one step toward him, then another, and another, until she was flying across the room and into his arms.

Enfolding her close, Royce whirled her around as applause thundered through the room. Setting her back onto her feet, he kissed her.

Pulling back, he cupped her face in his hands and gazed deeply into her eyes. "I love you," he rasped, his voice tight with emotion.

Blinking back tears, she gave him a tremulous smile. "I know."

Epilogue

One year later

Sitting in White's, enjoying his brandy, Royce bit back a groan as William and James approached him. He'd been looking forward to a peaceful evening.

"Evening, Royce," greeted William. "May we join you?"

"Yes, we're both in desperate need of some male companionship."

At James's announcement, Royce laughed, gesturing toward the seats. "Have a seat."

"Thanks," James returned as he beckoned for a brandy. "My life has so few peaceful moments these days."

William nodded. "As does mine. Such is the life of a husband and father." William rubbed his hand along his forehead. "I vow my head pounds at the end of each day while I listen to my child demand one thing after another."

"And my wife has become quite unreasonable

now that she is expecting," James added, leaning back in his chair with a huff. "Just last night, she expected me to head down to our kitchen and fetch her something to eat. Can you imagine?"

"At least you still see your wife at night," William retorted. "Mine is always so blasted tired from overseeing the house and the nanny that she wants nothing at all to do with me."

Taking a sip of his brandy, Royce shook his head. "The two of you are completely pitiful," he announced. "You lament about matters that could easily be taken into hand."

"And just how is that?" James asked, straightening in his chair.

"By creating a daily regimen within your home and ensuring that it is strictly followed."

Laughing, William slapped his knee. "That is a good one, Royce."

"I am utterly serious."

"It's beginning to sound as if another wager is in order," James said, "and if I remember correctly, you lost the last one."

"Indeed, I did," Royce conceded without a trace of embarrassment. "But I'm quite certain I'm correct in this matter."

"Would you care to make that a wager?"

James's question caught Royce's attention. "As I am not a father, I fail to see how I could accept the wager."

"Come now, Royce, surely you've figured out by now how this whole baby thing works," William said with a laugh.

Indeed he had, Royce thought, remembering his

wife's hungry hands just last night. If anything, it would certainly be a pleasurable pursuit.

Lifting his brandy glass, Royce smiled at his friends. "I accept your wager."

"... and that is how this wager came about," Royce told Laurel.

Smiling at her husband, Laurel just shook her head. He would never change. "So now you need my help in securing this wager?"

"I didn't think you'd mind the trying."

A shiver overtook her. "Not at all."

"Besides, the last wager I made turned out perfectly."

"After a few bumps," Laurel pointed out.

"True, but as I always say, nothing worth getting is ever gotten easily."

"Ah, but you're wrong, Royce." Laurel stepped closer to her husband and pressed a lingering kiss upon the tender skin beneath his ear. "It will be quite easy to catch me now," she whispered in sensual promise.

Tossing a smile over her shoulder, she sauntered from the room and up the stairs, fully aware of Royce's heated gaze following her every move.

Royce charged after her, catching her easily, and swept her into his arms. Grinning down at her, he murmured, "Let the game begin."

Return to
a time of romance...

SONNET
BOOKS

Where today's

hottest romance authors

bring you vibrant

and vivid love stories

with a dash of history.